# Meant to be Yours

# Meant to be Yours

*Sequaia*

www.urbanbooks.net

Urban Books, LLC
300 Farmingdale Road, NY-Route 109
Farmingdale, NY 11735

ISBN 13: 978-1-64556-318-1
ISBN 10: 1-64556-318-9

First Mass Market Printing July 2022
First Trade Paperback Printing July 2021
Printed in the United States of America

10 9 8 7 6 5 4 3 2

*This is a work of fiction. Any references or similarities to actual events, real people, living or dead, or to real locales are intended to give the novel a sense of reality. Any similarity in other names, characters, places, and incidents is entirely coincidental.*

Distributed by Kensington Publishing Corp.
Submit Orders to:
Customer Service
400 Hahn Road
Westminster, MD 21157-4627
Phone: 1-800-733-3000
Fax: 1-800-659-2436

# Acknowledgments

First and foremost, I thank God for all He's done and continues to do in my life. With Him, nothing is impossible. I want to thank my babies, Rique and Riqo: Mommy loves you two so much. To my love, Erique: thank you for your unwavering love and support. Also, to my family, thank you for supporting me. To my friends, who I'm able to discuss ideas with and receive motivational speeches from when I'm stuck: I appreciate you so much. I want to give a huge thank you to my super agents, N'Tyse and Diane, for your continuous support, motivational speeches, and just being two amazing genuine women. Thank you so much for all you've done and continue to do. I am so excited about where this journey will lead us.

To Granny, Marea and Keyon: this one is for y'all.

To those of you reading this: I am so excited for you to read Aúrea and Prentice's story, and I hope you enjoy it.

Thank you.

# 1

## *Aúrea*

Panic-stricken, I woke up sweating profusely. Looking over at the small Hello Kitty clock that rested on my nightstand, I peered at the time and exhaled deeply. It displayed 11:59 p.m. Taking deep breaths to steady my nerves, I tried coaching myself to pull it together. The time had come to get out of this house. I usually had about five minutes from now before he made his way into my bedroom.

"Please, God, don't let the door give out," I mouthed the words, referring to the makeshift lock I made using a rope tied from my doorknob to my dresser's handle. I hoped God heard me. He had to.

I waited with bated breath, silently continuing to pray that he didn't gain entry into my bedroom. My eyes shifted toward the light shining underneath the door, focusing on the shadow of his feet as everything seemed to go quiet. My eyes darted around my room, searching for anything to defend myself with if he happened to break down the door. As nothing came into view, his scoffing pierced my ears before I heard him say, "All right." Not a second later, a menacing laugh left his mouth, seeming to draw further from my door. I looked at the spot where his feet had once cast a shadow, relieved to see nothing other than light.

He was gone . . . had moved from the spot. I let out the breath I'd been holding as the house phone rang . . . loudly, buying me a little more time.

Nervously, I began chewing on the inside of my cheek as thoughts of my next move flooded my mind. Waiting around to be raped was far from a favorable option. Hence, the reason I popped two sleeping pills earlier, with hopes to sleep through the act or not wake at all. Just in case my lock tie didn't work. Was dying something I wanted? Of course not. It would've been an out, though. God clearly had other plans for me. So it was time to put in some work to take advantage of the chance given to me.

"Come on, Aúrea, you can do this." Finally finding my voice, I whispered the words meant to motivate me as my hands and legs shook as if I were standing in the middle of the North Pole, naked. Removing my blankets, revealing my black and pink pajamas purchased from Target, I inched my way off the bed. Picking up my messenger bag while easing my nightstand drawer open, I grabbed a few bras, panties, and my cell before tossing them into the bag, then slid my feet into my Nike slides.

"Okay, Aúrea, what next?" Talking to myself had slowly become a habit. Standing there, wringing my hands, I anticipated an answer that only I could give.

The doorknob shook again. My knees buckled.

"Shit," he cussed, rattling the doorknob before his heavy footsteps trailed off once again.

That was the final sign I needed. It was time to get the hell out of Dodge. Leaving was always a part of my plan, especially with my eighteenth birthday around the corner. Going tonight, however, wasn't. Apples and oranges, usually what life threw my way. So there was no reason to think now would be any different. For five years, my foster father had had his way with me. Routinely. At least three nights a week when my foster mother left for work. She departed the house at ten, and he waited until 12:05 a.m.; 12:06 a.m. at the latest, before entering—like clockwork, because around midnight, she'd call.

Unsure of what he was about to do next, I needed to hurry and make a move. I eased over to my window, sliding it up as gently as possible to avoid the raggedy window from making too much noise. This house was old. Even with the multiple streams of income coming in, my county check included, they still only did the bare minimum fixing this place. I exhaled, satisfied when it opened with a minimal clatter.

"Aúrea!" he growled my name. My heart just about leaped from my chest. I hadn't heard him come back and damn sure hadn't heard him open my door. Obviously, the rope hadn't worked. Wildly, my heart thumped as my eyes widened when they met his gaze. This moment reminded me of the scene from *Tales from the Hood* when the boy's stepfather came into his room as the "monster." Von, my foster father, was, without a doubt, a monster. Momentarily, we stared at each other. His unexpected entrance left me feeling paralyzed—until he moved.

All my senses seemed to come back, shooting through me as if I'd been hit with a defibrillator. Snatching up my messenger bag, I practically dove out of my window.

"Ahh!" My scream was loud enough to wake the block as the grip Von took on my hair jerked me backward. Tears immediately stung my eyes.

"Where you going, huh?" he gritted, yanking my hair tighter.

"Let me go, please . . . I-I won't run."

"You better fucking not, or there'll be hell to pay, and you know it." Releasing my hair, he shoved me forward. Had it not been for my outstretched hands, my face would have smacked against the wall. He promised there'd be hell to pay—as if this weren't hell already. With enough distance between us, I decided to take my chances once again.

I leaped headfirst out of the window, landing on my palms and belly. The rosebush my foster mother cherished so much flattened underneath me. Popping up, I scrambled a few steps away from the house before dusting myself off, removing the few thorns that stuck in me. My nights of cooperating were done.

I had had enough.

*Been* had enough.

Disgustingly, he made it a point to inform me the last time he'd crept into my room two nights ago that he would be getting some of my sweet little pussy until I was officially grown and walked out of their front door. The joke was on him, though. No way was I going to let him have that satisfaction. He would not get the chance to fuck me into age 18. He's been having his way with me since I moved into this home. Two nights ago, I deemed it the last time and began plotting my escape. Two nights hadn't been enough time to come up with a solid game plan. So right now, I was winging everything.

"Aúrea," the harshness in his whisper couldn't be mistaken, even in such a low tone. I spun around toward the window, my chest heaving up and down from the adrenaline and unsettled nerves. I peered into his dark eyes, glaring back at me. The sinister expression he gave me when our eyes met made my skin crawl. With his right index finger, he motioned for me to come back. The dingy wife beater he wore hung at the collar as if he'd stretched it. His skinny arms looked like small tree branches, with nappy armpit hair peeping from the sides. Von gave me vibes of the actor Michael T. Williamson when he screamed "raggedy bitch" to Robin in *Waiting to Exhale.* He grossed me out to no end. Could've possibly been a handsome man had he not taken it upon himself to violate me every chance he got.

I looked at him with wide eyes before scrunching my face and shaking my head in defiance, then took off for my safe place, the only place I could think to go right now, where I'd be okay for at least a little while until I figured out my next move.

My head was on a swivel as I walked as quickly as I could in the slippers I had on. It was late. I was alone.

I'd just escaped my molester—rapist, rather. There was nothing ordinary about tonight. When I made it to the block's nicest home, I paused briefly, looking around to be sure no one saw me approaching the house. It shocked me to see the light on in the room I hoped to be entering shortly. He was never up this late. Gradually making my way to the window, I did my best to see inside, but the curtain blocked my view. Tapping on the window, I waited what felt like forever before the curtain drew back, revealing his handsome face. Covering his mouth with his left hand, he yawned before opening the window.

"You were sleeping?" My eyebrows rose in skepticism. Why? I wasn't sure, knowing that if there was anybody I could trust, it was undoubtedly him. His bedroom light being on so late when I knew he typically didn't stay up this late had caught me off guard.

"Yeah, doing this assignment for history. Fell asleep at my desk. Come on." He extended his hand, assisting me through. "Aúrea, what's wrong, babe?" He asked me in the gentlest tone imaginable, even though the vein in his forehead protruded, alerting me of his frustration, his anger.

"I had to get out of there. I refuse to deal with him tonight—or any other night. It has to stop." I collapsed onto his chest, feeling safe instantly as his arms wrapped around me.

"Did he touch you?" I could hear the rapid pace of his heartbeat as he awaited my reply.

"I left. He didn't get to. But, Prentice," I pulled back from him, looking him in the eyes, "I can't live like that anymore." Half-truth, half a lie, I gave to him. Had he known that Von almost ripped my hair from my scalp, he'd go to my house and try his best to kill Von. That wasn't something I could allow.

"You won't. We'll figure something out. Come on. Let's get some rest and come up with a solution when we wake up, all right?" He took me by the chin and kissed my lips. And my heart sped up. This was the feeling that was supposed to come over me when I was kissed, not the vile feeling which always existed when my foster father put his lips on mine.

Prentice was everything to me . . . my best friend, my boyfriend, my confidant, my peace. With him was where I wanted to be, especially when he didn't turn his back on me *after* I confessed about my foster father, after making him promise not to tell a soul. Still, after all of that . . . He still wanted and cared about me.

"Okay." There was no reluctance to agree with him. His intentions for me were pure, even when my circumstances caused me to doubt them. My heart knew to trust him, so most times, I obliged what he asked of me. There was no doubt he would help me figure out what to do next. I knew I wasn't going to let Von hurt me any further.

"Prentice! Prentice!"

The sound of someone yelling his name woke me from my sleep. Whoever was yelling for him wasn't near. And the person shouting was undeniably female. Forcing myself to wake fully, I lazily rolled over onto my back, rubbed my eyes before stretching, and sat up. I almost forgot where I was until the photo of Prentice and me on his desk caught my eye.

"I know you didn't let that fast-ass girl sleep at my house. Did you have sex with her under my roof, with me home? I know you haven't lost your damn mind, boy."

Rolling my eyes at the sound of Tasha's voice, Prentice's mom, I contemplated lying back down. I was used to her voicing an unwanted opinion about me since most of what she assumed she knew about me was false, anyway. However, curiosity about the lies she would spew this time got the best of me. Standing from his bed, I sauntered over to his door to hear her extra ass better.

"Ma, I wish you'd quit talking about her like that. If you took the time to get to know her, you would actually like her," Prentice defended me.

"I know what I see, and the eyes don't lie. You two are lucky I didn't drag her ass up out of here. And *you*— you've always been respectful until she came along. Yet, you want me to give her a chance? Child, please, I've only seen you change for the worse, not better, since meeting her. Go get her fast ass out of my house," Tasha yelled.

I could imagine her neck rolling as she pointed her finger in his face. Tasha talked big and probably had hands, but she would have a problem if she decided to put them on me.

"But, Ma—"

"Prentice, go do what I said."

Footsteps drawing closer urged me to get my ass back into his bed and pretend like I hadn't heard a damn thing. I barely got the cover over my head when the door opened, then shut.

"I know you're not sleeping. We need to talk."

Taking a sharp breath, I withdrew the blankets just as he sat down, causing the bed to sink in some.

"I'm going to leave. No one should be at my house, anyway." I knew him needing to talk would only be to tell me to leave his home. I couldn't take hearing him speak those words to me, even if they weren't his own words. So letting him know I would leave was doing us both a favor.

"Leave and then what, A?" he quizzed.

"Go home, pack my things . . . Travel to Los Angeles, as I've always declared I would." Seriousness etched my tone because that's exactly what I was—spending another week or day under the same roof as my foster parents was not going to cut it. That was like me asking to be raped again. And since I refused to let that happen anymore, running away was the best option. Because if I didn't leave, I'd surely end up in prison for murder.

"You're serious?" his voice cracked as if he were afraid of my answer.

"I am."

"What about me, us?"

"Leaving you is not what I want to do, but I don't have any other option. I can't stay here, and I refuse to stay there."

"Can you stay with one of your homegirls for a couple of days until I can figure something out?" His pleading eyes tugged at my heart. Even though I had no clue what he was planning, my gut told me to give his plan a try.

"Then what?" I needed to know.

"Then I'll go to L.A. with you."

"Are you for real?" Tears pooled. My heart filled. This young man truly loved me. He had to if he was willing to leave what he had here behind. His life was far from fucked up, while mine was all kinds of shitty. He had no reason to go other than for me.

"I mean it. Let me stack some money and do some research first. Then we can leave. I'm not letting you go that far without me."

"Okay. I'll wait it out. At a *friend's* house." I had one person I could consider a friend, besides Prentice, although it felt like she only hung with me to get male attention since guys flocked to me because they thought I was easy. Outside of Von, Prentice was the only guy I'd been with. But big boobs and wide hips apparently equaled fucking. I'd been doing that since age 13, so I guess it was a reasonable assumption. I couldn't deny I developed faster than most of the girls in our community, though.

"Will you come with me to pack the rest of my things?"

Both of my foster parents should have been gone. Having Prentice with me was best in case they were there.

"Of course."

My eyes followed as he went into his closet and changed clothes before grabbing a pocketknife. He tried to pocket it discretely, then accompanied me home. When we got there, my bedroom window was cracked, and the cars were gone. I collected everything I'd need, plus all of my sentimental items, mainly the necklace that had been with me since being placed into the system. After gathering everything, I prepared to stay with a friend until he was ready to make our move.

# 2

## *Prentice*

"Hey, what you kids doing back here?"

My eyes shot open not just from the question but from the sharp poking in my side. It wasn't painful but being snatched from my sleep so abruptly had my heart pounding. Being treated as if I were some dead, dirty-ass dog had me on the verge of taking the stick and beating up whoever was poking me with it.

"Yo! What the fuck?" I said, sitting up and wiping my eyes. Defensively, my fists balled while my face scrunched into a mug. My girl hadn't moved once. She was a heavy sleeper, so her lack of movement didn't shock me. As my eyes adjusted to the light and reality of where we were, my head hung in shame . . . briefly, because the angry voice started again.

"Why y'all kids laying back here?"

I lifted my head to look him directly in the eyes. His expression indicated hurt and confusion, while his tone was one of a damn drill sergeant.

"My bad, man. I didn't realize we fell asleep. We'll move." I gently nudged Aúrea, trying to get her to wake up.

"Y'all want to eat?" His tone softened, as well as the expression on his face. I thought she was still asleep, but when she replied with "Food? Yes," she proved her ass was awake. I cut my eyes at her, knowing she was paying me no mind. She knew I was going to tell his ass no.

"Come on," he ordered.

"I got money. We don't have to eat your food for free." I was not looking for a handout, although him finding us back here looked foul. But I wasn't a homeless kid. We were back here by choice.

"Bring y'all asses on," he commanded, dismissing me.

I stood, helped Aúrea to her feet, and waited. Something about his fatherly approach got me up, a tone I'd been waiting to hear my entire life.

We followed him through the back door of his restaurant, where we had fallen asleep, which couldn't have been any longer than four or five hours ago. We were supposed to be taking a short break against the wall near the dumpster but evidently fell asleep.

"There's a washroom over here. Clean yourselves up. Meet me on the other side of this door." He pointed to the right where he said the washroom belonged, then straight ahead where he wanted us to meet him.

"Come on." Taking Aúrea by the hand, we stepped into a bathroom. I mean—a fully equipped bathroom, with a shower and everything. It made me wonder if he always brought in strays from off the street or lived here. I hadn't been in the back of many restaurants—none actually. Regardless, I doubted a complete bathroom in the back was how they came. Plus, he was too open to helping us. We could've been the young Black version of Bonnie and Clyde for all he knew, and still, he was willing to clean and feed us.

"Oh-my-God, babe, I'm about to take a shower." The smile stretched across her face expressed her excitement.

"Go ahead." After washing my hands, I stepped out. Honestly, I was eager to shower myself. I didn't realize how much I missed the luxury until now. Not to mention, sleeping by a huge-ass trash can did not produce a refreshing scent. I wandered toward the front and met the "Good Samaritan" at the stove, cooking.

"Have a seat."

"My name is Prentice." Introducing myself was my way of showing him I wasn't some bum-ass kid—just a young man with an identity who wasn't for no shit.

"I'm Mr. Lewis. I would say nice to meet you. Given your circumstances, I don't know if that's acceptable to say or not."

"Look, man . . . I mean, Mr. Lewis, we dozed off. After today, you won't see us again, so my bad if us being out there inconvenienced you." I relaxed in the chair, folding my arms across my chest. I was not in the mood for a lecture or sarcasm.

"What you running from?" He turned, placing a nice stack of pancakes on the table.

Instantly, my stomach took on a mind of its own and began doing somersaults and rumbling like crazy. Mr. Lewis glanced at me and chuckled before walking back over to the stove. I can't lie. Embarrassment is an understatement of what I was feeling. My damn stomach was performing as if it were a college marching band. The growling, the instruments, and the somersaults were the damn dancers. Within seconds, he was placing sausage and bacon on the table next to the pancakes. Self-control was a mothafucka at this point, but there was no way I'd eat before Aúrea.

"You gon' answer my question?" he challenged, looking me straight in the eyes. I don't know why I hadn't

noticed it at first, but OG reminded me of Uncle Phil
from *Fresh Prince,* a shorter, darker version. Anyway,
the resemblance was there.

"Who said we were running from something?"

"You gotta be, two kids as young as y'all. What, you
two can't be any older than 16 or 17? And you haven't
been on the streets that long. I know because you both
still look healthy, still got a little weight on your bones.
I've been around the block more than a few times and—"

"*And* you don't know us. Look, if this gon' turn into an
intervention or interrogation, we can leave."

"Noo, baby, I wanna eat. Ooh, thank you, mister. This
food looks so good." Aúrea entered in the middle of our
conversation.

Her timing couldn't have been worse. I was ready to
go, seeing where this was heading. Now, we wouldn't
be going anywhere. She walked to the side of the table
closest to the stove where he was standing. Like light-
ning, I grasped her arm, directing her to the other side.
Not roughly, of course. Mr. Lewis seemed cool, but I was
protective of Aúrea. If he were to attempt some slick shit,
he'd get to me before reaching her.

"It's fine, young lady. I made plenty of food. These
omelets are almost done. Soon, you'll be able to dig in.
By the way, my name is Mr. Lewis."

"Nice to meet you. I'm Aúrea," she introduced herself
in that friendly-ass voice of hers. She always sounded
like she was flirting when she wasn't. I knew it was just
one of the shortcomings of her upbringing, but I hated
that shit.

"Babe, that shower felt *so* good. You sure you don't
want to take one?"

I could have sworn she turned her nose up like she was disgusted or some shit.

"Nah, I'm gon' wait 'til we get to our next destination." I probably did stink. We slept next to a trash can, and for the past four days, we were sleeping where we could and taking ho baths. Four days ago, I committed to leaving with her. We had taken the bus to a city about three hours from our hometown, a bus station where we were sure my mother and her foster parents wouldn't find us. Besides, knowing my mother, she had an APB put out on me after the first twenty-four hours I'd been gone. I wouldn't put it past her to tell authorities Aúrea kidnapped me.

"It's fine, Prentice, I don't mind. Have at it," Mr. Lewis offered, calling me by my first name like we were cool and shit.

"I'm good," I responded with finality. Neither of them said anything about it to me again. I wasn't leaving Aúrea alone with him or any other man. He seemed all right; actually, he came off as a solid dude, but it took more than a hot meal to gain my trust.

Mr. Lewis placed a short stack of omelets on the table before telling us to eat up. Aúrea wasted no time filling her plate and digging in. I knew she had to be hungry. Hell, I was too, but damn. Her plate was lightweight embarrassing. Plus, she only left me with a little bit. It wasn't the amount of food on her plate that bothered me. Seeing her so hungry, not being able to provide for her fully, is what got me. We had only so much money to our name, and we were trying to get to California. We had to budget. The four days we'd been gone, we'd eaten just enough to get us through the day.

"Y'all eat up. There's more on the stove if you want it. I have to go straighten up the front before my place opens."

I nodded my head, and Aúrea thanked him again before he walked off.

"He seems nice, babe. Maybe we can get him to give us . . . well, loan us a few dollars."

My head shot up toward her so fast it was a miracle it hadn't dropped from my neck onto the floor.

"Is you crazy? That man is feeding us, and he doesn't have to. Now, you talking about getting some money? Nah, we straight. We don't need his money." I gave her a look that said, drop it. The dissatisfied expression on her face hurt. Still, I wasn't backing down.

I used my fork to cut a piece of my omelet and put it in my mouth. If this wasn't the best egg, ham, cheese, and some other stuff mixed in, I don't know what was. I was hungry, but my taste buds never lied. This man's food was like an explosion in the mouth, a good one—no homo. We ate, avoiding small talk. The echoes of our smacking were noise enough.

"Hey, Mr. Lewis, this food is amazing," Aúrea told him as he strolled back into the area where we were seated.

I watched as she got up and sexily stepped over to him. I know she has some wide hips, but my eyes weren't playing tricks on me. She was swaying those hips extra. When her ass brushed up against him, I was ready to flip. I knew what she was doing. One, I had already told her not even ten minutes ago that getting anything further than this meal was a no. Two, I wasn't in a relationship with a ho. Unintentionally, I slammed my hands on the table. It was the only thing I could do to simmer my frustration.

"Aye, let me speak with you real quick, Prentice," Mr. Lewis said to me, moving further away from Aúrea. He did so noticeably, and I respected that.

"Wait right here." I stood from my chair and followed Mr. Lewis to the front of his establishment. Instantly, I was mesmerized by the Harlem Renaissance vibe of the room. Yeah, I was on the run with my girl, but I was far from dumb. School was my thing. My 4.0 GPA confirmed it.

"I'm not trying to tell you how to live your life. However, I do want to tell you what I've observed. You tell me if I'm wrong." He paused, I guess, waiting for me to reply, so I nodded for him to continue.

"You aren't running from anything . . . but *she* is," he nodded his head in the direction of the back as if I didn't know who he was talking about. "You're very protective of her, which is how I came to my conclusion. I should have noticed it at first since you were asleep in front of her outside. It was also how you pulled her toward you when she came out of the restroom that gave it away. So you're running with her?" he asked again.

Instead of lying or answering him verbally, I shrugged. Figured if he knew so much, he'd come to his own conclusion, anyway.

"Like I said, I've been around the block more than a few times. We both know that I'm right. I respect you for trying to respect y'all's privacy. Let me tell you something I know, without a doubt, young man. You are not helping or protecting her by running. Young women like her will be running their whole life until they receive real help. Help that you can't give her. Whatever she's dealing with will eat her alive before she's able to bounce back. That's *if* you don't convince her to get the help she needs now. That girl will be running for a long time, and you can't change that, but if you take the journey with her, it will change *you*. If you care, and I can see that you do, don't help fix her situation by showing her it's okay to run. Fix it by teaching her it's okay to stay and fight." He stopped speaking, walked over to the cash register, and opened it.

"This is in case you decide to keep going. I hope you choose to do the right thing. That young woman in there is not a lizard. She won't be able to heal what's been chopped off, alone. She needs a team of people who care to share in her healing process, starting with you."

It took everything in me not to cry or acknowledge aloud that he was right—because he *was* right. I also made a promise to Aúrea that I had to keep. So against my better judgment, I pocketed the money he gave me and vowed to repay him one day. He nodded at me. I wasn't sure if it was a nod of approval or disappointment, and that bothered me. This stranger's support meant something to me. Hopefully, my next move would make us all proud.

# 3

## *Aúrea*

"Why are you slowing down? Our new life awaits," I sang, pulling Prentice by the arm. Suddenly, he seemed to be dragging his feet as if he were pulling a chain of bricks by the ankles.

"Aúrea, we need to talk," he said, pulling me back. I turned to face him, and his worried gaze scared me.

"Wh . . . What?" I stammered as a bunch of unfavorable scenarios flooded my mind. Something about his approach concerned me, and in a panic, I began scanning the area. Did someone spot us? The police? A family member? I wondered, looking around for a familiar or unpleasant face as my heart beat in my chest like conga drums.

"Babe, look at me."

His demanding yet gentle tone regained my attention. As I peered at him with questioning eyes, he took my hand and pulled me toward a nearby wooden bench. Sitting didn't equate to anything good. Still, I followed his lead as I had been doing and sat down.

"What's up?" I attempted to sound confident. Like, whatever he was about to say to me, I could take on the chin with no problem—even though I was doubtful as hell I could. I don't know what it was, but this was the first time since we'd left home days ago that I doubted this journey we were on.

Since leaving the restaurant, he'd been quiet. I was talking his ear off as always, and he hadn't said a thing. Not too unusual because when I ran my mouth, I hardly let anyone get a word in. But he knew how to shut me up. Or would at least try. He hadn't this time, and that indicated a problem. One I didn't care to see—until now. Excitement clouded my judgment, and now my gut told me that excitement was about to take a backseat. If there were one thing I knew, it was that my gut never steered me wrong when it came to fuck shit.

"Running to California isn't going to fix anything, A."

"I'm going to California, Prentice."

"Listen to me. You know I'll do anything in the world for you, would even die to protect you. But if we run, we're not making Von pay. We're only leaving the opportunity open for something else to happen . . . probably to someone else." His eyes were low like he'd smoked some good Cali Kush. Only that and agony could produce such dullness. Agony was the reason for the sadness in his eyes, which could be fixed if he stuck to our plan.

"I *tried* fighting, remember? A black eye I had to lie about. Then I tried again. Tried to get help, and nope, nothing." I shrugged. The day I attempted to tell my guidance counselor about Von came to mind. It was only last year, and she was no help. A victim basher, if anything. So if someone who was paid to help kids like me didn't care, no way someone else would care for free. "This is what will work. Besides, who'd believe a teen who stays getting in trouble and has had the fast-ass little girl reputation since junior high school? I'll pass," I said, yanking my hand away from him. However, he wasn't having that and pulled it back.

"I believed you. My mom would believe you. All you need is a support system, and you got that with me."

Those hazel eyes of his always got me. It was like looking into them made the world appear better.

Become better.

In his eyes, everything was perfect and would be okay. Just not this time.

"Tuh! Even your mother only sees what people say about me. She's not trying to help me or get to know me."

"She will. I will make her. She isn't mean to you all the time, either," Prentice defended.

"She tolerates me for you. I don't know what that man said to you at that restaurant. He doesn't know you, and he doesn't know me, so he can't give advice on our lives. We have a plan. I'm sticking to it. You promised you would too." I scanned his face, focusing on his lips, hoping they would expel the only answer that mattered to me.

"It has nothing to do with anyone else. I feel like a bitch if I run instead of handling this like a man. I'm supposed to protect you, and running ain't doing that," he raised his voice.

I jumped. I had this thing about loud voices. Being yelled at the majority of my life should've had me accustomed to loud noises. I wasn't, though, because when someone yelled at me, it never meant me any good.

"Oh, shit, babe, I'm sorry." He pulled me into his arms, hugging me securely. "I'm sorry," he whispered in my ear as silent tears escaped from my eyes.

We remained there, at least five minutes, him holding me, apologizing, as my tears stained his shirt. The fast beating of my heart echoed through my ears as he took the initiative and broke our embrace, taking my face into his hands.

"Look at me," he ordered, and as much as I didn't care to, I did. To my surprise, he had tears in his eyes, as well.

"I love you. I got you. Just stay with me. We'll work this out together," he pleaded while my mind was screaming, *Hell no*. I shook my head defiantly.

"You trust me?" he questioned. I nodded because I did, even though he wasn't my favorite person right now. "Then allow me to fight this battle with you instead of running."

"Nothing good will come from that. I'll end up in another home. Probably worse . . . or a group home where they'll treat me like I'm in prison. At 18, they'll throw me to the streets. I'm taking my life into my own hands now. The system ruined my life. There's no win for me, even if we get rid of Von. I love you, Prentice, and I am extremely thankful for you, but I'm not going back. It was unfair to ask you to leave when you're not the one with the issues. You have nothing to run from, only a future to run to. You should just let me go."

I felt pieces of my heart break with each word I spoke and fall into the pit of my stomach. I felt sick, but I had to do what I had to do. I wasn't new to making hard decisions. Truthfully, if everything would have gone as planned, I'd wonder what trick God was playing on me or what lesson he was trying to teach me. I didn't feel worthy of a happy ending but was damn sure trying to have one, though. Running gave me an opportunity that staying wouldn't provide. So it was a chance I was willing to take, even if it meant losing Prentice.

"You're serious?" he checked with furrowed brows.

"I am."

His head dropped in defeat, shielding his eyes. I knew he was hurt. So was I. Unlike him, I learned to live through the pain. Nodding, he dug inside his pocket and pulled out a handful of money.

"This is all the money we have—a little over $1,500. I'm going to get shit straight here; then I'm sending for you. *If,* by then, you don't want to come back, then I'll come to you." Sobbing, he forced out every word. I knew he meant what he said or wanted to mean it.

Taking the money from his hand, I dropped it into my purse before wrapping my arms around him and kissing him deeply until we both needed to come up for air.

"Come on." Taking him by the wrist, I led him toward a Porta Potty.

"Why are you bringing me in here?" He frowned. A stench filled the air, but seeing as he'd only done a quick washup before we left the restaurant after I begged him to do so, he didn't smell that great either.

Ignoring his question, I grabbed the buckle of his pants, unfastening them as I placed my lips on his. Massaging his manhood, I couldn't help hating that in a few years, when it grew a little more, another girl would get to enjoy him, and she would absolutely fall in love. At 17, Prentice was packing. This I knew because, against my will, I'd been able to experience the girth of a grown man.

"You want to do this in here? I'd never—"

I cut him off. "Yes, I do. Please don't ruin this moment with words."

Even though he smelled a few stenches better than a garbage truck, I wanted the last time I slept with someone to be consensual. I also needed to feel him, to hold me over, since there was no telling when I'd see him again—*if* I saw him again. I dropped my pants, panties included, turned, and placed my hands in a frisk position against the wall in front of him. Glancing over my shoulder, I could tell he was battling with his lust and morals. Those morals were going to lose. I was making sure of it. This was the last time we'd be together, and I wanted to feel him inside of me once more. He was the only guy I yearned for, which meant a lot. It said a lot. With Prentice, I had a choice.

I hiked my ass up, thrusting into him. He got the point. As lust won, he slipped into my warm silky walls, stroking my insides. It didn't last long, but still, it was worth it. Still satisfied to feel him this final time, I cleaned off with toilet paper before heading to get my bus ticket. We sat in the lobby holding hands, not speaking until the mention of my bus over the intercom.

"Prentice, it's time for me to go." With my right hand, I held it on the right side of Prentice's face. Our eyes bore into each other's as we both were silently engraving each other to memory. I didn't want to forget his hazel eyes, even though they were currently full of remorse. Or his perfect nose and full lips.

"I don't want you to."

"I know, but you can't stop me." My tone was as gentle as it could be with such a harsh truth as I removed my hand from his face.

"You call me when you get there. Don't get comfortable, either. I'm coming for you," he declared, embracing me, kissing my forehead.

"I know." I exhaled. "I hope you know I love you." I wasn't sure if I was trying to remind him or if I was confessing my love. Either way, I meant every word I spoke. I did love him. I do love him, which is why I was letting him go.

# 4

## *Prentice*

With my head hung low, feet dragging, I continued aimlessly on my path. I didn't know where I was going. As a matter of fact, I didn't know anything, not since Aúrea left, taking my heart with her. The minute the bus pulled off, regret consumed me, seemingly swallowing me whole. I couldn't think straight or even focus. The only thing I was sure of was, so far, every promise I made to her I had broken. Like a fucking failure was how I felt. Aúrea was going to do what she wanted, regardless. I knew this about her, admired this about her. Even with that in mind, I didn't fight for her.

The sun was beginning to set as I proceeded to walk with no plan or destination in mind. I found myself bumping into stranger after stranger, not offering an apology for the shit either. It was crazy nobody cussed my ass out or ran up on me for the blatant lack of respect. Then again, if I looked as bad as I felt, they probably felt sorry for me. Probably figured I was a kid who didn't have a soul in the world to call his own. They damn sure would've been right about that.

"Hey, Prentice? Back already, huh?"

I recognized the voice, though it didn't sound as sure and authoritative as it had the first time I heard it. As tempted as I was to ignore it, I couldn't. The same restaurant from earlier with the same guy from before was where I ended up. How ironic is that? We stared at each other, both standing outside of his place of business. His comment was a joke. It had to be intended to make me laugh when, right now, there was nothing funny. Crazy how fast life humbled me. It's what had me choosing to remain silent until my growling stomach betrayed me once again. And just like before, he was concerned, worried about me, when I didn't deserve his sympathy.

"Get in here and have something to eat," he instructed.

I hesitated before ultimately going inside. I wasn't in the mood to challenge Mr. Lewis. I was left behind for a few minutes while he headed to the back. When he returned soon after, he motioned for me to take a seat.

"I got them in there cooking something for you now."

"'Preciate it," I mumbled.

"What happened to Aúrea?" His eyes bore into me before he glanced around, assuming he thought she'd show up.

With nothing to say, all I could do was hide my face in my hands. It was the only thing I could do to avoid breaking down like a little bitch in front of another man. Bad enough I'd done the shit in front of Aúrea. Him? Couldn't do it. That was a type of embarrassment I couldn't handle.

"Is she okay at least?" he asked, and I could tell he cared. Only knowing us briefly, he cared what happened to us.

I exhaled, aware that I wasn't getting out of the conversation. I nodded, using my thumb and middle finger to collect the moisture building in the corners of my eyes.

"I gave it to her. All of it." I stretched my arms across the table, almost as if he could look at them and see how empty I was . . . my pockets included.

"That's fine."

"I'm going to pay you back," I reminded him, not wanting to look like the boy who came around for donations.

"I don't doubt it." He paused. His facial expression changed like he was trying to think of what to say next. It wasn't a long contemplation either. "Prentice, I can tell you're a good young man. Whatever you're going through, whatever you did or didn't do, isn't meant to break you. It's a stepping-stone into the next level of your life. This is simply a lesson, no matter how hard of a lesson it may seem."

"I guess." I could only shrug because he had no idea what I was going through.

"A hard head will always make a soft ass, young man. I know you wanted to help and save her. You cannot make decisions for her or anyone but Prentice. Quit being down on yourself. I promise once you do that, everything will fall into place. You don't see it now, but this all worked out exactly how it was supposed to."

I sucked my teeth, shaking my head at this fool. How was I feeling like this and her being out in the world alone for the best? How would this shit work itself out?

"How'd you meet her, anyway? You two seem like fire and ice. Heaven and hell." He chuckled, trying to make light of the grave situation.

"Opposites attract, don't they?"

"That's how the saying goes. I'd like you to elaborate, though."

I studied him, wondering if telling him anything further about Aúrea and me was a smart choice. We weren't his business . . . didn't know him from a can of paint. Yet, I could tell that Mr. Lewis genuinely cared. I felt this fatherly vibe from him. I wasn't an expert on that shit, 'cause my pops dipped years ago. Still, something told me I could talk to him. At least about something as simple as Aúrea and my meeting.

"Me and my mom had moved to Denver, into our own place, after having lived with my grandma down South. It was in the middle of my sophomore year. I wasn't looking to make friends or meet new people 'cause I hadn't wanted to leave behind the ones I had. Typical teenager stuff, I guess. Then she came along."

I smirked, remembering it as if it were yesterday. Aúrea was wearing a pair of shorts not too short, but because she was thick, they looked like she would pop out of them at any moment. She wore a grey Mickey Mouse T-shirt tied in the front, revealing her flat stomach and belly button. On her feet were some grey and black high-top Vans. Her hair was pulled into a ponytail on top of her head, broadcasting her beautiful, blemish-free face with its almond-colored complexion. I remember thinking, *Damn, she's the prettiest girl I've ever seen.*

"It took me some time to get up the nerve to holla at her. It wasn't until we slammed into each other at the corner store near our homes that I got the nerve to speak to her, and we clicked. She lived a couple of blocks from me, and it took that day in the corner store to build our friendship."

"Most great love stories start like that," he smiled.

"Can I ask you something?"

"Anything."

"What do you think about Aúrea?" Why did I care? I don't know. Maybe I needed one adult in my life to say something good about her—one person to see in her what I saw.

"I don't know her enough to judge. What I got from a first impression is . . . She has the potential to be amazing. I can see why you care about her and want to protect her."

He didn't say a lot, but I'd be damned if the little he said didn't mean something to me. To know he saw something in her like I did confirmed what I'd known all along. She was worth it. I knew her authentically. She allowed me in like she did no other. Aúrea had dreams. Goals. Heart. She also had pain and a lot of it. What she was dealing with at home, she hadn't just come out and told me, even when there was occasional bruising, bags underneath her eyes, and worry lines doing their best to imprint her forehead permanently. With all the obvious signs, something was going on. It still took time for her to tell me.

"Can I ask you something, now?" Mr. Lewis countered. I nodded my head, looking him in the eyes. "Why did she need to run?"

I didn't want to betray Aúrea's trust by telling him her business. I also didn't want to break the bond we were seeming to build by not being straightforward with him.

"She was having issues at home. Well, at her foster parents' spot. She turns 18 in two weeks, so she decided to dip early."

"Okay." He nodded.

I was grateful for him to leave it at that. "I know I was acting up before, so thank you. For real." How could I not let him know that I appreciated him? He'd looked out for me, way more than he had to. Displayed more of a caring spirit and personality than I've witnessed in a while.

"Don't mention it. You're a good kid. You'll do good things . . . only if you stop running and go home."

"Won't be running anymore. What I plan to do next requires me to be home and get on my sh—I mean, get my stuff together," I told him, and I wasn't lying. I was going to get to Aúrea eventually, and I was going to get Von's ass as well. Both were going to take time, so I had to plot and plan effectively.

# 5

## *Aúrea*

My head practically slammed against the cold window, jolting me out of my sleep due to the bus coming to what felt like an abrupt stop. The entire drive was a bumpy one because the driver swerved as if he'd been drinking the whole trip.

"Last stop, Los Angeles, California," the driver announced, and it felt as if my heart leaped in my chest. Nervousness and excitement were the two emotions flowing through me until I focused my attention outside the window. I didn't see the Hollywood sign nor any fancy lights or well-dressed people walking up and down the street. The view I had in front of me was nothing like I'd seen in the movies. Instead, I saw a raggedy building and few people moving around with luggage. I silently prayed this wasn't all L.A. had to offer. I mean, I knew it wasn't, but from the inside, looking out of this bus, it was discouraging.

Removing my phone from my pocket to check nothing other than the time, I, instead, was bombarded with text notifications, all from Prentice. He was checking on me, wanting to make sure I had made it safely. He also apologized again while telling me he loved me and to remember he was coming for me. And those were

only two of his messages that I read. The rest I ignored.
Reading the rest would continue to remind me what I left
behind—him, in particular, which was for the best, no
matter how bad it hurt. I also believed he would come for
me if he knew where to look. L.A. was a large city, and I
planned to keep my whereabouts unknown once I figured
out where I was going. Maybe I would send for him once
I became the star I was born to be.

Until then, I had to act as if he didn't exist, starting
with not replying to his text. Placing my phone back into
my jacket pocket, I stood and made my way off the bus
and waited at the side for the driver to open the cargo
compartment of the bus to unload my large duffle bag.
Standing on the curb, I gauged my extremely disappointing surroundings. I had to have been dropped off in the
hood because there was nothing clean about this area.
Homeless men and women, as well as what looked to be
hookers, lined the opposite side of the street. The bright
orange lining the sky let me know the sun was soon to set,
and I wanted to be off this street before it happened.

"Excuse me. Are you from around here?" I walked
up to a girl who didn't look much older than me. I was
aware asking a stranger any kind of question was risky,
but I was desperate. Besides, she didn't look crazy, nor
like a streetwalker, so I hoped I made the correct decision.

"Yeah, what's up?" she smiled at me, and I felt relief
wash over me.

At least she's nice . . . so far.

"Are there any hotels in the area not too costly and
willing to take a very-close-to-legal-aged young lady?"
She turned her nose up, not like she was in disgust, more
so as if she were in deep thought.

"Um, there is. I'm not sure if you'll like it, nor if it's even safe. But any hotel on this street should let you get a room."

"Thank you. Um, can you tell me a better area also? This is only for the night."

"Well, it's not gonna be the best area, but much better than this. Try the Figueroa area."

"Thank you so much."

"No problem. Be safe." She smiled right as a vehicle pulled up, and she got inside.

I removed the pocketknife I had and held it in my right hand as my left held tightly to my duffle. I was uncomfortable as hell but didn't want to get jacked, either. With my head held high, I started up the street trying to look confident, even though I was scared shitless.

The first hotel I walked up on was called Super 7, and it had entirely too much traffic. Men and women were hanging in the front, so I kept going, moving my legs as quickly as possible, ignoring catcalls which I wasn't sure if they were for me or not because I didn't bother to look back. I continued up for another block and decided to stop at Motel 6. Walking up toward the front door, I immediately recognized there was no one at the front desk. There weren't any people hanging around in front, which was significant enough for me to go inside and try my luck. When I pulled back the door, and it opened, I blew out the breath I'd been holding.

As I stepped inside, the office was eerily quiet.

Slowly, I made my way to the counter and rang the bell, hoping that it wouldn't take long for someone to come out and help me. It didn't take long for someone to respond to the bell. Heck, I heard whoever it was approaching before actually seeing them. The sounds of the sole of a shoe fighting to lift from the floor made its entrance before the short, white-haired man.

"Hi, do you have any rooms available? I only need it for the evening." I asked as sweetly as possible as he stared at me skeptically.

"You have ID?" His accent was strong, and his tone firm. His Asian ethnicity was apparent, but for some reason, I didn't expect him to sound so, well, I assumed he'd talk like me. Nodding my reply, I went into my purse, removing my identification from my wallet, and waited with bated breath as he examined it.

"Only one night?"

"Yes, tonight only." I'm sure my desperation showed through my pleading eyes and shaky voice. The sun had gone down in the short amount of time I'd been standing here, and walking the streets right now was not something I wanted to do. I'd find somewhere in the back of this hotel to sleep before risking being picked up by a pimp or pervert.

"Okay. One night, fifty dollars. You check out at eleven, no later."

"I promise I will. Thank you." Taking a fifty-dollar bill from my right sock, I gave it to the man, waiting for him to get me my room key. He looked at me oddly, more than likely because of where I retrieved the money. That was Prentice's idea. He knew the money he gave me was all I had to my name and would be it until something worked out for me while here. He explained that the first thing someone would go for would be my bag if anyone tried me. Knowing he was right, there was no hesitation to put the money in my sock as he suggested.

"Room 201. You be careful. Lots of bad people out there," he said as he handed me the key.

"I will. Thank you. Um, how do I get to the room?"

"You go up the front stairs right there." He pointed to my right. "Never the back because of bad people."

Nodding in understanding, I thanked him again, then made my way toward my room. Now I understood why this hotel seemed to be empty. Everyone hung out in the back. That's probably where he had been, watching them to make sure no one was doing anything crazy enough to warrant the cops.

My room was the second door from the steps. I looked over my shoulder multiple times before inserting the key and opening the door. There was no shame in my paranoia, and I refused to open the door—only to be shoved inside by an unwanted guest, so as quickly as I opened the door, I shut it behind me. I found the light switch pretty fast because most hotel layouts were the same. Besides the bed, a desk and chair were next in my line of view, so dropping my bags, I took a few steps, removed the chair, and planted it underneath the doorknob. Unless they broke the window, no one was getting into this room. Feeling slightly more comfortable, I picked my bags up from the floor, placed them on the bed, and sat beside them. My phone vibrating in my pocket prompted me to retrieve it, and seeing Prentice's face and name flashing across the screen didn't surprise me at all.

"Hello."

"Aúrea. Where are you? Are you okay? Why didn't you text or pick up for me?" He was worried. The way he babbled, sounding out of breath, it was apparent. His tone was also why I didn't want to answer the phone, why I didn't want to speak with him. But my heart, which controlled my finger hitting *answer,* had a mind of its own.

"I'm fine, Prentice. Just needed to get settled."

"Your bus made it almost an hour ago. You were supposed to call me as soon as you got there."

"Prentice," I exhaled, needing a moment. I understood him being worried, but it was I who took such an enormous leap, so his tone and questioning I didn't need right now.

"I'm sorry. This shit is hard, A."

"I know. But if we focus on our goals and what we want, it'll get easier."

"How, when what I want is you? I should've never let you go." His voice cracked. And he sniffled. And I felt my heart shatter.

"I love you, Prentice. You're one of the only people in this world who I love. We did not make a wrong decision with me being here and you being there regardless of whether you believe it. I need you to let me get settled. Trust that I'll be okay. I need to focus, and that's going to be difficult if you keep making me feel guilty."

Silence enveloped us. Surprisingly, he didn't have an immediate comeback. This was fine with me because it gave me the courage I needed to say goodbye again, but this time for the long haul. There would be no calls tomorrow or the next day or the day after that. We would have to learn to live without each other.

"I just want you to be okay and to know that you're okay until I'm there with you, at least."

"I am, and I will be."

"I love you, Aúrea."

"I love you too, Prentice. We'll talk again, okay?"

It was a promise . . . and a lie. The possibility that we'd meet again would always be an option. Hopefully, the stars aligned with me. Only saying goodbye would be for now and not forever.

"All right. Good night." He didn't wait for me to reply before ending the call, and I wiped the lone tear that fell from my eye while doing my best to ignore the aching in my chest. This was really the beginning of my new life.

I lied. Well, because it wasn't intentional, and maybe it wasn't a lie. Still, I didn't do what I said I'd do. So I guess it does boil down to me being a liar.

After my first night here at the motel, I could not find the courage to leave. Fear had reared its ugly little head and left me completely frozen. Mildly frozen. I left the room for a minimum of six minutes to ask for an extended stay and pay for the time extension requested. Today was day two. It was 12:09 a.m., making it another day of me being in this hotel and giving me only a few hours to decide if I would be leaving or paying for another night. As I stared at the time, I sighed. It was not a sigh of disappointment, nor was it a sigh of relief. I wasn't sure how to describe it because the only thing that ran through my mind as I pushed out my breath was what could have been or would have been happening at this time had I been back home. What I was sure of was that I was grateful, even in the midst of fear.

"Aúrea, you didn't come this far *only* to come this far." I reminded myself out loud as if I were advising a girl across from me because she needed not only to hear it but feel it too. And I did. I felt every word finally getting me to relax. I shut my eyes, praying for a sign and some sort of direction. I asked and prayed or prayed and asked until sleep finally came over me.

Yelling and the sounds of glass crashing against something woke me up. I should have been used to the chaotic sounds given where I was, but there was no such luck. People yelling and things breaking, and even some gunfire once or twice still had me shook. Even with the rag-gedy chair against the room door, I knew my safety was questionable.

"Really?" I grumbled after my stomach had done what felt like a triple somersault, double back spring, and a toe touch—if that's how someone describes gymnastic moves.

Slowly, I removed the blanket and threw my legs off the bed, inching toward the window to see what was going on outside and grab my bag to see what snacks I had left. My small food supply was why I didn't need to leave this room, other than to pay for the additional night. I had chips, a cup of noodles, salami, water, and a couple of sodas to hold me over.

As I peeped from behind the brownish curtain, a few people were lingering in front of the hotel, prostitutes and drug addicts, from what I could tell. The sun hadn't fully risen yet, so it was still business for them, as usual. I noticed at the hours the sun flourished, not too much commotion happened around here. Homeless people still lingered, but the pimps and hoes were harder to spot. I assumed that they either got to sleep in or the tricks went straight to the rooms. My stomach growled again, reminding me that food was my second reason for getting up.

Picking up my bag before sitting back on the bed, the weight of it, or lack thereof, let me know I was about to be majorly disappointed. There was no food left, not even a crumb from a chip. And with the way my appetite was set up on top of me being bored, it wasn't surprising that I'd eaten everything. My dilemma now consisted of what I was going to do next. Ordering in was out of the question, as I was sure no one delivered here, and it would bring attention to my room, which I didn't want. Besides, it was early, 6:03 a.m., to be specific. Grabbing my phone, I Googled food places near me and found a McDonald's less than a four-minute walk from here.

"You can do this." My left leg shook rapidly while I tried convincing myself to make the walk right as my stomach growled again, and it was also the moment the lightbulb went off in my head. Last night, a few hours ago, actually, I asked for a sign, a push. This had to be it. God knew hunger would always move me. If I could take this walk to McDonald's, then heading back to the bus station for a cab or Uber wouldn't be so hard. My eyes scanned the room, making sure there wasn't anything too valuable in the open. Positive there wasn't, I packed up the few things there before going into the bathroom to handle my hygiene. Once I completed that, I sat back on the bed, removed my money from my sock, taking only a twenty-dollar bill before putting the rest back. Less than four minutes was all the walk would take, but there was no telling how long I'd be inside waiting. So an executive decision had to be made.

Did I lug all my things or leave them? Taking them all would slow me down, and I couldn't have that. I would take whatever fit in my backpack and hide the rest. Two minutes later, I was out of my room, walking the street, looking like I stole something, or someone was after me. The fear in my body and the swift pace of my feet got me to my destination in two minutes. No one bothered me, thankfully, nor was there anyone around when I left my room. To be safe, I headed into the office first, so I'd appear to be checking out rather than give the idea that I only stepped out. I know I was doing extra and going through many emotions, but this was all new to me. Besides, being alone made me care more about being cautious than sorry.

"Hi, can I get three sausage McMuffins with no eggs, three hash browns, and a large orange juice?" I blurted breathlessly. Power walking took more out of me than expected.

"Anything else?"

I looked away from the cashier, who was pretty in a nerdy way. She was brown, wearing oval-shaped glasses, with a few moles on the right side of her face near her lips.

"That's it."

"Okay, your total is $9.58." She smiled, and I did the same, handed her my twenty-dollar bill and waited for my change.

I took a seat at one of the tables, anxiously waiting for my food due to hunger and worry about the few things of mine left in my room. Removing my phone from my jacket pocket, I checked my social media. Prentice's last post said he was heartbroken, and there was no doubt in my mind he felt that way because of me. We hadn't spoken since the night I asked him to give me space. Not talking daily was not our norm; twenty-four hours of no communication was unheard of. Yet, here we were.

"Welp, that's the end of that," I mumbled as I logged off and put my phone back into my pocket, promising not to check his or my social media for a while. I turned around in my seat, facing back toward the register just as some nicely dressed girl walked in. She couldn't have been from around here as she looked and dressed like someone I'd see on Hollywood Boulevard. Her style was fresh, a mixture of something I'd probably throw together but done so much better. She had on a

pair of black ankle boots, blue jean shorts with black
G stockings underneath. I'm assuming the G stood for
Gucci, but I couldn't be sure since I've never seen a pair
up close. Her shirt was hot pink, and her hair was laid,
not a strand out of place.

"Hey, girl." She turned to me with a large smile and
energetic wave.

"H-hey." Embarrassed, I shrunk in my seat, providing
a wave where I barely extended my arm. Oddly, she
seemed to take that as an invitation to join me.

"I'm Nijah."

"Aúrea."

"Ohh, that's a pretty name. So you're not from around
here, are you?" ·

"Number 97."

Saved by the bell. "That's me." I stood and headed to
grab my food. I intended to run for the exit, but Nijah's
smile and waving me back over stopped me.

"Um, you need something?" I asked, unsure of why
she'd call me back over.

"No, girl, just don't want to eat alone. Wait right here,"
she ordered, standing to grab her food, then taking the
seat across from me again.

"So, Aúrea, where are you from?" she was straightforward. Nijah didn't know me from a can of paint, and yet,
she sat so easily in my presence, starting a conversation
as if we'd be friends.

"I'm from Denver, Colorado."

"Wow, that's far from here. What made you come all
this way?"

"A fresh start."

"I've been there. Starting fresh can be gratifying. So
where you staying? You have family or something out
here?"

As suspect as her questions were, I felt at ease being open. Nothing about her rubbed me the wrong way.

"The motel up the street until I figure out what to do next. No family here, only me."

"Oh no, girl, you have to have someone here. These streets will eat you up and throw you away, especially in this neighborhood. I hardly ever come to this side of town, but my ass was hungry, so it was worth the risk. L.A. traffic was not gonna have me dying in my car from starvation. I do *not* play about my food."

I chuckled because what were the odds of running into a complete stranger who took food as seriously as me?

"I'm not gonna be in this area long."

"You sure aren't because you're coming with me."

"Excuse me?"

"Listen, I have a whole room at my place and no man, so there's no reason you should deny my offer."

"You don't even know me. I don't know you."

"I know enough. You also don't give off serial-killer vibes. You remind me of my younger cousin who lives in Texas, but that's my baby. Anyway, I insist you come and occupy the room rather than some weirdo found on Craigslist that I'll have to kick out in three months."

"I don't have a job. I can't pay to sleep in your spare room."

"You will be able to. So what do you say?"

I stared at Nijah, really doing my best to look through her. I needed to see what was beyond her eyes.

Von's eyes always looked like staring down a black hole. There was never any emotion. Patricia's eyes, my foster mother, always looked tired, and Prentice's were always full of love. If I could only see a glimpse in Nijah's eyes of what I saw in his, my decision would be easy. I'd also know my prayers had been answered. So I stared. Nijah stared back at me, full of patience, some confusion mixed in, but patience, nonetheless.

"I'll go. I still have stuff in my room at the hotel."

"That's fine. Ooh, I'm excited. This is going to be so much fun." She practically jumped out of her seat, bouncing with excitement, making me chuckle.

# 6

## *Aúrea*

A knock on the door caused me to put down the notebook I had been writing my list of goals in before looking toward the door as the knob twisted, and Nijah let herself in. This was nothing new. I'd been living with her going on a year, and since day one, she'd knock once, then walk right on in. Did it annoy me? Sometimes, because she didn't care if I was dressed or not. If she had something to say to me, she was going to walk in here and say it.

This was also her home, and I had yet to pay any real rent, so I could not complain. Now, after I paid like I was staying, I would initiate a talk about a little extra privacy. Outside of her lack of waiting for me to yell, "Come in," Nijah was heaven-sent. She was truly the big sister I wished I had growing up. She listened to me, gave me advice, supported me, and most importantly, didn't judge me when I told her my real reason for leaving home. It took a lot of convincing to keep her from booking a flight to Denver to kill Von herself. Telling her my story had been a gift and a curse. A gift because it brought us closer, and a curse because she became overprotective—overbearing and all; yet, I thanked God for her every day as I don't know where I'd be without her.

"What are you in here doing?" she asked as she plopped down on the bed next to me.

"I was writing out the things I wanted to accomplish this year."

"Yes, then I walked in here at the right time," she squealed, facing me as she crossed her legs Indian style. Nijah's smile could brighten any room, and I often told her that she was made for stardom. She was gorgeous, her personality was everything, and she had a heart of gold. Modeling and acting weren't her things, as she'd often remind me whenever I put the bug in her ear.

"I haven't finished writing them down."

"That's fine because I didn't plan to ask. I am in here about your original goal. You've been here for months, and besides the times I make you leave the house, you don't go anywhere. Since your birthday, we haven't had any real fun, nor have you started this modeling and acting journey that you came here for. You are legal in age now. You've learned the city pretty well, so now, it's time to kick ass."

She gave me this daring look like she knew I would protest or come up with some sort of excuse. To Nijah, that's what I've been doing . . . procrastinating and coming up with more reasons than a little bit as to why I hadn't gone out to pursue my career as an actress yet. What she saw as my being in my own way, I found my reasons to be valid. I had no job, no money, which meant no way of getting the things I needed to start. This is why getting a job was at the top of my list.

"Nahji," I whined affectionately, calling her the nickname I gave her. It also usually worked in my favor when I was ready for her to get off my back.

"Don't 'Nahji' me. It's not going to work this time, especially because I've already spent my money on this photoshoot you have in two hours."

"You didn't." Of course, she did. That was who she was, at least to me.

"I did. Look at it as a late birthday present. Besides, it wasn't as expensive as you think. You're doing headshots. The session is only for an hour, and whatever you get in the hour is what you leave with, so you better be ready to slay the fuck out of the shoot."

"I have nothing to wear, my hair looks crazy, and makeup isn't my thing."

"Do you want to take the pictures or not?"

"You know I do."

"Then get off this bed. Put on that cute dress you wore for your birthday, and I have your hair and makeup covered."

"Thank you, Nahji." I wrapped my arms around her neck, squeezing her as tightly as I could. "I'm going to pay you back."

"It's a gift, remember? But I will take a nice cashier's check when you become rich and famous," she laughed, hugging me back just as tightly.

"You got it." Removing my arms from Nijah's neck, I rushed over to my closet and pulled the cute black midi dress I wore on my birthday. I only wore it once, so it was still in top shape.

After laying it on my bed, I rushed to take a shower, making sure not to wet my hair. Tears of pure gratitude fell as I lathered up with my Caress body soap. Nijah had given me the key. Now it was up to me to open the door. I was going to slay the fuck out of this photoshoot, thankful that she'll be right there to root me on. A tap on the door pulled me from my thoughts as I braced myself for the invasion immediately to come.

"You do not have time for one of your hour-long showers, homegirl. Your hair and makeup are going to take a nice chunk of time, honey."

"I'm coming, Mom."

"Girl, bye." She slammed the door as my laughter carried behind her. She only needed to tell me once to haul ass, so I rinsed and exited, not even a full minute behind her. After drying off, I put on my underwear and robe, then met Nijah in her bedroom.

"So, I was thinking of a soft look to start, and if we have time, I'll add a bolder lip and eye in the middle of the shoot."

"That works. What about my hair?"

"Gonna flat iron it and give you a nice middle part. The point is to show off your beautiful face, so we'll pull it behind your ears to start, then change it up toward the end. I've been watching a ton of YouTube videos. I'm practically an expert on how to direct a shoot. You're going to have flawless photos."

It took her no time to complete my hair and makeup. Getting ready was a two-hour job in itself for Nijah, so to have me ready and flawless, might I add in less than an hour, was pure magic. The studio where my photos were being taken wasn't too far from where we lived, leaving us with a few minutes to spare when we arrived.

"I thought I was only shooting one of you—David, here." A slim yet tall man dressed in black slacks and a black button shirt spoke, approaching us. Once he was in arm's reach, he first extended his hand to me, then Nijah.

"You are only shooting one of us—her." Nijah's tone was clipped, causing me to wonder why she seemed irritated with this guy already.

"Hey, when two beautiful women walk into my studio looking camera ready, it's only right that I ask." He shrugged, then gave me another once-over. There wasn't anything creepy about the way he looked at me, but the lustful stare he gave Nijah let me know that he had to have some sort of crush on her.

"Okay, if you'll follow me this way."

"What's the deal with you two?" I asked Nijah once he walked off.

"Girl, we used to work together when I first moved out here. He's always had a little thing for me, but since he didn't give me a discount on this photoshoot, he can keep dreaming."

"Okay," was my simple reply before the two of us walked over toward the set. There was a white curtain behind a bar stool and lights on each side.

"Okay, Aúrea?" David's face scrunched slightly, letting me know he wasn't sure if he had said my name correctly.

"Yes."

"Good, I thought I was going to mess it up. Okay, so you can take a seat on the bar stool. Don't sit all the way back. Use the edge of it, just enough to where your bottom isn't hanging off. I want your legs turned away from us and your upper torso facing front, if that makes sense."

"I got it." With my head held high and his instructions replaying in my head, I took my seat on the bar stool as directed.

"Perfect."

I sat up straight with my hands in my lap and looked right into the camera. There was no smile on my face, but I was sure to smile with my eyes, as Tyra Banks would say.

"Yes, slay, A." Nijah's excitement forced me to blush right as the camera flashed.

"Okay, so from this angle, your only job is to serve face. Smile, don't smile, smirk, sad face, any and every expression you can think of," David directed, and I performed.

The hour went by rather quickly, and I had taken over fifty photos, which included hair and makeup changes.

"You were truly born to be behind the camera, Aúrea." Nijah practically screamed in my ear as she hugged me tightly before walking over to David.

"Hey, David, what's the best way for Aúrea to find castings and stuff?"

"Go grab one of those papers by the door. It has a list of websites and agencies. I only ask that she uses my name as a referral if she gets anything. It helps me get more work."

"No problem, I will." And I would. I was grateful that he so quickly provided me information that he didn't have to on top of taking some bomb-ass photos of me. Yes, my charisma, face, and being photogenic helped. But his skill with lighting and direction made everything so much better.

"Thanks again, David," Nijah said as she took the envelope of my photos he printed. She grabbed me by the arm, pulling me toward the door, barely letting me thank David as well.

"Girl, it was time to go before he started trying to ask for a date he'll never get. Besides, I want to hurry and get home so that we can check out these photos. Aúrea, you did that."

"Thank you. That was so much fun. I needed that. You have officially lit a fire under my ass."

\*\*\*

"We'll call you." I seemed to hear those three words continually after every audition I walked in. Even with the barrage of compliments I received, "We'll call you" was all I left with.

For the past few months, I've been going to auditions and doing what was called TFP photoshoots. TFP stood for time for prints, so I gave a photographer my time, and they gave me prints. It worked in both of our favor as I could use the pictures for portfolio building. Still, with the few connections I made, I was still struggling to be chosen.

With my folder full of my photos in my hand, I walked into a café not far from the last two auditions I just had. One was for an agent because since things hadn't been working out with me doing this all on my own, I figured getting an agent would help me land some gigs. What I didn't expect was the price tag. Apparently, the agents around here knew that aspiring models needed them more than they needed the model, so they were charging exorbitant prices from their clients and client hopefuls. When the application asked how I would be paying, and "in prayer" wasn't an option, I had to go with the next best thing. The agent would get paid when I got paid. In my opinion, that's how it should work anyway, but as I watched a few men and women shake hands with agents who handed them contracts, I knew the "we'll call you" statement meant I wouldn't be hearing from anyone. When I left there, I auditioned for a commercial. It went well as far as I'm concerned, but I didn't leave with any paperwork again.

"Hi, can I get you anything to drink while you look over the menu?"

I lifted my head from staring at the table and began staring at the waitress. "Sure. Can I get a Sprite?"

"Coming right up," she smiled and walked off.

Since today hadn't gone the way I expected, I made my way to something that would surely brighten my day: food. I'd been gone all morning, only eating fruit because I didn't want to look bloated behind the cameras. So, needless to say, I was starving. Scanning over the menu, I saw that the prices were right within my price range, and everything looked amazing. The crowd in this place couldn't have been for the atmosphere, so there was no doubt I'd find the food excellent.

"Here's your Sprite. Have you had a chance to look over the menu?"

"What's popular here?"

"Girl, everything. We have specials every day. Today is Wednesday, so the special for today is garlic noodles and shrimp with sourdough bread. It's amazing. And because it's the meal of the day, it's way cheaper than it would have been yesterday."

"That does sound good. I'll take it."

"Okay, I'll put your order in."

"Thanks . . . and um . . . "

"Chanelle."

"Chanelle, are you guys hiring?"

"We need to be. I'll send the owner, Ms. Jackie, over here, and she can help you. Between you and me, I hope she does hire you because, as you can see, an extra hand or two won't hurt." She winked at me, then walked off.

It was time for a job. Modeling wasn't going how I expected, and I was broke. Nijah was the reason I had money right now, and I was over getting money from her. It was time for me to face reality. My dream was not going to take off overnight, no matter how ready I was, and I couldn't keep going on auditions without money. It was time for me to put as much effort into job hunting as I had been putting into modeling.

"Hi, young lady. You wanted to meet me?" The most pleasant voice I'd heard in a while grabbed my attention.

"Yes, ma'am." I made my way to stand, which she halted by raising her hand, and instead, she took the seat across from me.

"So, how can I help you?" Her smile was inviting, and she reminded me of a dark-skinned version of Debbie Allen.

"I wanted to know if you were hiring."

"Do you have reliable transportation, and can you adhere to the schedule I set for you? Including overtime?" The sweet tone she used moments ago had transformed entirely to no-nonsense. Ms. Jackie cared about her business, and if I weren't ready to commit, she would not hire me. My foot tapped against the floor as I contemplated my answer. Currently, I had all the free time in the world as I wasn't doing anything but going to auditions and sitting in the house. The downside, however, was most of the auditions I went on were sporadic. Some, I didn't find out about until the night before. If I took this job, that meant I'd have to prioritize it over my dream.

"So, are you still interested?"

"I am. I can get here."

"Okay, I'll grab you an application. Fill it out before you leave, and I can have you on the schedule as early as next week, possibly."

"Thank you so much."

"You're welcome, sweetie. What's your name anyway, and how old are you?" she chuckled, and so did I because those are the two things we probably should have gotten out of the way first.

"Aúrea, and I'm 19."

"Okay, Aúrea, I'm Ms. Jackie, and it's nice to meet you. Make sure you get the application to me before you leave."

"I will."

"Chanelle, give Aúrea the employee discount for her meal," Ms. Jackie told her as she got up from her seat and left.

"Hey, girl, you're in. And your meal is free."

"Huh?"

"That's the employee discount. We get free lunch." Chanelle shrugged.

"Oh, wow, thanks."

"It gets hectic around here, but Ms. Jackie is like a mother to all of us. This is a business, but we're like a little family . . . most of us anyway." She placed my food down, then walked off, quickly returning to bring me the application and a pen. I enjoyed my meal, and since this one was free, I placed a to-go order for Nijah and me to eat at home. Even with things not going as planned today, getting this job was the silver lining.

# 7

## *Aúrea*

Excitement rushed through me as I laid my uniform on my bed. Tomorrow would be my first day working at the café, and I was ready. Finally, I would be making my own money. Nijah never complained nor cared about all the extra help I needed. She helped me and gave to me with no reservations. But at 19 and having lived with her for over a year, I needed to make my own money and take care of myself.

My cell ringing caught me off guard. No one called me because only Nijah had my number. I'd terminated my Colorado number, opting for a California one because this was home now. Changing my number was also my way of making sure to leave everything and everyone behind me. Prentice had reached out, and I ignored him. This was extremely hard to do because I wanted to tell him all about Nijah and how she invited me to live with her, but I knew he would want to come here, something I knew he couldn't do. So to avoid it, I avoided him, then changed my number, which, in a way, erased him.

I saw the 213 area code, and my brows furrowed in confusion as the number was not familiar to me at all. Curious about who was calling, I hit *answer*.

"Hello."

"Hi, I'm looking for a Ms. Aúray Shepard." the woman's voice on the other end of the phone was pleasant, though she also sounded unsure of the pronunciation of my first name. That was likely due to how she'd just butchered it.

"This is Aúrea," I politely corrected before releasing a light chuckle. No one had called me Aúray before. Not everyone got my name right, yet this woman's pronunciation was a first.

"My apologies. Aúrea, that's very pretty."

"Thank you."

"Well, my name is Katherine, and I'm calling from Gates Studios, where you auditioned about a week ago for the clothing commercial."

"Yes, I remember." My lips had spread so wide that the corners were possibly inches from my ears. I had no clue what this woman wanted, but my gut told me she wouldn't be calling if it wasn't for something good.

"Great. Well, the casting director loved you and would like to give you the job."

"Really? Yes, yes, I'll take it." My voice had reached an octave even I hadn't known it could extend to. I heard Katherine snicker, and it did not bother me one bit. Hell, she'd laugh until her stomach hurt if she were able to see how I was going to celebrate *after* we ended this call.

"Awesome. The shoot is tomorrow morning. You need to be here at the studio at 7:00 a.m. sharp. You don't need to bring anything other than yourself, as a hairstylist, makeup artist, and wardrobe are all provided."

"Tomorrow at 7:00 a.m.?" My tone was still full of enthusiasm, even though my heart dropped to the pit of my stomach. I start my new job tomorrow, and Ms. Jackie made it crystal clear that she didn't play. No way could I not show up on the first day.

"Yes, will that be an issue?"

"No, not at all. I'll be there. I do have a question, though."

"I'm sure I have an answer for you. It's good to get your questions out of the way now because once filming starts, they'll be less time to ask anything."

"Oh, okay. Well, do you mind telling me what to expect and if there is anything specific I should do?" That wasn't my original question. I wanted to ask how long the shoot would last to gauge how late I would be to my first day of work or if I should call Ms. Jackie and tell her I wasn't going to make it. The way Katherine asked if I was okay with the time frightened me a little. There was no way I wanted her to think that I couldn't show up.

"Sure. The shoots last a few hours, usually. The length of time really depends on how well the shots go. If it takes you too long to catch on, the shoot could last all day. So be sure to pay close attention to everything people tell you to do. You'll be paid at the end of the shoot as well. Oh, and you will also receive a call or email when the commercial airs."

"Thank you. I'm excited." And that was putting my emotions lightly. Hopefully, I'll get to meet her at the shoot. If not, this call was still cool. I really appreciated her taking the time to explain how things should go when I doubt she had to.

"I'll more than likely be the person checking you in. Have a good rest of the day. See you tomorrow."

"Same to you."

Removing the phone from my ear, I looked at the screen to make sure the call had ended. Seeing my home screen, I tossed the phone onto my bed and began dancing like I'd caught the Holy Ghost. Tears immediately began to fall from my eyes, but I did not stop stomping my feet nor waving my arms. This moment I have been waiting for—no matter how bittersweet of a moment it was.

"Girl, what is going on with you?" Nijah asked, inviting herself into my room as usual, minus the knock this time.

With tears still streaming down my face, I turned to her and smiled.

"Um, what's going on? I'm not sure if I need to hurt somebody or have you committed."

Laughing, I used the back of my hand to wipe my tears before walking closer to Nijah, who had the nerve to back away from me. Maybe I *was* looking deranged.

"I did it, Nahji."

"Did what?" Nijah's tone was full of skepticism.

"Got my first modeling gig, and I'm being paid for it." There was no need to make her guess or have her sitting around in any more suspense than necessary. I was too excited to even play around like that. This kind of news deserved an immediate announcement.

"Yes," she screamed and began jumping up and down. "Wait, with whom? What's the job? Tell me everything." Nijah grabbed my hand and pulled me to sit with her on my bed, anxiously waiting for me to give her the rundown.

"Aúrea, that is *big*. I'm so proud of you, and I'm going with you. I will sit my happy ass in the parking lot in my car with no problem."

"Really?"

"If you think I'm missing out on this, you have lost your mind."

"Good. It'll mean a lot to me having you there even if you're not in the building. Knowing you won't be far is comforting. Plus, I'm going to need your NASCAR-skilled driving ass to get me to the café after the shoot."

"Oh, shit, you are supposed to start your new job tomorrow. Are you sure you're going to make it? Maybe you should consider not going or asking for one more day."

"That's not something I can do, Nahji. You've met Ms. Jackie. She don't play, and even if I'm late, it's better than not showing up at all. Letting her down isn't an option. This is only one acting gig. Who knows how long it'll be before I get another. I need to keep this job."

"You're right. Tomorrow is going to work in your favor. You're going to kick ass in the commercial *and* make it to work on time. When you get off work, we'll celebrate." She grinned before wrapping her arms around me, an embrace I not only welcomed but also I reciprocated.

"We have to be there at 7:00 a.m., so I want to get there no later than 6:55."

"We can get there at 6:30. Why you bullshittin'?"

"Thank you, Nahji." Hugging her tighter, I made a mental promise to knock tomorrow out of the park. I was going to slay the commercial and be the best waitress I could be right after that.


Six forty, that was the time on the clock of Nijah's car. I planned to sit with her until that forty turned into fifty, but my adrenaline was booming. I couldn't stop my legs from shaking. My palms were sweaty, and sitting in this seat was becoming harder and harder.

"Girl, just go," Nijah laughed.

"I'm about to. Just pulling myself together."

"You're going to do fine. Go in there and show them they made the best choice."

With my head held high, I exited the car, making my way toward the building with wobbly legs because I still hadn't gotten my nervousness and excitement in order. I coached myself to feel every emotion flourishing through my body because once I got in front of the camera, there was nothing for me to feel other than the character they needed me to be.

"Hello, I'm here for the commercial." I walked up toward the front desk, and a Hispanic woman with deep red hair and heavy makeup, which included a handmade mole above the right side of her lip, smiled at me.

"Aúrea." Her greeting was one of expectation.

"Yes."

"I'm Katherine. Nice to meet you, and you're early. Let's get you to the back so they can start on hair and makeup. Your promptness is going to be appreciated." She stood from the desk, motioning for me to follow behind her.

When we made it into the studio, the setup wasn't different from any other shoot I'd been on. There were curtains, stage lights, chairs, and props. I'm not sure why, but a part of me expected to walk into something much more extravagant.

"Hey, Monica, this is Aúrea. She's here for the commercial." Katherine introduced me to a petite Black girl with a short curly 'fro and flawless makeup.

"Nice to meet you. Have a seat, and I'll get started." She pulled the chair back, and as instructed, I took my seat. There was no small talk, only silence as she stood in front of me and applied my makeup. A few people came in and out of the area where she worked on me, asking my size, and one lady tossed my hair around. She made a comment, which I'm sure she didn't think I heard about being happy that I came with my hair already straightened. That bothered me slightly, but if she were happy about it, I would be too because, hopefully, that meant I didn't have to worry about her burning my tresses with whatever products she used. Plus, she wasn't Black, and though that may not mean much, not everyone knew how to handle the kinks of a Black woman's hair.

"Okay, you're done. I'll walk you over to Annabelle, who will do your hair."

She smiled finally, more so at the job she'd just done on my face than at me. Hell, I smiled too because she had really done well. She didn't cake the makeup on my face, which still gave me a natural look, and I didn't look as if I had aged two years within minutes.

Once I was in the chair for my hair, things changed. Annabelle was a talker and a bit heavy-handed. My hair had come out cute, and she had my baby hairs laid to perfection. Half up, half down was the style she gave me, and it was dope.

"Okay, girlfriend, you look good. Tell Tina she better be careful not to mess up your hair when she has you changing clothes. No, I'll tell her myself. Anyway, you're going to look amazing in front of the camera. The director, Abe, he's a little over the top, but he means well. Follow his directions, and everything will go smooth."

"Thank you."

Annabelle took my hand, practically dragging me to the other side of the room, where clothes were lined up against the wall. I thought Nijah had a lot of clothes. This room looked like its own boutique.

"Hi, I'm Tina. We're going to pick out four outfits for you, and you'll be shooting in all four. We'll start with the more casual look, then go from there. Each change will be fast, so do not get used to the pace we're about to go now. It's not at all what you're going to experience when it's time to switch things up. Got it?"

"Yes." The information she'd given me wasn't hard to understand. She painted the perfect picture that had my ass nervous all over again.

"Okay, let's get you dressed for your first shot." Tina walked over to the rack of dresses, pulling off a navy-blue, thin-strapped maxi dress.

"Do you need a bra? What size do you wear?"

"I'm a 36D. I've been able to go without, so I guess it'll be what you think is best," I shrugged.

"Well, try without first. I'd rather use tape than a bra anyway because of the neckline of this dress. Step behind that curtain over there and put this on." She extended the dress to me before nodding in the direction of the curtain I was to go behind. I removed the romper I had on and my bra, balling them up before throwing them into my tote and slid the dress on. The dress fit snug from my belly button up and hung loosely at the bottom. It was comfortable, and though I had yet to see what it looked like on, I felt good in it.

"Cute! And your boobs still have some perk to them, so no tape is needed. However, when moving around the camera, be mindful of a possible nip slip." she tugged on the straps before giving me one final once-over.

"All right, honey, it's showtime."

"Is this my girl?" A short, white-haired man who looked more like an English professor than a TV director approached, pulling me by the arm, not waiting for a reply.

"Yes, Abe, that's her," Tina yelled, shaking her head as I was whisked away and practically thrown on the set.

"Have fun. I want to see if you're a natural behind the camera. Show me what you got, and I'll see how much direction you need. You got three minutes to impress me." He stepped back and lifted the camera, giving me only seconds to digest what he said.

I shut my eyes, took a deep breath, and got to work, smiling, posing, dancing, acting like I was the only one in the room. The silence made me feel that way. No one said anything . . . not a good job, no little cheer— nothing. I had no idea if I was doing good or not, but I kept going until he told me to stop.

"Not bad. Go change."

Once again, before I could reply, someone whisked me away. Tina took me back into the dressing room, giving me a pants set to put on that I changed into in record time. Once I was back in front of the camera, Abe gave me eight lines to say. "*You too can look good on a budget.*" I recited those lines at least fifty times in each outfit change. When I finished, everyone applauded me, and even Abe said I did a fantastic job. When I made it to the front desk, even Katherine, who I had no idea could see what I was doing in the studio, told me I was a natural behind the camera as she handed me a check for $1,500. It took everything in me to contain myself until I got into the car with Nijah.

"How'd it go?" Her smile was large, like she knew I had done a fantastic job.

"Great! They all clapped for me when it was over."

"I told you. I knew you were going to kick ass."

"Guess how much I got paid?"

"You know I hate guessing."

"You can be a party pooper sometimes, you know that? Anyway, $1,500." My joy had me bouncing in the seat, waving the envelope in the air with my check.

"Oh, look at you, little Ms. Hollywood. *That's* what I'm talking about. They knew better than to give you chump change because, honey, you're a star."

"Nahji, I had so much fun. I can't wait to do it again."

"You will. But I know what you won't do, and that's work for Ms. Jackie if we don't hurry up. We have less than twenty minutes to get you to the *other* side of town. You're going to be late but not *that* late."

"Shit, I almost forgot about starting my job today. This is the one time you won't hear me complaining about how fast you drive," I promised as I crawled into the backseat. Nijah pulled off as I used her backseat to change my clothes. Though she made it to the other side of town in record time, especially for L.A. traffic, my ass was still late.

"I'm sorry I'm late, Ms. Jackie. We left early, and traffic still caught up to us." Nijah was hungry, so she came inside with me. I hoped having her with me made Ms. Jackie go a little easy on me, but I should have known better.

"Looks like you spent time in the mirror that you could have spent on the road. Don't let it happen again, Aúrea." She gave me a look that let me know she was not playing with me.

"I won't."

"Chanelle is going to train you. I need you to catch on quickly because you can't follow her around all day."

"Okay."

"I'm proud of you. We celebrate tonight." Nijah gave me a quick hug before I rushed off to find Chanelle. I didn't lose my job and had the time of my life acting in my first commercial. Today was a good day.

# 8

## *Aúrea*

"I feel like I hardly see you anymore," Nijah complained as I packed my uniform into my bag and gave myself one last once-over in the mirror. I had to work today, *and* I had an audition, so I was pressed for time.

"We still see each other."

"Not like we used to. You've been busy with work and auditioning or sleeping. And I miss you." she poked her lip out while making her way toward me, wrapping her arms around my waist and resting her chin on my shoulder.

She was right. I had been busting my ass at the café and going on more auditions. After landing the commercial over a year ago, I thought that the jobs would be pouring in or that agents would be knocking down my door to work with me, but that was far from my reality. Getting an agent and getting into acting school cost way more than I was making, even with Nijah telling me I didn't have to help with the bills. What I was bringing in still wouldn't be enough. She was fine with that. I wasn't. I couldn't be okay with making money and not helping.

"I'm off this weekend, and I don't have any auditions lined up, so how about we go out and have some fun?"

"You sure you won't be too tired?" She gave me this look that told me she felt like I had unintentionally become the old lady of the house, and maybe I had.

"I could use the extra sleep."

"Like hell, you will. We're going out."

"That's what I thought."

"How are you getting to the audition?"

"Uber."

"I'll drop you off. You can Uber to work."

"Thank you. I'll be ready in five minutes."

"Cool." She left my bedroom, and I made sure to gather everything I needed.

This audition was for a small role in a movie. An extra, to be exact. I more than likely wouldn't have any lines and would only sit and look pretty, but if I got it, it would look good on my résumé. Hell, it would be something else added to my résumé other than the *one* commercial and TFP photos I participated in. At this point, I decided to take what I could get. I was getting older, though I still didn't quite look my age. I *was* older, and that was not going to work in my favor, according to the last photographer I shot with. Once I hit my twenty-second birthday, he told me that I should take a year or more off my age to have a better chance of booking work.

"Ready?" Nijah asked, sticking her head in the door.

"Yup." I grabbed my things and followed her out of the house.

I took her phone and added the address, then sat back with my eyes closed as she drove. Due to the lack of success I'd been having on these auditions, the thrill of the audition was barely there anymore. I tried to remain positive and optimistic, despite my efforts, but it was hard. I had gotten back to the "We'll call you" before I left every door only to, of course, receive no phone call. The laughter and pep talks that Nijah and I used to have on my way to casting calls had diminished at my request. Now, I preferred to sit in silence, talk to God, and talk myself into continuing to try.

"We're here."

Instinctively, I looked at Nijah instead of out of the window because her tone was full of uncertainty.

"What's wrong?"

"Are you sure this is the right place?" she pointed, directing me to look out of the window. At that moment, I saw her concern. There were scantily dressed women hanging around. Some guy had at least three women on his arms, and the building looked nothing like any of the other studios I'd been in. In fact, this was a warehouse of some sort.

"I mean, there are women out who I'm sure are here for the casting," I shrugged.

"I don't feel right leaving you here. If you want to do it, I'll wait, but I also think you may want to let this one go, Aúrea."

"It'll be fine, Nahji. And you don't have to wait for me."

"At least make sure you're in the right place. If this is the place you're supposed to be at, I'll leave you here. If not, I'm dropping your ass off at work."

"Fine. Give me a second."

As I exited the car, the confidence I was portraying on the outside was nothing compared to what I felt on the inside. I was scared shitless, and my gut told me that maybe Nijah was right, and I should take my ass on. But being my stubborn self, I ignored my feelings because getting this part meant more to me than some ill feelings.

"Hey, are you here for movie casting?" I walked up to one of the women who had on more clothing. She was the most dressed out there, and I had more than likely missed her in the slew of women who looked like prostitutes. Though her attire was different, she was too small to stand out.

"Yes. I was nervous that I wasn't in the right place, but the woman inside assured me that I was."

"Thank you." I turned on my heels to head back to the car when she stopped me.

"Are you leaving?"

"No, I'm only grabbing my purse and telling my big sister that she doesn't have to wait for me."

"Okay, good. It was getting boring not having anyone to talk to while I wait."

Offering a look that told her I understood, I made my way back to the car, opening the door to grab my purse.

"This is the right place. I'll be fine. You can go." Her facial expression told me she was not convinced but was going to respect my wishes.

"Call me if you need me. The minute anything doesn't feel right, you get your ass away from here."

"I hear you, Mother."

"When you talk like that, I have no problem leaving your ass."

"Yeah, right. I'll call you when I get in my Uber." I shut the door, then made my way back to wait in line.

"Are they all ahead of you?"

"No, they are waiting for one more girl to come out. When she comes out, I'm next, then you." Right as she said that, the door opened, and out walked a girl whose dress would barely stay above her ass. It was evident as she held it down while she walked. My eyes unintentionally followed her toward the crowd of women as she stopped in front of the guy. From Nijah's car, I couldn't really see what he looked like, but now . . . Damn, was he fine. He had bad boy and stay the fuck away written all over him at the same time. He was very easy on the eyes. When our eyes met, he smiled at me, and every nerve in my body awakened. I hadn't been with a man, well, boy, since Prentice. No dates, no texting, no male connection whatsoever, even though guys had hit on me a lot. Especially at the café. Someone always asked for my number or offered to take me out. For one, I didn't really have time to date, and for two, I didn't feel anything with any of the guys who approached me. I needed to feel some sort of spark to render someone worth the little time I had.

"Are you the only two left?" A lady who looked to be in her midthirties asked, poking her head out of the window

"Yes," the girl whose name I had yet to learn and I replied at the same time.

"Come on then." She instructed both of us inside, and we followed. There was a desk at the entrance and a door right behind it, which she told us to go through. There was the usual white curtain and lights I'd become accustomed to when out on castings.

"You two can wait over there, and Mike will be right with you," the lady advised, leaving us.

We inched our way over to the lit area of the room and waited. Within moments, a huge, dark-skinned man with long dreadlocks came into view. He was dressed in a plaid shirt and blue jeans and loosely held the camera in his left hand. He approached us, looking us both over before he spoke.

"Thanks for coming, but you don't fit the description listed in the casting flyer," he spoke to the girl I'd been waiting with. Though he wasn't talking to me, her confused expression matched mine because there was no description request if I remembered correctly.

"I didn't see one. If you give me a chance, you won't regret it," she practically pleaded.

"We'll have another in a week. Come back then. You'll be perfect for that role." That seemed to make her feel better. Her entire body language shifted, and her shoulders were no longer slouched.

"Okay, thank you. Good luck, girl." She smiled at me, then waved as she walked out of the building.

"What's your name?"

"Aúrea."

"Aúrea, I'm Mike. Let's step over here. I'd like to take a few photos of you if that's okay."

"Sure." I set my bag on the counter before standing in front of the curtain, putting together a couple of mediocre poses while he took my photos.

"I don't think you took a bad photo," he complimented me, putting his camera down and walking closer to me.

"Thank you."

"Aúrea, I'm not sure if you know the kind of pull I have in this industry. I've worked with some of the best. I also know a star when I see one. You showed up to this casting with hopes of becoming an extra, but if you're willing to really put in some work, I can get you a supporting role."

"Of course, I'm willing to work. I don't expect anything to be given to me, I assure you."

"That's exactly what I wanted to hear." Slowly his hand made its way to my shoulder, and I froze. He started massaging my right shoulder, and as uncomfortable as I was, I could not move.

"Can I kiss you?" His question awakened every sense that had shut down on me, jolting me back.

"What? No." My tone wasn't the only thing to show my disdain. My facial expression did as well as I felt how deeply the frown on my face was.

"You just said you were willing to put in the work." He approached me again, backing me into the counter, closing me in with both of his massive arms. Well, massive was putting a lot on his build, but he was still bigger than me, and I felt threatened.

"I didn't think you were talking about anything like this. I'd like to leave now, please." I tried moving his arm, but it wouldn't budge.

"Nah, you knew exactly what I meant. You don't get to play these kinds of games with me. Now, do me this favor, and I'll make you a star." He leaned into my face taking his tongue, gliding it from the bottom of my cheek to the corner of my eye, and I lost it.

"Stop. Get off me." I flailed my arms, screamed, and it only seemed to excite him more. He even had the nerve to pick me up and sit me on the counter.

"Stop, please." Tears were streaming down my face as he tried prying my legs open. Thank God I didn't wear a dress.

"Be quiet. Don't fight it, and I'll make you a star."

"No, let me go." My entire body shook, and my vision was blurred, but I didn't stop trying to get out of his grasp.

"The fuck going on in here?"

Mike froze, backing away from me as I fell to the ground, shamelessly crying my eyes out.

"Nothing. I'm not seeing any niggas for casting today, so you can get up out of here."

"Aye, did he hurt you?" My head was still down, and when I felt a hand on my shoulder, I jumped to my feet, coming face-to-face with the fine-ass man from outside.

With all the reservations I had about him when I obviously prejudged him by only looking at him earlier, right now, I felt safe enough to answer him honestly.

"He tried to."

"Man, that ho's lying. Either way, both of y'all can get the fuck out of my place of business." Mike wasn't intimidated in the least.

I grabbed my purse, pulling it into my chest, and looked at my savior for a sign of what to do. I mean, hauling ass was at the top of my list, but I didn't want to leave without him because there was no telling what Mike would try. Handsome Face nodded before turning and knocking Mike right on his ass. He struck him hard.

"Bitch ass, bet not never catch you trying this type of shit with another woman," he told Mike as he motioned for me to come near him.

"Fuck you and her. She just ruined any chance she ever had working in this industry," Mike yelled, holding his nose, which was leaking blood.

"Let's go." He took me by my elbow, not forcibly, and I walked out with him.

"You all right?"

"No, but I will be, though. Thank you so much. Who knows what would have happened if you didn't come in there when you did."

"Let's not think about that. The worse *didn't* happen because I *did* show up." He smiled, and my heart melted.

"I'm Aúrea." Introducing myself seemed like the right thing to do, given he just saved me from a fucking pervert.

"I'm Adrian, Aúrea. It's nice to meet you. Wish it had been under better circumstances, but the pleasure is still all mine."

I wasn't sure what else to say to him, so instead, I removed my phone from my purse, deciding now was the time to get my Uber. I'd walk up the street a couple of blocks to get as far away from this building as possible.

"You need me to walk you to your car?"

"Oh, I didn't drive. I was gonna call Uber."

"Nah, I can't let you come across any more strangers today. Let me give you a ride. I'll take you anywhere you want to go. All I care about is you making it to your destination safely."

"That's okay, really."

"It's not, so come on." He extended his arm, and without hesitation, I took it. I'm not sure what kind of spell this man had cast on me so quickly, but I was going to trust him to get me to the café safely. From there, I'd have Nijah pick me up. There was no way I would get through a day of work after what I dealt with today.

"Do you know that guy?"

"Who, Mike? Nah, not personally. I mean, he's a big deal and one of the people to see out here if you're looking to make it in Hollywood."

"So, when he said I'd never work, he was actually telling the truth?"

"Pretty much. I mean, he can really make it hard for you to get acting or modeling gigs."

"Well, I guess I'll never work because if whoring myself off is what he or anyone else expects from me, then they are gonna always be disappointed, and I'll always be blackballed." I sat back in the seat of his car and folded my arms across my chest.

"I mean, I know some people and wouldn't expect anything from you. Here's my card. You can also use it to call me just because." He winked, extending the card to me right as he placed his car in park.

"I'll keep that in mind. Thank you again."

"Is this where I can find you?"

"This is where I work."

"All right." He smiled at me again, and, boy, did my knees get weak. I knew right then that this would not be my last time seeing Adrian.

# 9

## *Aúrea*

"And where do you think you're going?" Nijah asked with a huge grin on her face.

I was admiring myself in the full-length mirror in my bedroom when she knocked once and came in. Though we had our talk about giving me a little more privacy, mainly because I was able to contribute to the bills now, it was apparent that old habits would die slow. At this point, I didn't even care anymore. If she stopped, I would probably assume something wasn't right between us.

"On a date, remember?"

"Hmm, I do. And you're going out with hero boy, right?"

"Hero man, because he's older than both of us. But his name, Adrian, will work just fine. He helped me out of a jam. Calling him hero boy or hero period is a bit much."

"It was a joke. Is he picking you up from here?"

"I mean, he can. But I wasn't sure about that, so I told him I would meet him at the restaurant."

"This is your home too. Why would you not find it okay to get picked up here?"

"It's not that." Blowing out my breath, I took a seat on my bed, and Nijah did the same.

"This is all new to me. I haven't dated or had a boy-friend in years."

"Girl, going on a date is like riding a bike. You never forget how to do it. You just have to hop on to be re-minded," she laughed.

"Maybe you're right," I shrugged.

"I know I'm right. Don't overthink it. And make sure you tell him to pick you up from here. I've yet to meet him and need to lay eyes on the man taking my little sister out. Ms. Jackie has made a few comments about him. I need to see if she's right."

"Ms. Jackie is still old school. She's judging him based on how he dresses. He's always respectful when he stops by the café."

"As he should be. Still, Ms. Jackie has seen way more than our eyes can imagine. I'm sure the woman is seasoned, okay?"

"I know you did not just call her old," I laughed.

"That word did *not* come out of my mouth."

"Honestly, I had a few reservations about Adrian, but he kind of wore me down. He gave me his num-ber, which I didn't use, and he still came by to check on me . . . something he didn't have to do. It's like he knew how traumatic that experience could be or had been and wanted to make sure I was okay, genuinely."

"You have a point. Him checking on you is sweet. I don't know; it's not horrible for you to give him a date. I only want you to keep your eyes open."

"I got this. I'm never not following my gut anymore. I could have avoided the whole Mike situation had I left with you that day. When I met him, it was obvious something wasn't right about him, and I should have left. After going through all I did back in Denver, I knew better. But I ignored the signs."

"Shit happens. It's what you do with the lesson that matters." She gave me a reassuring smile before pulling me into a slight hug.

"Thanks, Nahji."

"Anytime. Now, tell that man to pick you up from here."

"Done."

Nijah left my room, and I sent a text to Adrian with our address. He informed me he'd be here within twenty minutes . . . And I'd never known twenty minutes to go by so fast. I didn't want Nijah to have enough time to ask Adrian a whole lot of questions, so after introducing the two, I ushered him out of the house. He took me to a nice restaurant in downtown Los Angeles, and the food was delicious. Our conversation flowed smoothly, and I was really enjoying myself, so much so that now that we were sitting in front of Nijah's and my home, I didn't want the night to end.

"I had a good time." I turned in my seat, looking Adrian directly in his handsome face. Those eyes of his were so mesmerizing. I could get lost in them and not be in a hurry to find my way back.

"So did I. Hopefully, this means you don't plan on running from me anymore," he grinned.

"I wasn't running from you. My focus has been work, that's all. Focusing on that is easier than thinking about other things."

"You know that dude won't ever fuck with you again."

"Yes, I'm sure of that. But he is still in my way. I won't be able to get any casting jobs out here because of him, and it was hard enough trying on my own without any kind of reputation."

"I told you not to worry about that either. I got you if you let me."

His words sounded sincere, but I didn't know anything about how much pull he actually had in the industry. He would have to show me.

"Aúrea?"

The delicacy in his tone as he called my name made me shudder in a good way.

"Yes."

"Can I kiss you?"

The last time I was asked that question, I was almost a rape victim again. Those words grossed me out and made me want to run away in fear. Oddly, this time, all I wanted to do was let him.

"Yes."

Adrian wasted no time, gently taking me by the chin and placing his soft, full lips on mine. His kiss started slow, a couple of pecks to gauge my comfort, I assumed, before going in. Once his tongue entered my mouth and brushed against mine, I thought I would lose it. He had my body on a level of fire it never experienced before. Then he pulled away.

"You should probably go inside." He tried adjusting his pants subtly, but I saw him, even saw the bulge in them too.

"If it's okay, I'd like to go with you." Where did those words come from? The voice didn't sound like mine, but only two of us were in this car, and his lips weren't moving.

"Nah, that's not what you want, and I don't want you to feel like you have to do anything with me."

"It is, and I don't. Let's go."

Adrian started the car and pulled away from the curb, proof that I didn't have to ask him twice. Truthfully, if he hesitated any longer, I would probably change my mind and take my ass in the house where I probably should have been going anyway. My legs shook the entire ride. To say I was nervous was an understatement. Underneath the nervousness, excitement brewed too.

"We're here." I looked up at the nice brownstone home as he parked in front. Adrian exited the car first, walking to my side and helping me out.

"You live here alone?" It seemed like a lot of house for only one person.

"Yeah," he chuckled as I looked around the living room. Furniture was there, but the walls were bare. The typical male pad, I guess. I didn't get to look at much else as he took my hand and led me to the back of the house where his bedroom was.

From the moment my feet hit the carpet of his room, Adrian was on me. He gently lay me on his bed, hovering over me, alternating between pecking my lips and gazing into my eyes. This man had me on the verge of climaxing, and he hadn't penetrated me yet. I couldn't tell if my yearning for him came from not being with a man in years or if Adrian really made me feel that way.

"Is something wrong?"

"Nah, I'm just thinking that if we do this, you're mine, and I'm yours."

"What do you mean?" No, I wasn't that naive, but his commitment seemed to be a bit over the top.

"Look, Aúrea, you know I like you. A lot. I can't see myself sleeping with you just to do it. If I need pussy, I can get it from anywhere. You're not the kind of woman who should be fucked without commitment or on a whim.

Many niggas would do you like that, but I'm none of them, though. So if we gonna do this, I need to know that it's the start of some real shit. You belong to me, all right?"

"All right," I said breathlessly. Why I had agreed so quickly, I didn't know. It only felt right to agree, so I did. Adrian smiled before leaning back in, kissing me with so much passion that I knew things were only about to get better.

He went from my lips to my neck and did this swirly thing with his tongue and had my body lifting from the bed in pure pleasure. I had no clue about this spot on my neck, so how he found it was unbeknownst to me. He continued making his way down, taking time to pleasure each of my breasts, kissing my belly button, and removing my panties. When his tongue introduced itself to my clit, I felt my soul leave my body. I'd only had pleasurable head from one guy, Prentice, and since we both were young, who knows if he was doing it right. What Adrian was doing to my body was different. And within a matter of minutes, I came. Hard.

"Damn, Aúrea, this pussy tastes so good."

A lazy grin was all I could produce as my chest heaved up and down. I had never had an orgasm that left me breathless, even the ones I gave myself.

Slowly, he slid back up my body, hovering over me as the tip of his manhood poked at my entrance.

Years. That's how long it's been since I had any form of penetration, and from the sight of Adrian's bulge and what I was feeling from him only poking at my entrance, I knew I was in for a huge surprise.

"You sure about this?" he checked again, which I appreciated.

Making eye contact with him, I nodded and gasped loudly as he entered me.

"Shit." Adrian cussed, pausing to put his forehead on mine. I assumed he was pulling himself together. If I knew one thing about myself, it was that my lady parts were intact. I also knew what this kind of reaction from a man meant, and he hadn't been expecting me to feel like I was feeling to him.

He kissed my forehead before sucking in some air; then he moved. Slowly, deep, deliberately. Adrian's stroke was out of this world.

"Ahh," my moans were loud enough to wake the dead. My body had never felt this way.

"Aúrea, I mean it. Shit. you belong to me." Adrian spoke through clenched teeth.

"I'm about to come."

"Shit, me too. Come with me, Aúrea," he demanded. Or coached. Whatever it was, his words were all it took for my floodgates to open. Not even five full seconds later, Adrian went stiff before collapsing on top of me.

"Damn," he complimented breathlessly, and we both chuckled. "Tonight was the start of something beautiful," he told me, and I smiled. After the pleasure he just gave me, there was no reason not to believe him. I lay in his arms for I don't know how long before I finally looked over at the time. It was going on two in the morning, and I knew Nijah was up having a fit even though she hadn't blown up my phone.

"Hey, do you think you can drop me off at home?" I asked in the softest tone possible because I didn't want to offend him.

"Why you trying to leave me? I thought you were mine now," he frowned.

"I am. That's not it. Nijah expected me to come back home tonight. This is new. I want to ease in these kinds of changes. I can't stay tonight. I will next time, though. I promise."

Adrian's body froze, and I watched as his eyes went dark before they transformed to their original color. It happened so fast that maybe I only thought they changed. What there was no denying, though, is that Adrian released the hold he had on me.

" All right, I'm going to take you home."

"Are you upset?"

"Nah, baby. You're mine." He kissed my forehead, and I felt at ease.

# 10

## *Aúrea*

"I need you to do this for me, just this one time. Besides, it'll help you prepare for this movie role I'm trying to get you."

"What movie role?" This was my first time hearing about me having a possible part in a movie, mostly since I haven't done an audition in months.

To be honest, I hadn't had to audition much because Adrian had gotten me a couple of gigs like he promised. They weren't ideal, nor did they pay anything, but I gave him credit for doing what he said he would do. I knew it was hard to find work for me since I pissed that last director off refusing to sleep with him, and then Adrian turned around and knocked him on his ass, which did not make things any better. I was blackballed before I could even really get started. So the work Adrian got me, no matter how small, was appreciated and made me feel like I owed him.

"The one I have lined up for you. You trust me, don't you?"

"Yes." It wasn't the absolute truth, nor was it a complete lie. I trusted him because I had to, and even though Nijah and Ms. Jackie hated him, just as I felt indebted to them, I felt the same toward Adrian. So I prepared to

go out and do this one thing for him because he needed
me to. As crazy as it may sound, he was the first person who needed something from me. Since I arrived in
Los Angeles, someone had practically been taking care
of me, so it felt good for someone actually to need something from me. Adrian wasn't a saint, and he had all the
obvious warning signs that told me to be cautious, better
yet—to stay away. But he stepped in when I needed him.
He did to that director what I secretly hoped Prentice
could and would do to Von for abusing me. So though he
wasn't a true knight in shining armor like the fairy tales
would describe, he did at least save me. Therefore, I was
going to do this for him. It was only a one-time thing anyway.

The entire room was dim. Had it not been for the
small lights on the other side of the thick burgundy velvet
curtain I stood behind, I wouldn't have been able to see
the stage.

The stage. I was to step out there in less than two
minutes and show these strangers what I was working
with. And I was far from ready.

"You got this shit, Rae, baby. Here, take this last shot.
I want you relaxed, not pissy drunk. Go out there, imagine you're dancing for me, all right?" His pep talk was
meant to provide me confidence, and oddly, it did, knowing what I was doing would please him. With one hand
on the small of my back, he used his free hand to give me
the shot glass of brown liquor.

Quickly, I took it, tossing it back, grimacing from the
burning sensation it provided as it slid down my throat.
My entire frame shuddered as I tried shaking away the
nervousness that was refusing to disappear. My breasts

just about leaped from the small red bra that had already left little to the imagination. My movements mimicked a boxer loosening up before a fight.

"Look at me," he commanded, and my eyes landed without reluctance on Adrian's beautiful amber-colored orbs, drawing nearer as he pecked my lips. A small smile formed from the gesture.

"You can do this. You're doing this shit for us, for me. So make it the best damn performance you've ever put on. Consider this shit an acting gig, baby. Reenact Diamond from *Players Club* if you got to. Got it?"

The beating in my chest felt like my heart rate was auditioning to be in the *Guinness Book of World Records* for the fastest beating heart as I nodded my understanding.

"Good. Go do your thing." The sting from the slap he landed on my ass jolted me forward, and I just about flew out of the curtain. Instead, I used it to prevent my fall. He chuckled, walking away toward the front to watch the show.

"You can do this," I reassured myself as I withdrew the red thong from the crack of my ass, only for it to settle right back.

"Coming to the stage, she's a newbie, but fine as fuck, fellas. Give it up for Sunny Rae!" The DJ announced me, and the tune of Beyoncé's "Dance for You" came through the speakers. Adrian had my stage name covered. He'd started calling me his Rae, or Sunny Rae, not long after we made things official.

Slowly, I strutted from behind the curtain, swaying my hips, simultaneously doing a belly roll. Adrian wanted Diamond, but I would give him and every other man in this building her *times three*. No shade, but my moves were better, and movie role or not, I. Could. Act! Making it center stage, I spun my back to the crowd, closing my eyes tightly. I mouthed, "and scene," before reopening my eyes and going off. Pulling up on the pole, sliding down into a split, twirling around, removing my bra, and the men went wild. By the time I finished, the stage was covered in cash, and I was ass naked. It was all good until the reality of what I'd just done set in, causing me to feel sick to my stomach. It took me some time to collect my money with one hand while I used the other to cover my chest. Once it was all inside the black trash bag, I bolted off the stage, right into a bright-eyed Adrian, grinning like a Cheshire cat.

"You did it, baby," he cheered. "You were everything I knew you'd be and more, babe." He lifted me off my feet, spinning me around as the other women looked on with smug expressions I chose to ignore. The butterflies in my stomach were fluttering like crazy. Adrian's enthusiasm made it somewhat easy to ignore them. His open affection made me feel good.

"You damn sure gonna get that role in the movie." For some reason, when he told me that, I was taken back to the day he rescued me from Mike. I trusted Adrian because up until now, he hadn't given me a reason not to. But something about what I'd just done to get a role I still wasn't positive I'd get made me feel uneasy. I promised Nijah that once my gut told me something wasn't right, I'd follow it. I felt liberated and accomplished moments ago, and it changed so rapidly. There was nothing ordinary about that.

Standing in the bathroom of Adrian's home, I leaned forward over the sink to get a good look in the mirror. I examined my face, zooming in on my right eye. The blood vessel that had burst, leaving me with red scarring, was finally barely noticeable. And the blue and black bruise that once decorated that same eye was now a light red against my butterscotch complexion. It was light enough so that I could cover it with makeup, which I was thankful for. I had been off work for almost a week, nursing my bruises, and I was more than ready to get the hell out of this house.

Opening my makeup drawer to the left of me, I removed my Fenty foundation and applied it to my face. Crazy how I'd gone from not knowing how to do makeup because I didn't wear it to damn near a pro with applying it to my face. The new skill wasn't by choice. It was due to necessity. Wearing large shades to hide bruises drew more attention to my face. The same thing I would be trying to hide became the same thing to make me more noticeable.

After watching a few YouTube tutorials, makeup became my saving grace. Even with makeup, I hated that I didn't feel as beautiful as I knew I was. I always received compliments on my butterscotch complexion, hazel eyes, and thick, curly hair. As beautiful as all my features were on the outside, years of abuse prevented me from fully embracing them on the inside. Stepping back from the mirror, giving myself one last glance, I exited the bathroom toward my closet.

"What you about to do?" Adrian's voice boomed from behind me, making me jump. Shutting my eyes tightly while I clasped together the last two buttons of my white uniform shirt, I took a deep breath to settle my nerves.

I slowly turned around, and my sad eyes met his cold ones.

"I'm going back to work at the café today."

"Is that right?" He sucked his teeth, and I watched as his amber-colored eyes darkened.

"Yeah, it's been a little over a week since I've been. I want to go back, so I don't lose my job." My voice cracked as I spoke, afraid that he was going to flip out on me. The café was my sanctuary, though he didn't care for me working there. Today was the last day that Adrian would see me. After stripping in the club for him, I promised myself that I would back off of him, and I did. I didn't tell Nijah why I was putting a halt to our relationship, just that I wanted to get back focused on me. Of course, she was happy, and I felt good about my decision. So why did I fall for his crying and pleading a week ago? He called, wanting to apologize in person for making me feel like he didn't care and asking me to strip, blah blah blah. And I let him pick me up. The night started well. Then he lost it. He yelled, telling me how much he'd done for me and all that he sacrificed for me and how I owed him . . . The moment I tried to leave, he knocked my ass out. When I came to the next morning, I looked exactly how I felt . . . like I had gotten my ass beat. He cried, apologized, and begged some more, and though I had no intention of staying with him, whatever we had was over. But I stayed for this past week because I didn't want Nijah or Ms. Jackie to know. Yeah, it was stupid of me to keep them out of it, but they'd done so much for me already that I didn't want them in this kind of drama, and if he didn't hesitate to kick my ass, I didn't want to chance him hurting either of them.

A wolf in sheep's clothing, that was the best way to describe Adrian. It was either that, or he had been pretending to be this guy who cared for me for over a year— only to show me the complete opposite. I trusted him, cared about him a lot, and now I couldn't wait to get as far away from him as possible.

"Rae, baby, you love me?"

His question caught me off guard, and unintentionally my face revealed my confusion and disdain. Loving him was the last thing on my mind. However, he asked a question, leaving me no choice but to answer in a way that would make him happy. Before the answer could leave my mouth, the back of his hand met the left side of my face.

Covering my stinging cheek with my left hand, I put as much distance as possible between us before the wall prevented anymore.

"You didn't even give me a chance to answer," I cried, crouched down against the wall, holding myself like a frightened child.

"If you couldn't respond right away, the love ain't there. You were getting ready to lie to me, Rae, baby, weren't you?" He leaned down over me, leaving no room to escape if I wanted to.

"Noo," I whined. "And I do love you. I just can't take you hurting me." Half of what I said was true. The other half—a lie. The love was gone. The hurt I absolutely couldn't take anymore.

"I'm not going to hurt you anymore, all right? That was the last time. Don't call yourself ignoring me again, and we'll be good."

"Okay." I conceded with no reluctance, though it wasn't an answer I believed in. Honestly, I hadn't felt real love since Prentice.

"Good girl. You know you can never leave me, right?"

"I don't want to. I only want the man I first met to come back."

Nodding his head, he chuckled as if I just told a joke. Adrian kissed my forehead before walking away.

I sat there, not feeling sorry for myself but determined. When the front door shut, my nerves settled, encouraging me to my feet. Sitting on the bed, I removed my phone from the nightstand, sending a text to my Nijah for a ride, as my screensaver snagged my attention. It was my very first professional headshot, taken after my first year here in L.A. It was also the headshot that landed me my first and only commercial a year after that. That commercial was supposed to be the beginning of my acting and modeling career, but, of course, it was a one-and-done kind of thing.

Sighing, I shook off thoughts of my failed career, knowing if I further indulged in the ideas of what could have been, I'd drive myself crazy. Not a full minute passed before Nijah replied, "Okay," as I knew she would. I hadn't seen her all week, so I knew she would have a ton of questions when she picked me up. I wasn't in the mood to answer any of them, and I wouldn't until I was ready.

Nijah: I'm outside.

Reading the text, I stood, slipped on my shoes, grabbed my purse, then headed out the door.

"Don't look so thrilled to see me," Nijah said sarcastically, looking me over with a stank face.

"I'm sorry, Nahji. Today isn't a good day," I explained, using the nickname I gave her.

"You had better days when you weren't with that fuck nigga," she stated, gaining an eye roll from me. There was no question of whether she cared for Adrian. He didn't care for her either.

"Not today, Nahji," I groaned, laying my head against the window.

"Then when, Aúrea? Because I know you have to be more tired of that nigga than me. He's not good for you. I don't know how you went from coming over here to 'hear him out' to staying for a damn week."

"Well, you don't have to worry about Adrian anymore. I'm really done with him. Like it's over for real. The week here did nothing but make me realize he was never who I thought he was."

"Good. I'm holding you to those words."

# 11

## *Aúrea*

With the pen and notepad in hand, I followed an older couple to their booth waiting for them to sit comfortably before taking their order. Today was going smoothly for a Thursday, which was unusual because it was usually the busiest day of the week. Ms. Jackie cooked her famous pot roast, mac and cheese, and 7Up cake. I can't even lie. It was good as hell, and like the customers, I couldn't wait to dig in. Ms. Jackie put her foot and soul into everything she made, and the patrons knew it, which was why they kept coming back. Plenty of celebrities frequented her establishment, making it one of the most popular places on the West Side of Los Angeles.

What I loved most about this place was that no one was better than the next in here. It didn't matter one's stature in the streets or corporate building. Everyone gave respect, and everybody was equal in here, no matter what. Ms. Jackie was the second person since Nijah was the first to tell me not to be so down on myself when I became depressed, not landing any more acting gigs. Working here kept me grounded and independent.

After taking the couple's order, I gave the order to the cooks before excusing myself to the restroom. I didn't even have to use it. I just needed an excuse to get off my feet for a moment. I pulled the toilet seat down and sat on it to gather myself. I hadn't sat a good four minutes before the door opened.

"Aúrea, you in here?"

Rolling my eyes, I stood and flushed the toilet for nothing before stepping out of the stall, making my way to the sink to wash my hands.

"What's up, Chanelle?" I forcefully greeted my nosy-ass coworker. She meant well, but I didn't really mess with her because she was nosy and talked too damn much. I knew so much about people who came in here, and *none* of them told me their business. After she trained me, I thought we would build a genuine bond, but she wasn't the type of woman I wanted to call a friend.

"Your order is up, and I think your man just walked in here."

She peered at me with a sly smirk. Her ass didn't "think" anything. She knew exactly who Adrian was, and it was also obvious she had a thing for him. Most of the girls here had a thing for him because he was fine as hell. Still, looks were very deceiving. I was sure sis didn't want them problems. Hell, neither did I, which was why I was done with him.

"Thanks," I threw over my shoulder, leaving her standing there. When I walked into the kitchen, I grabbed the food for the couple at my table and headed their way. My eyes landed on Adrian, who was also seated in my section, and before I could make it over, Ms. Jackie stopped me.

"Aúrea, you know I don't do drama in here. I also won't allow him to disrespect you. Now—"

"There won't be any mess, Ms. Jackie. We're good." I cut her off, hoping I was being honest. I hadn't told her that I was done with Adrian yet, but I guess she could tell from my body language that I wasn't happy to see him. I forced a smile, then stepped to my table, putting the food in front of the customers.

After being assured they didn't need anything else from me, I made my way to Adrian.

"Took you long enough to get over here," he spat before rising to kiss me on my cheek.

"I had to finish with my customers first." My tone was low, wanting to keep wherever this conversation was going between the two of us.

"I guess." He shrugged. "Look, Rae, baby, I wanted to apologize for the way things went down at the house. You pissed me off."

"Really?" With furrowed brows, I glared at him. I knew this boldness I felt came from being in a room full of people. It also stemmed from the conversation I had with Nijah. Adrian was full of shit.

He looked me in the eyes, and as always, when I was pissing him off, their amber color darkened.

"Yeah, really." He sucked his teeth while cocking his head to the side.

"Since we've been together, Adrian, I submitted to you, doing something I never wanted to do because you asked me to." As soon as the words left my mouth, I regretted them. Adrian lunged at me, taking me roughly by the wrist. He scared me and caught me off guard. My high-pitched squeal drew attention to us.

From across the restaurant, Ms. Jackie loudly cleared her throat, forcing Adrian to look around to see where the sound had come from. Releasing a light chuckle, he let go of my wrist by practically throwing my hand down.

Glaring at me, he spoke. "We'll finish this when you get home. Yo' ass is mine," he threatened through clenched teeth. The joke was on him because there was no reason for me to return to that house, and I wasn't.

My eyes followed him as he exited the café, feeling a sense of temporary reprieve . . . which was short-lived as I noticed all eyes on me. Ashamed, I hurriedly made my way to the back of the café to the break room. Surprisingly, no one came in to bother me, and I appreciated having the time to myself. Sitting at the table, I bit my nail as my foot shook nervously. I knew I messed up.

"What to do, what to do," I mumbled, biting my lip, my legs shaking. I would have to figure out a way not to have to deal with him anymore.

"You can't hide back here forever."

With joyless eyes, I peeked up to see Ms. Jackie with a smirk on her face and hands on her hips. Should've known that she wouldn't let me stay back here forever.

"Sorry about Adrian."

"Child, never apologize for the actions of a man. If you find yourself doing so often, then he's not the man for you. Now, we've had multiple conversations about your situation, so it's not going to be discussed now. You'll know when you've had enough. Only *you* know when you're ready to bow out. I just pray it won't too late. Chanelle's about to go to break. You have two minutes to pull it together because your section is full." She walked over to me, providing me with a motherly hug before walking out. She was right. And I had had enough. Times like this, I missed the one guy who would never hurt me.

Prentice.

# 12

## *Prentice*

Driving through the front gate of my home, I sat in my car for a minute, staring at my crib in awe. Three years in this bitch, and I still was marveling at the fact that it was all mine. All five bedrooms, three-and-a-half baths, and 2,000 square feet. Not to mention the acre that was my backyard. Exiting my Tesla and hitting the alarm on my key fob, I made my way to my door. My hand moved to my waistline as a precaution where my .38 was tucked before opening my door.

"Alexa, turn on all the lights," I directed, locking the door behind me. Not many people knew where I lay my head, and no one was crazy enough to try me in my home. Still, I could never be too certain. So I always made sure to keep my gun at my side. After I told Alexa to turn on all the lights, I waited for my trusty sidekicks to meet me at the door. No sooner than I thought about them, they were rushing toward me.

"What up, Rocko and Chuck?" I grinned, swatting their happy asses down. Rocko was my blue nose pit bull, and Chuck was my Rottweiler. They were the most loyal niggas I've met in my 23 years.

Since they were so happy to see me, as usual, we played around for a few minutes before heading to my bedroom with their asses trailing right behind me.

Stepping into my walk-in closet, I removed the Js on my feet, placing them in their rightful spot. Shoes were my weakness, and with as many as I owned, I could easily fill my own Foot Locker, front and back inventory. I removed the only chain I wore from around my neck, a diamond-crusted cross, placing it inside my jewelry box in my closet before removing my True Religion jeans and a white tee and tossing them, along with my boxers, into the laundry bin. The shower was where I found contentment, the only place I could think without any distractions.

As the warm water fell over my low, curly cut, I smiled, reflecting on the moves I made today. I paid off the restaurant for Mr. Lewis on top of securing a new connect and made my most trusted worker, who happened to be my best friend, the next nigga in charge. I could officially sit back, collect money, and step in only when necessary. Shit felt wonderful. I worked myself up from a corner boy to the HNIC within three years. This wasn't the life I had planned, nor was it the life that chose me. But after losing my heart and balls five years ago, I needed to do something to prove to myself that I wasn't the bitch I felt I was at the time.

Soon after, I graduated high school with honors and a few full-ride scholarships to college. I decided it was time to man up. Like most young, Black males, I took to the streets to get my balls back. Fighting, gun-toting, and selling drugs was how I proved that I could hold my own and take care of matters when necessary. My hands were never a problem, even though I never fought much in school. The few times I'd been tried, I made examples out of my opponents, and no one else my age wanted to square up. It was in the streets amongst other hustlas and gangstas that I had to show why niggas didn't want to fight me. A couple of TKOs under my belt in the hood and I earned respect while instilling a little fear as well. After the cops picked me up for selling weed, my mom was done with me, so I went back to the only person who I knew wouldn't judge me—Mr. Lewis.

Who would've known that him finding two kids behind his restaurant five years ago would make him a permanent and positive fixture in my life? He was the only person I listened to outside of my mom, and I listened to him more. When I got caught up, he cussed me out and smacked me upside the head a couple of times. Then he told me to take my ass to school and not leave until I got my degree. Telling me that if I thought selling drugs would be enough to improve my life, then I was dumber than a mothafucka.

Taking his advice was the best thing I'd done. Obtaining my business degree laced me with the biggest group of weed and pillheads I'd ever encountered, making my pockets fat. Those were the only drugs I sold, and they made me a grip of money. Selling drugs was my primary source of income. Investing in Mr. Lewis's restaurant, owning a consulting firm, and my mother's medical spa also had me cool financially. Still, something was missing. Monetarily, I was straight. It just couldn't fill the empty spot in my heart.

I rinsed off, exited the shower, then wrapped a towel around my waist. Heading to the sink, I brushed my teeth before looking myself over in the mirror. I was still cut up like a fresh-out felon. Though a little pudge was growing at the bottom of my six-pack, a result of the free food I consumed frequenting at Mr. Lewis's spot, a dietary menu was going to be added to the suggestion box next time I rolled up because I couldn't be walking around like I inhaled beers all day.

Stepping back into my bedroom, I hit the remote on my nightstand, powering on my sixty-five-inch plasma that hung on the wall a few feet from my bed. I dropped the remote with my mouth wide open, shocked as hell from what I saw on the screen. I'd know that smile, those eyes, that sexy-ass butterscotch skin from anywhere. Like a lovesick nigga, my knees just about gave out. My mouth was still opened somewhat as I stared at the screen so hard that my eyes started to burn. After the commercial ended, I was still stuck, staring.

"Aúrea." Her name left my lips as a smile spread from them while shaking my head. Baby girl had made it, and I couldn't have been prouder. That's what she craved . . . to be on TV. To become a superstar, and though this was only a T.J. Maxx commercial, it seemed she'd done what she set out to do. "She's okay," I whispered in confirmation.

For five years, I beat myself up for letting her go, being too much of a coward to run to L.A. and look for her. When the money started rolling in, a private detective was on my list of people to hire. I just didn't hire one. She dipped. Not once had she tried to reach out. Not via social media, shit that I hardly used now. Not a text, when all these years I still had the same number. There were a million reasons in the world for me to find her. Yet, the few that told me to let her go were greater in weight, so I did just that.

Seeing her on TV, in good spirits, looking as beautiful as I remembered, reminded me there was one last thing I could do for her. Her bitch-ass foster father hadn't slipped through the cracks. He became a distant living memory. Trying to push her out of mind resulted in him being removed. It was his bitch ass that drove her to leave, made me lose my girl. I wasn't a skinny, 18-year-old boy anymore, either. It was time for Von to meet Prentice, the man. His ass was one wrong I was about to right, even if Aúrea never came back after all this time. And I doubted she would. But at least Von's ass would be taken care of—one less bitch nigga sucking the good air from the real niggas.

# 13

## *Prentice*

Rocko and Chuck's aggressive growling at my front door woke me from my nap, causing me to roll off the sofa onto the floor.

"Shit!" I grumbled, not expecting to have fallen on my ass. Blowing out a frustrated breath, I leaped up. My body full of aggravated tension, I made my way to my cell, resting on the coffee table.

"What the fuck?" I wasn't expecting company, so I had no clue who was at my front door.

Opening the Ring app on my phone, I saw my girl, a term I use *very* loosely. Brittney was on the other side of the door, looking irritated as hell. Releasing a light chuckle, I thought about leaving her ass out there since, once again, she thought it was cool to show up unannounced after I told her on multiple occasions that wasn't how I got down.

"Rocko, Chuck, go lie down." Both dogs whimpered before doing what the hell I said. They actually had the nerve to look sad, like *I'd* done something to them. I took my time walking to the door.

"*Really,* Prentice?" Brittney grumbled, pushing her way inside.

"Really *what,* Brit? It ain't like I knew you were on the way." I looked at her, not moved at all by her thick, bushy brows that she furrowed, or the pout gracing her plump, pink lips, one of my favorite parts of her body, as they always provided me a special kind of comfort when wrapped around my manhood.

"Well, as your *girlfriend,* I should be able to come and go as I please."

"Who gave you the title as my girlfriend, Brittney? You or me? Keep it real too." It took everything in me not to laugh in her face as embarrassment washed over it. I watched as she used her hand to straighten out her long weave, shifting her body weight from one side to the other.

"Every time I think you care, you prove me wrong," she pouted, shaking her head dramatically.

"I didn't say I don't care, Brit." I inched closer to her, grasping her by the waist. Other than being rough around the edges, Brittney was a cool girl. Just not the girl for me. I mean, not the girl meant to be my girlfriend—my wife. If I were to end up with Brittney, it would be me settling for someone I really didn't want, and I refused to do that. Brittney did look good on a nigga's arm. Her weave was always done up. I still didn't know if she had any real hair up under that shit. I mean, I guess she had to have enough to tag that fake shit on the top. Her body was shapely, her stomach kind of flat, and for me, she stayed wet. All that, and still, I couldn't see a future with her.

"Are you ever going to commit to me? Are you ever going to be more to me than what you are? I mean, to me, you're my boyfriend. I don't want to be with anyone but you. You don't feel the same about me, and it sucks."

"Probably not. So we can keep doing what we doing until one of us don't want to do it no more. Or you can cut your losses now." This repetitive-ass conversation still managed to hurt her feelings. Not sure why she thought my mind would change.

"I don't know why you keep fighting me when you and I both know there's not another woman who can make you feel like I do."

She let the jean jacket she had on fall to the floor before taking her hand and massaging my dick through my basketball shorts. Instantly, I hardened because getting me there was never an issue of Brittney's. She leaned in, pressing her lips to mine, and I obliged. We didn't kiss often. Kissing wasn't my thing. It was too intimate and couple-ish since we weren't on that. I usually dodged her lips. Tonight, though, since her feelings were already hurt and I wasn't trying to cock-block myself, I let the move slide.

"Mmm," she moaned into my lips as she pushed my shorts down. Swiftly, I stepped out of them, then led her over to the couch. By now, my dick was as hard as a brick, and taking her upstairs to my bedroom would waste too much time. Breaking our kiss, I kept my eyes on hers, helping remove the black crop tee she wore. The knee-length skirt she had on, I wasted no time lifting above her ass before twirling her around and bending her over the sofa. She didn't have on panties, which let me know she came over here to start some shit and get fucked. Slowly, I eased into her wetness and stood there just for a second, collecting myself. That initial entry with Brittney was always toe-curling. Then after about five strokes, the shit was just cool 'cause she ain't know how to throw it back.

"Prentice," she cried my name, sounding like she was out of breath. I had barely begun to stroke her.

"Throw that shit back, Brit," I urged, slapping her on the ass.

"I can't . . . You-u-you're too big," she moaned, causing me to roll my eyes. Maybe this was the other reason she couldn't be my girl. She was as cute as Laura Winslow from *Family Matters* but couldn't handle me in the bedroom. Damn deal-breaker.

Gripping her hair, I forced her head up, placing my lips to her ear. "You telling me you came all the way over here to get fucked and can't handle it? You should be used to this by now, Brit."

"You make me feel good, Prentice. But you know I can't take it all," she pushed out, taking a breath after each word.

"I do, huh?" My reply was sarcastic as hell. Indeed, I knew she couldn't take all that I was packing. She never missed a beat to remind me when I was inside her.

Tugging her weave a little tighter, pounding faster, I felt myself getting ready to reach my peak.

"Prentice, baby, I'm about to come," she moaned.

"Come," I ordered. And within seconds, Brittney's entire body was shaking. I stroked her a few more times before pulling out and releasing on her ass as she collapsed over the couch.

"I'll be back." Glancing down at her, I chuckled, knowing she wouldn't be able to move right away. I went into the bathroom, grabbed a towel to wipe myself, then another for her.

After she cleaned up, she sat down, getting comfortable, with her shoes removed and feet on my couch resting underneath her ass. *Coo',* I thought, taking the seat next to her.

"I really care about you, Prentice. Like enough to love you," she told me, resting her head on my shoulder. There was no reason to reply because she knew what was up, regardless of her playing like she didn't.

I picked the remote up from the end table and powered on the TV, turning to the sports channel. Besides releasing a little scoff from her lips, she ain't say anything else.

"Hold up." I lifted her head from my shoulder as I stood to answer my phone.

Brittney sucked her teeth, and I shook my head as I slid the *answer* button to the right.

"What's up?"

"That package you wanted to be delivered has made it to its destination."

"A'ight, hold tight. I'll be there to grab it shortly."

"It's all good."

The excitement surging through my body was hardly containable. I put the order in a few days ago, and already my guys had come through. Talk about perfect-fuck-ing-customer-service.

"You're leaving?" Disappointment could be heard in Brittney's tone and seen on her face once I turned back toward her.

"Yeah, something came up. You can stay or go, but I gotta dip."

"If I stay, can you put the dogs away?"

"This they shit. So, no. They not thinking about you. Decide now because I gotta get going."

Anxiously, I placed my Nike slides on my feet with black socks on. Real niggas wore socks and slides, no matter what.

"Fine. I'll just wait in your room with the door locked. They scare me."

"Nah, you can wait right here. You not about to be in my room going through my stuff, Brit. You not slick. The blankets are in the hall closet if you get tired. I'll be back."

"Fine." She sat that ass back on the sofa, arms folded over her cantaloupe-sized breasts, pouting.

"Chuck, Rocko, go to your rooms," I yelled out before eyeing Brittney.

"They gon' chill, but the moment they hear you moving around and shit like you ain't got no business, they gon' come and check yo' ass, believe that." It was up to her if she took heed to my warning. If she didn't, she would learn the hard way that my dogs weren't to be tested. This was my first time leaving her here alone, and it would be the last. Because of the call I received, she was getting a pass. I knew I was making a mistake, contradicting myself like a mothafucka by letting her stay.

"All right." Defeat was prominent in her reply.

"Don't wait up," I threw over my shoulder, heading out the door.

"Guess you not goin' to see another bitch, since my pussy juice is still on you," she mumbled, but I heard her ass.

"Damn," I muttered at the realization of what she just said as I walked out the door. I had wiped off, but only a shower would guarantee all residue was removed.

Being pressed for time was causing me to slip. I needed to make this run quick. Brittney being alone at my place for one minute was already too long. I looked up at my door again before jumping into my car, headed to my package.

The drive to my package was going smoothly until I got caught by a red light about a block ahead of my destination. While stopped, my hand tightly gripped the steering wheel, issuing a mild pain through my fingers. Crazy, I wasn't aware of how tight I was grasping it until I felt numbing. I loosened my grip as the light turned green, and I hit the gas, causing my car to jerk as the tires spun a bit. *Relax, nigga,* I chastised myself as I pulled into the lot of the storage unit. I was as excited as a kid on Christmas morning, and if I wanted this shit to go right, I had to pull myself together and calm down. It had been a minute since I had to put in this kind of work, but this would be a sweeter score settled than any other.

Stepping out of my ride, I locked my doors, then rubbed my hands together in eager anticipation. At the door, I tapped twice, and my entire demeanor shifted as the door slowly opened.

"What up, boss man?" my worker, Nick, spoke, extending his hand for a pound.

"My package still intact?" I inquired, following behind him.

We stepped into another room, lit by a small lamp. The lamp was right over the person I was there to see. My package. Aka Von's bitch ass. Underneath the chair he was sitting on was plastic to contain the mess that would be made.

"Who's there?" He attempted to sound unafraid, though the lack of vibrato in his tone proved otherwise.

I chuckled angrily as I stepped toward him. He had the nerve to be afraid. Guess fear only mattered when he was the one on the other side of it.

"Yo' bitch ass scared?" I stepped into view. His eyes met mine, and they were wide as saucers when he recognized me.

"I . . . I know you," he stuttered, and I smirked.

"You do, huh?"

"Ye . . . Yeah, you're my daughter's friend. Or used to be." He sounded relieved now. I guess he thought recognizing me and associating me with someone we both knew wasn't his daughter would help him.

"Who's your daughter?" I slowly asked, keeping eye contact with him. My hands twitched, itching to wrap around his neck, but I was gonna keep my cool a little longer.

"Aú . . . Aúrea," he spit out.

"That's your daughter, huh? Then tell me, what kind of sick mothafucka rapes his own daughter for over five years?" I slapped the shit out of him before he could respond.

"I never touched her."

Cocking my head to the side, I looked at him as if he'd just spoken to me in Portuguese. "Look, man. You gon' die tonight no matter what you say. Best thing for you to do . . . is be real. Clear yo' conscience and shit before I send you to hell. Now, what would make a man rape his daughter?" I asked again, much firmer this time. The blow to his face should have let him know I wasn't playing.

"She's not my real daughter. Plus, she asked for it. I didn't mean it, though. I feel bad. Horrible. If I could apologize, I would."

Tears were streaming down his face, but they didn't move me in the least. He never cared for Aúrea's tears. Then he had the nerve to lie about her.

"Well, you will never get that chance, but she *will* have justice."

I reached behind my back, removing the gun I had tucked away, shooting him in a kneecap.

"Ahh, shit! Please," he cried as blood spilled from his leg like a broken fire hydrant.

"Why'd you do it?" Closing in on him, I put my gun underneath his chin.

"My wife is sick, man. She's dying. Please don't kill me. She needs me," he begged, and I laughed. I mean, a hearty laugh like Kevin Hart or someone had just told me a joke.

"Why did you do it?" Slow and deliberate was how I delivered the words. I needed to know what possessed him to do what he'd done—and for all those years. However, if he tried to bullshit his way through the answer again, he'd die with his reason.

"I was sick, man. I know it was wrong, which was why I did my best to find her."

"You looked for her?" I asked, looking at him, confused as hell.

"Yes," he breathed out, taking in a huge gasp of air. "I never found her. No idea where to even look. I wanted to apologize. I knew what I did was wrong, man. I don't deserve to die for it. I've changed, been going to church. God—"

"God forgives—but I don't. Your sin is too great. Have a nice life in hell." I pulled the trigger, sending his brain splattering everywhere.

I've waited for this moment since the day Aúrea told me what he'd been doing to her.

Back then, I was mad enough to kill him, yet was still unsure if taking a man's life was something I could do. When they say timing is everything, I understood that more than ever now. 'Cause if I could, I'd bring his ass back from the dead, just to kill him again.

*Pow!*

I turned to see Nick's gun smoking and pointed at Von. "What the fuck?" I hissed.

"My fault, boss man. I couldn't help it. I know you killed his bitch ass, but my trigger finger was itching, though. It takes a bitch-ass nigga to do what he did. I got a daughter, man. Niggas like him deserve to die a thousand times."

"Clean this shit up. No evidence," I ordered, removing my shirt and putting the gun inside of it. Those two items I would get rid of myself.

"Got you, boss," Nick assured me.

I nodded and headed to my car. The drive to Mr. Lewis's place was slower than usual. I was riding dirty and had to make it there without any hiccups. Once there, I used my key and went inside. I headed to the master grill, lit the fire just like he taught me when I worked for him and threw both items inside. For twenty minutes, I sat there, waiting for the shirt to become ashes and for the gun to be as damaged as possible before I tossed it in the lake near my home. When he opened shop in the morning, he would know I'd been there. Mr. Lewis never missed a beat when it came to this place. I looked around, making sure I left nothing behind before turning everything off and exiting.

I hoped like hell Brittney was sleeping when I got home because I wasn't in the mood to deal with her any further tonight.

# 14

## *Aúrea*

I sat on the thin mattress of the bed made of metal in the women's shelter I'd been in for two days. Never in a million years did I imagine myself sleeping in a place like this, but here I was. With my back against the wall, I looked around at all the women and children heading toward the cafeteria to eat. Luckily for me, I had already eaten and had enough money to feed myself whatever I wanted. I also had leftovers from the Chinese spot I stopped at before coming back in here. The two days I'd been here weren't as horrible as I thought they would be. Oddly, I was okay with being here until I figured out my next move. Adrian wouldn't think to look for me here, and if he did show up, he'd be arrested on the spot.

Saving Grace provided protection and shelter to women of domestic violence situations. They took their jobs seriously, and though they cared to help all women, they were only interested in housing women trying to get away from their violent men. The day I showed up here, they were ready to turn me away. I guess because my face wasn't black and blue, I didn't read "victim." But when I presented the bruise Adrian left on my arm the day he grabbed me at the café and the bruise left on the left side of my back from one of his outbursts a little over a week ago, they proved I needed help. Then came his calling and threatening me via speakerphone, which I let the receptionist hear. That was the icing on the cake, and almost immediately, I was ushered inside and given a bed within thirty minutes of walking to the back.

That first day, I was impressed. The place was clean, there weren't any funky smells, and despite there being a ton of beds in one room, it was spacious. They had a few individual rooms, the receptionist told me, which were reserved for women who had children under 1 year old. The area I was assigned to had four rows of beds, about ten in each row. The first two rows were all twin-sized metal bunk beds, and the last two rows were single twin beds. Everybody had a thin mattress and a dark green comforter with the Saving Grace logo, a simple S&G. Though the mattresses were thin enough to feel the bars coming through, the blankets were nice and thick. The far right of my bed area was the security window. It was huge and allowed a full view of the room, where two people were at all times keeping an eye on things.

When I found this place on Google, I didn't expect any of this, not that the reviews were terrible or anything. It was the simple fact that I never expected to be in a shelter—period. When I got off work from the café, going home to Adrian and our apartment was the last thing on my mind because I knew there would be hell to pay. He was embarrassed when he left Ms. Jackie's place. I disrespected him in front of a room full of people. Adrian was probably going to kick my ass within an inch of my life the moment I stepped through our front door, so I didn't go there. I took my ass to a hotel. When I didn't show up at the house within an hour of clocking out, he blew up my phone because he knew my schedule like the back of his hand.

Nijah told me he showed up at her house looking for me. His going to her place was the nail in the coffin for me. So I found myself asking Siri to search for things a woman could do to escape an abusive relationship. The things that were coming up during my search didn't really fit me. Or I was too embarrassed to admit that they *all* fit me. Denial almost convinced me I could take one more ass whopping. Then, I thought about him sending me back to the club, and that did it. When my fingers scrolled upon Saving Grace, I knew it was a sign from God. So here I was.

As I observed the women in line, my eyes widened at the sight of Anna. She was beautiful and had been one of the girls I met through Adrian. It had been awhile since I'd seen her, and even though she was underweight, had matted hair, and a bruised cheek, she still looked the same. I didn't plan to make myself known to her. We wouldn't be playing catch up in this place because although I wasn't sure what my next move was, I knew I wouldn't be staying here long.

My phone chimed in my hand, alerting me I had a DM. Because Adrian's petty ass shut my phone off, I could only connect through Wi-Fi and social media. I opened the IG app and read the message from Nijah, who was making sure I was okay. She didn't know where I was because I didn't want her to let it slip to anyone, especially Adrian if he continued to harass her. I doubted she would, but just in case. It was better to be safe than sorry. I replied, letting her know I was okay and promised to see her soon. She whined through the message. I know I couldn't hear her, but I read the message in her voice, and it sounded like whining to me. Right now, at least.

After checking the rest of IG, I logged into my fake Facebook account. It had been a minute since I logged in. I was honestly surprised that I hadn't forgotten the password. It was a page I made about a year after moving to L.A. I still had my personal page but was afraid of all the "Come home" and "Where are you?" messages I was sure to have, so I avoided logging into it. This page was because I was homesick. Well, Prentice sick, to be more specific, and the only way I could catch up with him was via social media.

I also added my foster mother and a couple of friends to be nosy. Well, I wanted to see if my foster mother, Patricia, cared that I was gone. And whether she even looked for me. Clarise Monroe was my fake name. Funny. It was also the name I claimed as my alter ego. The name I vowed to see in bright lights one day. No one knew the name, not even Prentice, so it worked perfectly. Anyway, I found an artsy photo from a webpage, and they all fell for it, accepting my request like it was nothing. Prentice barely logged on, and when I noticed he waited months on end to check his page or post, I stopped caring to login. Besides, the friends I thought I had stopped caring about me after the first year. Even Patricia, so I just forgot the page.

Until now.

I could only use my current situation as the reason I cared so much to check up on the people who had probably forgotten all about me. I'd been gone for five years. Surely, I was a distant memory.

I went to Prentice's profile first, and my heart thumped heavily. He made a post a few days ago that simply said, "Blessed." He hadn't updated his profile picture in a while. I wondered why he was so blessed. What happened to him recently for him to post something after so long? My mind raced. The thought of a baby or a girl-friend entered my mind, and jealousy washed over me.

"Damn," I mumbled. Selfishly, I hoped neither was the case as I went to check his relationship status. "Single." I know it was probably fucked up, but the smile stretched across my face had my cheeks hurting. I knew relation-ships weren't supposed to be solidified via a post, but unfortunately, we were living in a time where it was. It was working in my favor at the moment, so I was gonna ride the bandwagon . . . this one time. If I happened to check later and the status was changed, I would hop right off the wagon. I went through the few pictures he had up and admired the handsome man he'd become. Prentice was always fine, but now, he was very hand-some. Moments like now, looking at his pictures made me miss him. I guess I never stopped. There were mo-ments when I'd miss him to the point of it hurting.

I know I did the right thing leaving him, but it didn't mean it felt good . . . especially for me to end up with someone like Adrian. The shit he's done and does to me, Prentice would never do. I got too caught up in old feelings and started to feel like it was best to log off. Yet, something told me to check Patricia's page.

Sorry for your loss. Reading the words, I thought my eyes were playing tricks on me as I read the many messages of condolences.

"Who the hell died?" I whispered while scrolling. My heart began to race again, and my palms started to sweat. I was a ball of nerves, and my eyes began to sting. I was getting emotional, and I didn't even know who died yet.

Shutting my eyes tightly, I was trying to tell myself that it didn't matter. I should leave well enough alone.

I just couldn't.

I opened my eyes, and my ass went right back to scrolling. I finally found what I was looking for.

Patricia, my condolences to you and your family. I know it's been a rough year, you being diagnosed and all, and now, Von. I pray you find strength and healing in your time of need.

I read the message. My foster mother had been diagnosed. And Von? What happened to Von? I opened the post to read the comments.

What happened? someone named Stephanie asked.

Von was killed. It's been all over the news. Just pray for Patricia.

Patrice wrote. She was Patricia's sister, who hardly came around. Far as I knew, they barely got along. In the years I lived there, I could count on one hand the number of times I'd seen or interacted with Patrice.

Immediately, I logged out of the page. I hadn't noticed I was crying until my tears made a puddle on my phone screen. I shook them off and wiped my eyes with the back of my hands. But they just *kept* falling. And there were a lot of them. They just wouldn't *stop*. With my phone in my hand and my purse, I hurried to the bathroom. I rushed into the stall, sat down, pulled the bottom of my shirt up to gag my mouth as much as possible, and cried hard. The sounds were muffled because of my shirt, yet still discernible. If anyone came in or stood near the door, they would definitely hear me . . . and with my luck, the door opened.

I kept trying to pull myself together.

Kept trying to stop crying.

I just . . . couldn't.

"Hey, are you okay in there? It's Rebecca, the counselor," she announced herself.

Rebecca was a nice woman. Right now, I was too embarrassed to face her. I'm sure she'd dealt with worse situations, but to tell her my emotions were on ten because the man who raped me consistently for years was killed just sounded crazy even to me.

"Aúrea, I know it's you in there, sweetie. Please come out and talk to me." Her tone was soft and inviting.

I nodded my head as if she could see me while sniffling. Slowly, I moved, unlocking the stall door, and when I came out, she placed her arm over my shoulder, leading me out of the bathroom and into her office.

"Are you afraid for your life?" she asked as soon as we were both seated.

I guess I was because it was more than likely lights out for me if Adrian got a hold of my ass. I couldn't say yes because I didn't want her to think that was why I was crying. So I shook my head.

"Okay, well, I had to ask in case I needed to make arrangements for your safety and all of our guests. Now that I know that, whenever you're ready to talk, I'm right here."

I wiped my eyes and took deep breaths to pull myself together. "Today, I found out my foster father died."

"I'm sorry, Aúrea," she said, and I saw the sincerity in her eyes.

"No," I stopped her quickly. Von didn't deserve her compassion, just like he didn't deserve my tears.

My statement caught her off guard. Her facial expression showed it.

"I lived with him and his wife for five years, and as soon as I got comfortable, he started raping me. I had been there for about five months when it started."

"I'm sorry, Aúrea."

"It's okay. I mean, it's not, but I could've said something—told my caseworker, the authorities, or someone. They were the first family I felt comfortable with and were nice to me. Not the greatest, but compared to the places I lived prior, it was like I finally had a family. I knew if I said something, I would be moved and probably placed somewhere worse. So I kept my mouth shut. It wasn't until the year before my eighteenth birthday that I told my boyfriend at the time. Then right before my birthday, I left and ended up here in L.A."

I know she didn't ask me all of that, but I swear, it felt good, amazing, even, to get all of that off my chest.

"You know what he did *wasn't* your fault, right?"

"I do. And then again, I don't. My not speaking up kept it going. I know I can't control anyone but myself. So how isn't it my fault if I didn't take control to stop him?" Saying that out loud stung. I felt like I took a needle to the heart and started crying again. Well, my tears never stopped flowing, really, but the sobs had. They were back now.

"Aúrea, you can't blame yourself. And if I have to remind you, repeatedly, it wasn't your fault until you get it, I got all night." She smiled. Not the most pleasant-looking smile because my tears distorted my vision. Still, it warmed my heart. "You being here isn't your fault either."

I nodded fast, trying to assure her and myself that she was right.

"Can I ask what knowing he's dead is doing to you emotionally? Like, if you could put it into words, how would you describe what you're feeling?"

I wiped my tears and gathered myself. I forced my shoulders to stop shaking and finally found my voice through the sobbing.

"Angry."

"Understandable. Anything else?"

"I'm upset. I didn't get to take my power back from him by beating his ass. I'm so sick of men taking advantage of me. Tired of being treated as an object."

"You still have your power, Aúrea. And the parts you feel that you lost, you can get back."

"How?" It was a serious question. I really wanted the answer. I *needed* the answer.

"Well, for one, you're here. You got out of the abusive relationship you were in when you decided to step foot into this building. Has your foster father been buried already?"

"I don't think so. No. I highly doubt it. The way I found out seems as if the news just spread. Why do you ask?"

"Because you can go back to your hometown to face him."

"He's dead, Rebecca, and I don't *want* to go there." I scrunched my face at her as if I could taste the bullshit she just fed me.

"You don't want to go back, or are you afraid? If you're afraid, you allow him to keep power over you. He doesn't have to be alive for you to go give him a piece of your mind."

"I-I . . ." My shoulders slouched in defeat because I didn't know what to say. There wasn't a comeback I could think of. Maybe she was right. Shit, she *was* right.

"Think about it. That may be the closure you need. In most cases, we don't recommend women face their abusers, but yours is gone, and he can't hurt you anymore unless you let him."

"You're right. I'm going to think about it. Thank you." I stood, leaving her office with a lot on my mind. I was already homeless here. I'd absolutely be going back to nothing there. Here, I had nothing but clothes on my back that I purchased from the thrift store. Luckily for me, I left my most valuable items at Nijah's house when I moved in with Adrian. So if I decided to go back for Von's funeral, my valuables would be the least of my worries. Money and my clothes were few, so I would have to think of a way to sneak into Adrian's apartment before leaving. I had every excuse why I couldn't go when the reality was . . . Rebecca was right. I *needed* to go.

# 15

## *Prentice*

It had only been a few days since the news spread about Von's murder. The case opened and closed as quickly as the news spread. That wasn't a surprise to me, though. Detectives weren't getting any awards to solve cases of murdered Black men. For all they knew, Von died from a drug deal gone wrong. That's usually how they noted the shit. Someone found him in a dumpster near one of the city's known drug- and murder-infested areas. When his wife's sister spoke on their family's behalf on the news, she tried to make him sound like a good dude who took care of his home and wife. She claimed he never did drugs, but you know, if it looks like a duck . . . Seeing her on TV speaking that nigga's praises made me laugh, then pissed me off all over again. If he were such a good man, how could he rape the same girl he was supposed to take care of for five years?

If Von were a good man, I'd take my chances with a fucked-up nigga any day. At least his wrongdoings would be expected. I whipped the corner in my Tesla, putting Von's bitch ass out of my mind. Long as they had no suspects, I had no reason to dwell. I pulled into my mother's driveway, cut off the engine, and sat there staring at the door. I wasn't in the mood to be over here, but it had been a minute since I stopped by, and I felt terrible about it. More so because of my little sister Prima. She was only 3 years old, and she and I had a bond tighter than a mothafucka. When my mom told me she was pregnant with her, I was pissed.

I felt she was too old to be having another baby and shit, plus, I was already grown. Selfishly, I kept thinking if something happened to my mom, I'd be stuck raising a baby 'cause the daddy for sure wasn't going to do it. Not that she purposely chose a deadbeat—'cause her ass did. Still, even if dude weren't a deadbeat, my sibling would be coming with me—period. Luckily, though, Moms was doing her thing, and little sis was my world. I couldn't imagine life without her.

I exited my car and strolled to the front door like I owned the block. I was lightweight feeling myself today. Dressed in dark blue Gucci jeans, a white, red, and gold Gucci tee, and a fresh pair of black-and-white Ones by the man Jordan, of course. Issey Miyake cologne, one four-carat diamond earring in my right ear, and my chain around my neck . . . All simple shit, but I was expensive and fresh. Not to mention the fresh cut I got yesterday. My waves were on swim.

I rang my mom's doorbell, even though I had a key. She fussed at me, telling me it made no sense that I refused to use it, but it was a form of respect. Yes, this was my mom's place. I even helped pay for it. I didn't live with her anymore, and since I didn't want her or anyone else just walking into my shit, I tried to give the same respect, not to sound messed up, because my mom had a key to my spot as well. I preferred her announcing herself before showing up unless it was an emergency. It only took one time for her to walk in on me having sex with some girl to establish that rule.

"Why don't you use your key, boy? I had to walk away from my gravy to answer the door," my mom spat upon stepping to the side and letting me in.

"If you used the security system I put in here, you could've seen me standing at the door and told me it was coo' to come in. *Then* I would have used my key," I chuckled, pulling her small frame into me and kissing her cheek.

"My phone is in the bedroom charging. Plus, I'm still not up to date with all that new technology stuff. If anyone comes in this house, I know it's either you or Gerald."

"Nah, that's not true, Mom. Yeah, you in a good neighborhood, but that doesn't mean anything. We don't expect people to do crazy things . . . but with crazy people in the world, you never know," I told her. Sometimes, I forgot that the time I spent running the streets, my mom was working. Because of that, she wasn't hip to a lot of the shit I was hip to. My mom really lived a square life, and I would have too had I not decided to enter the school of hard knocks.

"All right, son." She dismissed my ass smoothly, making me release a light chuckle.

"Preeeetisss!" my little sister yelled, mispronouncing my name and running up to me. I scooped her up in my arms and rained kisses all over her cheek.

"What's up, my baby?" I tickled her, feeling my heart swell at her infectious giggles.

"I missed you, brother," she told me.

"Well, why you didn't call me?" I asked her, still causing a tickle fit.

"Um." She placed her index finger on her chin as if she were really in deep thought. I mean, all the giggling and goofy antics utterly stopped. And I knew at that moment, my little sister had the qualities of a con artist.

"Prima!" I called her name, reclaiming her attention.

"I forgot. My iPad needs plugged."

She meant charged. I knew that. Chuckling, I placed her back on her feet, following behind her as we headed to the kitchen where my mother had gone. The aroma of her cooking hit my nose instantly, causing my stomach to growl. I didn't even know I was hungry until I stepped inside her kitchen. I took a seat at the small table and helped Prima onto my lap.

"So, son, how have you been?"

"Cool. Chilling and working. Working and chillin'."

"Settled down yet?" she inquired.

"Now, you know if that were the case, you would know."

"What about the girl you've been messing with for the last year or so?"

"Brittney isn't my girlfriend, Mom. Won't be, either."

"It's wrong to string that girl along, Prentice."

"I can't string her along, Ma, when she knows what it is. I promise you, she does."

"Listen here, son. I may not be all street-savvy, but I *know* women. Keep at it with that girl, and you will have *A Thin Line Between Love and Hate* situation. No woman sticks around chasing behind a man if she isn't crazy or full of hope that she will one day have her happy ending. She feels that way because the man's actions tell a different story than his words."

She gave me a look that dared me to tell her different. Something I wouldn't do 'cause I couldn't. "Okay, Mom, I hear you."

One thing about me, I did take heed to the lessons my mom taught me about women. There was only one woman in the world she couldn't tell me nothing about, and that was Aúrea, even though Aúrea leaving me made me wonder if there was some truth to the words Mom spoke about her when she left.

"What else has been goin' on with you? I know you said working, but which *job* are you speaking of?"

"The only ones I talk to you about. Why am I getting the third degree?"

"Because you stayed away too long. Now, I need all the tea, as you young people say . . . So spill it."

"I've been between Mr. Lewis and my consulting business." I hoped the information presented pacified her curiosity because her digging for more details would only lead her to a dead end. If she didn't know what I did in the streets, she couldn't tell the law nothing.

"So, I was wondering if you could take your sister home with you next weekend? I'm going to a business conference, and, of course, she can't come."

"You know she can stay with me anytime. I gotta ask, though, is her pops goin' with you?" I knew the answer was no. Still, I had to ask.

"He's not going, Prentice. If it's a problem—"

"Mom, I just said it wasn't. Prim can come live with me, and you can have a hot girl summer if you want. I love my sister, and as long as I'm here, she don't need a daddy, stepdaddy—none of that." My eyes bore into my mother's as I spoke, so she could see how serious I was. "You either," I informed her.

"Well, she has a father, just like you. Speaking of, when was the last time *you* spoke to yours?"

"Cool way to change the subject." She wasn't slick, and I was gonna let her know it.

"Think what you want. At the end of the day, *I'm* still the parent, and *you're* still the child. Now, you're watching Prima *and* about to tell me the last time you spoke to your father."

"You still feelin' that man, Mom?" I raised my brow in question. It was an answer I wanted. My mom had this thing about choosing shitty men. My father was one of 'em. I hadn't laid eyes on my pops since I was 8 years old. Just occasional phone calls and gifts now and then. Other than that, pops was a no-show. I think that's why I gravitated to Mr. Lewis so quickly. He parented me in the way I had been looking for my whole life. Well, after my first eight years, that is.

"Boy, no. I have been over that man. Because I don't deal with him doesn't mean you're not supposed to."

"I spoke to him last week. He's good. Our conversations haven't changed much. He still asks me the same questions he did when I was a kid." I shrugged.

That was the truth. My pops didn't know how to hold a conversation with me, which I chalked up to his guilt of not being there for me like he should have. Not only that but I also probably didn't make the calls easy, being that I usually was dry as hell when we spoke. I have to give it to him, though. He always called me. I never dialed him, so he was trying. It was apparent that he wanted some type of relationship with me.

"That man never learned how to communicate. At least, he still tries," my mother acknowledged, removing plates down from the cabinet.

Nodding my head was my way of silently agreeing with her. I also decided to be more open with my father and begin speaking to him in a nicer tone. Maybe if I talked to him like I talked to my mom, he'd get more comfortable. When we spoke, the awkwardness between us was preventing him from seeing how really dope I am and me from getting to know who he is.

"Did you see the news? They found the body of the man your old girlfriend used to live with. Such a shame," my mom spoke, interrupting my thoughts.

"Yeah, I saw it."

"You think she'll come out of hiding? I heard she stole from them before running off and—"

"Mom, let's talk about something else."

"Tinc." She placed my plate on the table.

I rubbed my hands in front of me, well, in front of Prima, who was still sitting in my lap, ready to dig in.

Moms always threw down in the kitchen. Tonight's dinner consisted of carne asada smothered in gravy, topped with onions and mushrooms. On the side was white rice with butter and a little bit of sugar, just how I liked it, and corn with a slice of Texas toast.

"Ooh, eat," Prima said with a huge grin on her face, damn near slobbering on my food. This was how I knew she was my sister. We had the same appetite.

"Mom, make your daughter a plate 'cause she not sharing mine," I said seriously, placing her on her feet. I pulled out the chair next to me and sat her down on it before tickling her.

"Oh, I made my baby her own plate. I swear you'll share everything else with her but yo' food."

"That's right." Picking up Prima's fork, I fed her a small piece of steak.

"It smells good in here. Where my plate?"

I looked up to see my mother's baby daddy walking into the kitchen. What irritated me about this nigga was he could step in and out of this bitch like he paid for it. I would probably be okay with it if he paid a bill, but his bitch ass couldn't do that. He felt he had some sort of reign because he was Prima's father. Yet the reality was—Prima's big brother would beat his ass.

"That ain't how you greet my mother or my sister, bro." That was something I shouldn't have had to tell the dude.

"I thought that was your car. What's up, Prentice?" He didn't deserve a reply, so he didn't get one. My eyes remained on him as he kissed my mother on the cheek, then walked over to do the same to Prima. His ass knew I wasn't playing, so when he took his seat, I went back to my plate.

"Brother, help me," Prima demanded, holding up her fork.

"What you need, baby girl?"

She pointed to her meat, and immediately, I cut the rest of it up to make it easier for her.

"Daddy can help you, Princess," Gerald's bitch ass chimed in.

"She asked the right person."

"Prentice!" my mom attempted to chastise me.

"It's okay, Tasha. Let the boy say what he wanna say."

Chuckling, I cut my eyes at that nigga, and if looks could kill, he'd be just as dead as the cow my mama got this steak from.

"I'm a grown-ass man. Only boy in this room is the nigga I'm looking at. Ol' goofy broke ass. You better remember my pockets' heavy, and my name holds weight in the streets. So you might wanna think twice about the next thing you say to me 'cause I have no problem mopping the floor with yo' face in front of my mom and sister. *That's* how I give it up. If you ready for it, let me know." The venom and seriousness weren't only laced in my tone. I was positive the look in my eyes showed it too. I wanted nothing more than for his ass to jump stupid so I could pop his ass right back into some sense.

"Watch your mouth in front of your sister and me. You won't be mopping a damn thing in this house unless it's with a real mop. Shit."

"You know what? I'm about to dip." I pushed my plate forward and stood. Gerald kept his eyes on me, and I can't lie. I was ready to leap on his ass just to see him jump out of his seat in fear.

"You don't have to leave," my mother told me. I knew that. I could've easily made Gerald's bitch ass leave. The fact remained that this wasn't my house. Plus, Prima saw me as this big ole' teddy bear. I never wanted her to see the actual beast that lived within her brother, and if I stayed, she would get a front-row seat.

"I know. I got something to do, though." I kissed Prima on top of her head. I love my sister, but no way was I putting my lips on her in the same area as her dad.

"Bye, brother." Prima smiled before wrapping her little arms around my neck and kissing my cheek. When she released me, I stepped to my mom, kissed her forehead, and left.

I drove around for a few minutes with no destination in mind before deciding to head to the block. It's been a minute since I made my way to the hood. There was no need for me to be out there. Not even to collect my money. Still, going through today was just something I wanted to do.

When I pulled up on Ninth, only a few people were out. A couple of youngins and my right-hand, Sonic. That's not his real name but a name he earned from being quick. He was quick as hell, the fastest on the track and football teams. He had a future in sports until he hurt himself, trying to dodge bullets not meant for him. He was depressed for a minute, then realized an injury was better than death. Plus, he still was the fastest nigga up out of this county. So Sonic still fit. I parked my car, then hopped out, making sure to leave my doors unlocked and gun on my hip.

"Yo, look who the cat done drug in," Sonic laughed, extending his hand for a shake.

"You got jokes, huh?"

"Nah, just ain't expect to see you out here with us regular folk."

"You know to expect the unexpected with me. What's poppin', though?"

I leaned up against Sonic's car with him. Even though he and I were having small talk, my eyes were on every part of the area, watching my back 'cause even though I felt safe here, I could never be too sure. If I wanted my mom to be aware at all times, no way I couldn't follow my own advice.

"Man, ain't shit. You see it's dry out here. I don't even know why I haven't taken my ass in the house yet."

"Aye, who's that?" I asked, noticing a smoke-grey Honda Accord pulling up on the block. My hand went to my hip, and I started regretting coming over here. All I needed was to get caught up in a shoot-out in broad daylight.

"Oh, shit, that's Janae," he said with a smirk on his face.

"Janae?" The name wasn't ringing a bell. Whoever she was had Sonic's ass ready to risk it all. Confirming it was a female, I relaxed a little. Not totally would I put my guard down 'cause females could be grimy too, but I could breathe a little easier.

"Yeah, she went to high school with us. Used to hang with yo' ex-girl, the one who ran away."

"Janae." Her name slipped from my lips quietly as my eyes grew in recognition. I knew exactly who she was, and I couldn't stand her ass. I had a feeling she kept in contact with Aúrea, which she always denied. After that, she became invisible to me.

The door to the car opened, and Sonic and I kept eyes on her as she got out and headed in our direction.

She damn sure wasn't invisible right now. I could see why my boy was smitten. I'd sleep with her. Well, in another lifetime, but still, she was doable. Janae had grown up. Her hips were wide, ass phat, and titties big. She was probably what society called a BBW. Yet to me, she was just thick in all the right places. If I had to estimate her size, my guess would be about a size 13/14, and that wasn't fat at all.

"Hey, Sonic," she flirted. She grinned hard, and her eyes concentrated solely on my boy.

"Ain't nothin'. What's up with you?" He shrugged his shoulders like a shy-ass schoolboy, and laughter erupted from the pit of my stomach. I wasn't trying to block nor embarrass him, which was why I composed myself quicker than a mothafucka. My laughter took Janae's attention from Sonic, and her eyes landed right on me, widening in recognition. Sort of how mine probably looked a few seconds ago when I realized who she was.

"Prentice Mayor?" She looked at me, and I couldn't tell if she was asking or telling me who I was.

"What's up, Janae?"

"Wow, it's been years. How have you been?"

"Good, and you?"

"I've been good. I just moved back. I moved to Florida temporarily to go to college. Had my son there. His dad wasn't shit, so I came back here to be with my family."

"That's what's up."

"Yeah, being home has been cool." She hesitated. I could see in her body language that she wanted to ask me something.

"It is."

"Uh, did you hear about what happened to Aúrea's foster dad?"

"It's been all over the news. Everyone has heard about it, I'm sure."

"Yeah, that's just sad, man."

I shrugged. It was sad for those who cared. I didn't care. Plus, I sent him to the other side, so there was absolutely no reason for me to feel anything outside of joy.

"Aye, I ain't know you had a son," Sonic cut in, and I was thankful for him.

She confirmed being a mother for him once again and even told him her son's age, but I had tuned them out. A text message from Brittney currently had me listing the pros and cons of seeing her tonight. After what my mom said earlier, it was probably smart for me to back off her for a while.

"Prentice," Sonic spoke my name, regaining my attention.

"What's up?"

"I'm about to run in here and take a leak. Don't leave, nigga. I'ma follow you up out of here."

"Don't take too long. I'm ready to go."

"Man, that ho gon' wait for you," he laughed.

I couldn't even think of a comeback for his ass because though he didn't know who had my eyes glued to my phone, he was right. She would wait for me.

"Whatever, nigga. Don't be all day. You probably gotta shit, stanky ass," I teased.

"Fuck you," he laughed, heading for one of the fiend houses on the block.

I held my phone, still debating on whether I was going to message Brittney back.

"Oh my God." Janae's gasp brought my attention back to her.

Honestly, I forgot she was right there. Her tone had me slightly nervous, so I furrowed my brows before asking, "The hell you do that for? What's wrong?"

Mouth agape, she looked at me. "The dead has arisen," she told me, not giving me a clue about what the hell she meant.

"What are you talking about, Janae?"

"Your precious Aúrea. She messaged me on Facebook."

My brows, I'm positive, were deeply furrowed. I could feel them by the tension in the middle of my forehead caused by the amount of pressure I felt.

"Come again?" I needed her to repeat herself. I wasn't sure I heard her right. The mention of Aúrea had my heart beating so fast that it felt like it was banging against my chest. My ears were pounding, and I wasn't sure how that was possible.

"Aúrea. She messaged on Facebook," she repeated.

Sure that I heard her, my expression changed as if asking, "What the fuck?" Shit, it was a what-the-fuck moment.

"I know this seems weird, and back then, you didn't believe me when I told you that she and I didn't communicate after she left, so this looks bad. But I promise you, this is my first time hearing from her since she's been gone—"

"What she say?" I cut her off. I didn't even care about that shit no more. I just wanted to know what she said and where she was.

"She asked me if I could pick her up from the bus station."

"When?"

"Uh, looks like in two days. I mean, she said in two days."

"Let me see yo' phone." It wasn't a question, which was why I extended my hand for her to give it to me.

As I read the message, I checked to make sure this was real. *It was.* Aúrea was writing from the page she had in high school, the same page I messaged multiple times, getting no reply. I kept looking and reading. She still had the profile photo of her at 16 from the school dance.

*Why she ain't hit me up?* I wondered as jealousy took over. I passed Janae back her phone and went right to my social media account. I ain't logged into that shit in forever, but I needed to see if she tried to contact me.

*She didn't.*

"Aye, tell her you'll pick her up. Get the bus station name and time."

"Prentice, I . . . It's been so long since I've seen her, I—"

"You won't be picking her up. I will. Get the information and don't say shit." I dug into my pocket and peeled off ten $100 bills. I wasn't trying to buy the agreement. It was just a small compensation for her agreeing. She'd have to 'cause if not, I'd take her phone and do it myself.

"Okay, Prentice," she agreed like I knew she would and took the money.

Damn, in a couple of days, I'd have Aúrea back.

# 16

## *Aúrea*

"Be still, my beating heart," I mumbled as I exited the bus. How ironic was it that the same form of transportation that took me away was the same form that brought me back? I couldn't even afford a plane ticket to come home after all this time.

With my suitcase on wheels, backpack, and duffle bag, I stood in front of the bus stop looking as homeless as I was. Before leaving L.A., Nijah and I snuck into the apartment I shared with Adrian and snatched up as many of my things I could get my hands on. Then we stopped by the café so I could say goodbye to Ms. Jackie. I wasn't sure whether I would be back to California, but I knew for sure that I was not resuming my job at the café if I returned. That would be a suicide mission. Adrian's ego wouldn't allow him to ignore all that transpired between us, as well as me successfully leaving his ass.

I still had dreams and a goal to become an actress. Maybe New York would be my next destination to try to make my dream come true. For now, I had to focus on confronting my past so that I could truly move on. After another long talk with Rebecca, I felt better about coming back, as well as motivated to get my life back on track. The setbacks I faced were only there because my comeback was meant to be so much greater.

"Where is this girl?" I looked across the street, behind me, and back in front of me. She told me she would be here to get me, and I was surprised she agreed. I don't even know what made me reach out to her. And now that I'd been waiting a good three minutes already, I felt like I should have just taken an Uber to my hotel and never reached out at all. No one had to know, nor needed to know I was here anyway.

But, of course, a conversation with Rebecca prompted me to reach out to a safety net from my past. Prentice had been that. After leaving him the way I did, though, there was no way I could reach out to him and ask him for anything. Plus, he hadn't been on social media any time I checked, and Janae stayed on her page like she got paid to post.

So, by default, she won. I removed my phone from my pocket. I was still using it on Wi-Fi because Adrian controlled the account, and I couldn't turn it on. Nijah offered to get me a phone by adding me to her plan, but I refused. She did enough for me—more than enough—so I wasn't taking anything else from her. Once I got settled and decided on what to do next, I would get a phone, a prepaid one at least.

"Aúrea?" the sound of my name caught me off guard. Not because I wasn't expecting it, but because of the voice behind it.

Why was a man checking for me? I wondered, and I was sure my face showed it. Slowly, I turned around to see who it was.

Deaf.

I swear I had temporarily gone deaf.

The loud honks. The sounds of tires moving along the pavement. The loud chatter from the patrons outside.

The sounds of suitcase wheels being pulled. The every-few-seconds announcements made over the intercom of the bus station . . . all ceased. I, literally, could no longer hear anything. That valuable sense had gone MIA on me. My eyes were working, though, possibly playing tricks on me, but they worked. I mean, they were temporarily paralyzed, stuck on the figure directly in front of me. But I could see.

I breathed in and held my breath for three seconds, exhaled, and did it again. This was the breathing method I learned to help with anxiety.

"You all right?" he asked me.

No response to give, I just continued to breathe. Then my eyes started working. I felt them fluttering damn near about one hundred flutters every five seconds. My mouth wouldn't work, though. In my head, I said I wasn't okay, but verbalizing it didn't seem possible. He kept coming near me, closing the small space there had been between us.

It had been five years. Last time I saw him, we were standing in this same spot. Well, maybe not this exact spot, but we were at a bus stop. He was taller than me then. He towered over me now. He was cut up then, skinny and defined. Today, he was chiseled. Wide. Well defined. Cut up. From what I could see, his once-smooth baby face now had a light mustache sitting perfectly above his full lips. His lips—*whew*. Sexy, plump, kissable, and suckable. His sexy, light brown eyes peered into mine. And unconsciously, I licked my lips. *Damn,* I crushed on him then, but I was in heat behind his ass now.

"Aúrea," he spoke my name a little more aggressively this time.

"Prentice. Wh-what are you doing here?" My words had finally made their way to my throat and exited.

"That's how you greet me?" He smiled, broadcasting all thirty-two pearly whites, straighter than I'd ever seen on a human.

"I mean, no. I didn't expect to see you, that's all." *Janae, where the hell are you?* I thought as I began looking in every direction, avoiding him. She needed to hurry the hell up. His presence was too much. I didn't want to see or face him right now. I planned to make this trip, not seeing his face at all.

"Well, here I am, and ain't no getting away from me now."

"I was actually about to leave. My ride should be pulling up any moment."

"Your ride is here, Aúrea."

I scrunched my face, not in disgust, in confusion. I didn't see Janae anywhere. I knew what she looked like, and none of the people around looked like her. Hearing Prentice chuckle brought my attention back to him.

"Give me your bags."

Damn, I don't remember him being this authoritative. It was kind of a turn-on . . . well, would have been if I hadn't just left a relationship with a damn dictator.

"Why would I do that? I just told you, I'm waiting on my ride." Now, *I* had an attitude. How dare he think it was okay to tell me what to do? The purpose of this trip was for me to take my power back. I had no problem doing that, starting with him.

"Because *I'm* your ride, Aúrea. I know it's been a min-ute—"

"Exactly. I don't know you like that anymore, and you don't know me. So to think you can just tell me what to do, well, you must be tripping."

His brown skin was starting to become flushed with red undertones as his brows furrowed as low as they could. He was frustrated. Angry possibly, and the weird part of it was I wasn't afraid.

"Maybe we have changed, but what's for certain is I would never hurt you. Janae isn't coming. I know that's who you're waiting for, and I came in her place. So can you please let me take your bags and follow me to my car?" The frustration I saw on his face only moments ago was gone. He looked sincere with his handsome face and pleading eyes.

Rolling my eyes toward the heavens, I tried to suppress my smile as I handed over my bags.

"Still the most beautiful girl," he complimented me, and I felt my cheeks heat up. I extended my bags to him except for my purse and backpack, not bothering to reply to his compliment as I followed behind him to his car. Watching him walk was like watching a piece of art leave an art gallery. Swag dripped from him, and it didn't look like he was even trying.

We hadn't even taken many steps before I watched him open a trunk to a navy-blue Tesla with white trim. His car was wet as hell. The paint job was immaculate.

I stood to the side as he placed my bags into the trunk, then came around, opening the passenger-side door for me.

My ass sank into the seat, and I felt like it was made to fit the mold of my body. He walked around the front of the car, and my eyes followed him until he got inside and sat sexily in the driver's seat.

"I reserved a room downtown at the Hyatt." Well, I didn't reserve it. It was a gift to me from the women's shelter. They paid it up for three days, and I was okay with that. After the three days were up, a Motel 6 would be enough for me.

"All right." He spoke without looking at me and pulled off. As he drove, nodding his head to what I assumed to be the new Khalid album, I stared out of the window. Not much had changed. Besides a few building remodels, my hometown looked as it had before I left. We jumped on the expressway, and I was relieved to see he was following my directions heading downtown. It wasn't that being around him right now was horrible. I just still wasn't ready.

I could tell that Prentice had done . . . well, had been doing pretty well for himself, from this expensive car to the clothes on his back. He was rocking a pair of Jordan's while everything I had on came from Plato's Closet, including my Converse shoes. A women's shelter had to pay for my hotel. I barely had money when I decided to leave Adrian and was thankful that Ms. Jackie gave me what she called a *bonus* on my last check. I left him and had nothing to show for it. Seeing Prentice now proved that I at least made the right decision by leaving him here. Had he come to L.A. with me, there's no telling who he would have become. And instead of being open to giving me a ride like now, he'd probably resent me or want to kill me.

"How have you been?" he turned the radio down and asked.

Rolling my eyes again out of his line of vision, of course, I provided him a short answer.

"Okay," I lied, easy to do since I wasn't looking him in the face.

"What brings you home?"

If he was trying to make small talk, that was the wrong question to ask. Although Prentice knew about what I experienced at the hands of Von, for me to say I was here because of him felt weird. How would he look at me for saying that when he knew I left because of that man?

"Not something I want to talk about right now."

"That's fine. What would you like to talk about then?"

"Nothing. I don't want to talk about me right now," I snapped. It wasn't my intention, yet my emotions weren't too stable at the moment.

"It's cool. We can talk later." He sounded hurt, and guilt washed over me. This trip was about me, and I felt terrible for hurting him.

*Why did he have to pick me up?* I wondered with my eyes shut tight.

This was not what I imagined for this trip. The crazy thing is, I don't know why I hadn't expected something to happen. Monkey wrenches had been thrown my way since I was born. Why would now be so different?

Even though I knew he wasn't too happy with me shutting down us having a conversation, he turned the music back up and said nothing. I was good with that. Grateful for it, even. So we rode in silence. And I just got lost in my thoughts. It wasn't until he turned off the highway that I noticed he missed the exit for my hotel. Miles ago, he had passed it.

"Uh, where are we?" I questioned as I saw an area I wasn't familiar with. It had to be fairly new 'cause I would have known if I'd been here before. Beautiful houses lined up for blocks—all the same beige or brown.

He kept driving, and soon, he was putting a code into a gate system that opened and led to another row of big homes. These homes were spread farther apart and were much larger.

"I asked where we are," I repeated, taking it upon myself to turn his stereo down since he wanted to act like he didn't hear me.

He pulled the car up a wraparound driveway of a huge house, pulling right in front of the door.

"We're at my house," he spoke like it was no big deal.

"I told you I was staying at a hotel." Sucking my teeth, I folded my arms across my chest and looked at him.

"I know what you told me . . . *I* want you here."

"You don't get to make that choice, Prentice."

"Since I'm the driver . . . I do." He chuckled, and my anger rose.

*How dare he?*

"This is kidnapping."

"It's not. It's me making sure you have someplace comfortable to be instead of a damn hotel. There's no reason for you to be in one when you have me here."

Shaking my head, I took my attention from him. My eyes were beginning to feel heavy. Water was slowly pooling at the bottom, and he didn't need to see me cry.

"Aúrea, please, look at me." He placed his hand on my knee, and I jumped. Not a small jump either. I jumped so hard I damn near leaped from my seat through the front windshield. His hand retreated from my knee.

"I didn't mean to scare you." His voice shook, and for the first time since I'd reunited with him, he sounded like Prentice, *my* Prentice.

"It-It's okay. You didn't scare me," I lied.

I turned to him. Tears still holding court in my eyes had yet to fall because I was holding on like hell for them not to.

"Look, it's been five years since I've seen my girl—my best friend. I will take you to your hotel if you really want to be there. Just know, I want you here. You're safe here with me. I won't even speak to you if you don't want me to. You being here is enough. For the first time in five years, I feel whole again."

*Dammit.* That did it. My tears spilled out of my eyes.

Nodding my head, I gave him what he wanted—agreeing to stay here with him, not the whole time, though. Tonight, at least. I'd contact the hotel and say I needed a late check-in.

Pleased, Prentice exited the car before popping the trunk, retrieving my bags, and assisting me out of the passenger door. Slowly, I followed him up the three broad steps to his front door, and as he stuck his key in the lock, it dawned on me that this was a huge house for just one person.

"You live alone? Does your mother stay here with you?" Two questions I should've asked before getting my ass out of the car. If I didn't like his answers, getting back inside of his vehicle, demanding to be taken to my hotel wouldn't be an issue either.

"I live alone. My mother and little sister stay way across town," he assured me.

"Little sister?" That caught me off guard. Tasha's mean ass getting someone to knock her up a second time had to have been a magic trick.

"Yeah, depending on . . . Well, you'll get to meet her. She's my heart."

Hearing him refer to his little sister as his heart warmed *and* iced my heart. There was no reason for me to be envious of someone else occupying space there, but I was. He continued, opening the door, and I followed him inside.

"Wow," I whispered as my eyes darted around the massive foyer with an elegant chandelier hanging above my head.

He shut the door, and the sounds of heavy feet heading our way had my ass backing right into the door, ready to run for it. My heart pounded as a big-ass pit bull and Rottweiler happily jumped at him with wagging tails.

"They do bite. They won't bite you, though. Sit," he informed me before sending over a command to the dogs, which they promptly followed.

"Two big-ass dogs. I'm sure they *do* bite," I laughed. "At least you're honest," I told him as I bent down to pet them. Seeing their tails wagging and their overly friendly nature, I wasn't afraid.

"Shit, you know people love to ask if dogs bite when they first see them. Of course, they bite. They got teeth, and they dogs. The question people should start asking is if the dog will bite *them*."

"And if asked that, what would you say?" I quizzed.

"Shit, I'd tell 'em that I don't know. It's a chance they gotta be willing to take," he shrugged.

"So, how did you know they wouldn't bite me?" I paused from patting the dogs' heads and turned to face him.

"Because they wouldn't harm who or what I love. They're too loyal for that." He winked at me, and I promise, my clit jumped, and my heart skipped a beat at the same time.

*Did he just declare his love for me?*

*How could he still love me?*

*I mean, do I even still love him?*

"Um, what are their names?" Quickly, I changed the subject.

"The pit bull is Rocko, and the Rottweiler is Chuck."

"Rocko and Chuck. Those are cool, I guess."

"What would you have named them?"

"I don't know, but now that you said their names, they look like a Rocko and a Chuck."

"Man," he dragged before laughing. "They like you. They usually don't take to people so fast."

"Probably because other people show that they are afraid of them. Dogs can sense fear."

"You weren't scared? I remember you being scared of the little wiener dog that Mr. Hank had."

"Because that dog was evil. I was shook when I first saw these two, though, but I wasn't gonna show it because then, I'd been dog food."

"Not at all. As much as I love them, they'd be dead first."

*Wow. Who is this man? How does he still wanna protect me and not wring my neck?*

"This is a nice home." Again, I changed the subject. I went from not wanting to talk to having to be a conversation shifter.

"Thanks, come on. I'll give you a tour and show you to your room."

"My room?" I frowned.

"Yes, your room. You're gonna be here for a while," he stated like he was so positive.

"Says who?" I sucked my teeth before placing my hands on my hips.

"Still beautiful," he complimented me again, picking up my luggage.

"Prentice, I'm not sure what you're thinking as far as me staying here, but it won't be for long. I'm not moving in." I trailed behind him up the flight of stairs.

"This right here is my room." He opened the door, and I peeped my head inside. Truthfully, I was anxious to go all the way inside and look around. I refrained from doing so, however. From what I could see, the room was decorated in black and grey. Bachelor decorations and relief washed over me.

"This is your room." He led me to a room directly across from his.

"You mean the room I'll be sleeping in," I corrected him. I don't know why he was trying to move me in.

Chuckling, he told me, "If that's what you want to call it."

Stepping inside, I saw a huge room. I mean, it was almost the size of the entire front entry of Adrian's and my apartment. Like, the living room, kitchen, and dining area put together.

This room was decorated in beige and burgundy, much warmer and more welcoming colors, so I assumed this room was used strictly for guests. He walked over to the closet with my luggage and placed it on top of what I assumed was a folding table. The closet was huge as hell as well . . . rows of drawers, hanger space, and shelves.

"Let me show you the bathroom."

I followed behind him and walked into a huge bathroom, the biggest I'd ever seen. There was a Jacuzzi tub, walk-in shower, his and her sinks, a linen closet. The shower and bathtub were decorated in burgundy and gold marble.

Breathtaking.

"If you go straight through this door, it'll lead to the small lounge area in my bedroom."

"So, this is your bathroom too?"

"No, the master bath is on the other side. I had this bathroom connected to my room, just in case." He shrugged like I was supposed to get it. Like I was supposed to know what the *just in case* is for.

"Just in case what?" I inquired.

"I had a kid and wanted him or her to be close to me."

"Oh, so you don't have any children?"

"Not yet. And if I did, this room would be occupied," he spoke as I followed him back into the bedroom. I took a seat on the bed as he walked back into the closet.

"What are you doing?" I questioned as he opened my suitcase. Had he been facing me, he'd see the meanest mug my face could muster.

"Putting your clothes away," he said like it was no big deal. Standing with force, I marched a couple of steps to him and snatched my favorite Mickey tee from him.

"No one asked you to do that. I prefer to grab what I need from my luggage because it'll be much easier to keep up with. Besides, I have underwear in here, and I would prefer you *not* pick up my panties."

"It makes no sense in you living out of your suitcase when you have more than enough space in front of you to put your things away."

"Stop, please," I yelled at him. I didn't mean to yell, but I was becoming annoyed. Frustrated.

Why did he keep trying to make me do stuff? Why did he want me here so badly? My tantrum didn't faze him much as he gently took my hand, leading me to sit back on the bed while he stood in front of me.

"Aúrea, I know it's been years since we've seen each other. I know so much has changed in both of our lives. I promise you that my heart beats for you just the same. I'm still your friend before anything else, so you can trust me. I only want what's best for you; always have. Just give me a chance to show you that."

The sincerity in his eyes was all I needed to know that he was telling the truth. His tone proved it before his eyes—still, fear of giving him my trust after so long consumed me. Years had passed. No way was he the same person. I sure as the hell wasn't. And he wasn't. This new Prentice had swag, was a bit rough around the edges, and was getting money . . . from where I had no clue, though everything about him screamed paid hustler.

Looking at him, I contemplated a response, and one didn't come to mind, not verbally at least, so I nodded.

And he smiled. He smiled wide, showing all thirty-two pearly whites. His smile was infectious. It shot right over to me, making me smile as well.

"There she goes. You're beautiful, Aúrea."

"Thank you. You can stop saying it now." I knew I was blushing, and the compliment felt good. It was just becoming overwhelming.

"Okay, so since the mood has lightened up some because you were tryin'a act like a nigga was a serial killer or something, how about we go out to eat? Can I take you out?"

I raised my right brow in skepticism. He needed to slow his roll once again.

"Not as a date; just two friends catching up. Relax, girl. Sheesh." He shook his head.

Maybe he was right. I had to relax because as much as I was fighting being here, I wasn't ready to leave, well, ready for him to kick me out. I was playing harder than a motha, but his constant organic reminders of him still caring about me, wanting me here, had chipped away the hardened parts blocking my heart.

"Sure," I smiled . . . genuinely, and it felt good.

"Cool. What you have a taste for? Well, you wanna try something old or new?"

"New," I answered without hesitation. I was back home to deal with the old and moving forward. I wanted everything new, and we could start at dinner.

"Cool, I know just the place. Give me a minute to make our reservation. You can get comfortable for a li'l minute if you'd like," he instructed, standing.

"Thank you."

"No problem. And, Aúrea," he said as he stood at the door of the bedroom.

"Yes?"

"At some point, you should realize that you can still talk to me about anything. I care why you're back. Not as much as me caring *that you're back*. I've missed you. Thought about you every day since the day you left. I'm not trying to pressure you into anything. A nigga a little extra 'cause I'm happy you're back." He winked.

"Thank you," I smiled as he walked away.

Why did I have to run into *this* Prentice? I mean, the first one was great, but Grown Man Prentice was doing something to me, and I didn't like it because I wasn't here for this. I wasn't here to fall in love again. However, seeing as Janae stood me up and had yet to reach out, might I add, it looked like Prentice was also a part of my past that needed fixing.

"You straight?" he asked, coming back into the room.

"I came back to go to Von's funeral. I ran for so long. I need to face him, take back what he took from me. My power," I told him. I wasn't too fond of this form of expression, but this was the first step.

"Damn," he mumbled, coming over to take a seat next to me. Taking both of my hands into his, Prentice urged me to look him in the eyes. "That's big of you, A."

*My nickname. He called me by the nickname he gave me.* I bit gently on the inside of my mouth. It was the only way to prevent my cheeks from spreading into yet another smile. Fighting off the grown man that he was— was becoming hard. He was so damn attractive.

"You don't have to go alone. I'll go with you if you'd like."

"You will?" I checked because that was the last thing I expected him to say.

"I will. When is the service?"

"In two days, according to Facebook."

"That's how you found out?" He looked at me as if he couldn't believe it.

How else was I supposed to find out, though? I lost touch with everyone. "Yes, it's not like I speak to anyone."

"How are you feeling?"

"Like this is something I have to do. I mean, before I got here, I had a bunch of emotions, and now that I'm here, I guess I'm just numb. Not to mention, tryin'a keep you in your place has been a distraction," I chuckled.

"What you mean, keep me in my place?" He smiled so sexily, making my palms feel like I'd just put them in a puddle and pulled them out.

"Because you keep telling me that I'm moving in . . . and I'm not."

"I never said you were moving in. Since you said it, though, it doesn't sound like a bad idea," he laughed, and I shook my head. This new Prentice was slowly growing on me.

"What's that?" The sound of his dogs barking like crazy just about made me jump out of my skin.

"My dogs—hold up."

He rose, and I could see the tension in his body.

What kind of shit was Prentice into? I speculated as I calmly stood from the bed and crept to the door. I was probably safer in the bedroom if something were to pop off because I didn't know where any other exit was beside the front door where we came in. My curiosity got the best of me, and I wanted to know who or what had his dogs barking like madmen.

I held my breath as if my breathing could be heard way up here, listening as intently as possible. The barking had stopped, and I heard the front door shut. It was quite still, so I moved farther out of the bedroom, yet close enough to get back into the room and lock the door in two-point-two seconds.

"Prentice, can you please tell your dogs to back up?"

My ears perked up, and I was sure that was a woman's voice I heard.

Prentice did what she asked, and I heard the patter of their paws rushing across the floor.

"What are you doing here, Brittney?" He was annoyed.

"Why is it always an issue with me showing up?"

"Why is it always an issue with you doing what I ask?" he shot back.

I rolled my eyes, an inch away from being pissed. *Did he ask me to stay here, practically move my bags in, and he has a girlfriend?*

One thing I wasn't going to do was be in a place where I wasn't wanted, nor was I about to disrupt what he had going on. I'd love for him to go with me to Von's funeral still but not at the expense of drama. Plus, if he really wanted to go, I didn't have to stay with him for him to go. They were going back and forth, and I wasn't sure what they were talking about as I went into the room and grabbed my luggage. Without hesitation, I made my way down the stairs, walking right into Prentice and a pretty girl, Brittney, I'm assuming because that's the name I heard him say.

"A, where are you going?" he asked, taking me by the arm, stopping me before I could get to the door.

"Prentice, who is this?" she asked with a full-blown attitude, looking me up and down like I wasn't shit.

"Don't worry about it," he told her flatly, and I can't lie; *I* was offended.

"Prentice, I didn't come here for this. You could have told me you had a . . . situation—"

"There was nothing to tell you. There isn't a situation."

"You're right. We're more than that. I've been with him for over a year," she snapped.

And my heart sank. *Why did I care?* To hear he was sharing himself with her for over a year did something to my feelings, and I didn't like it.

*Fuck that.*

"Brittney, you have to go. You doin' too much right now," he stated.

"You're *really* gonna put me out for her? Who is she anyway? Prentice!"

As I looked at her, I could recognize the pain in her eyes. It was the pain of a woman wanting to be loved by a man who just didn't love her. I doubted he was anything like Adrian. Still, I remember having that same look in my eyes while with Adrian, knowing that if he truly loved me, he wouldn't have been beating my ass and putting me through all he had.

"I am. *No one* comes before Aúrea in my life."

My face, I was sure, was as frowned and showing confusion as Brittney's was. My ears couldn't have heard him right. She no longer mattered—her standing there no longer mattered. I was too busy trying to wrap my head around what he just said. Did he *really* just say that?

"What?" she asked fairly above a whisper, obviously not expecting him to say that.

"Still?" I asked. My voice wasn't as low as hers had been, though there was definite uncertainty in my tone.

Turning to me, focusing on my eyes, he spoke. "Still."

# 17

## *Prentice*

Today was the day I would be sitting inside of a church to watch the homegoing of the man I killed. I can't lie. I was nervous—scared shitless. I knew there was a special place in hell for men like Von, but what about dudes like me? I guess I would find out. Experience was one of the best teachers, and this was possibly the most fucked-up lesson I'd learn. I shut my eyes tightly and said a silent prayer, asking for exemption and understanding. He knew why I did what I did. But showing up to see the effects of my handiwork was wrong as shit. I released a light chuckle, imagining myself walking inside, and my hair starts smoking like Eddie Murphy's did when he played Preacher Pauli in *Vampire in Brooklyn*. Damn, that would be some shit. Still, being there for Aúrea was important, so I was willing to take the risk of that happening . . . or worse.

Thankfully, she was still okay with me accompanying her after the incident with Brittney's ass. Speaking of Brittney, she's been blowing my phone up since I put her out of my house. I know it was fucked up of me to do her like that, and I have every intention of making things right with her. Well, right by way of apologizing and explaining myself a little bit. My main concern then and now . . . was and is . . . Aúrea. When I saw her with her bags heading for the front door, I panicked. She may not have seen it, nor did Brittney. Internally, I was melting like ice in front of a fire. I knew if she left, I wouldn't see her again, and that was *not* an option.

After Brittney left, Aúrea and I had a long talk, and I did my best to convince her that Brittney was not my girlfriend. Though she said it was okay, my gut told me she didn't believe me. If she gave me time, though, I would show her I wasn't lying.

Someone knocking on my door pulled me from my thoughts, and as I looked over my shoulder, Aúrea was walking into my bedroom. She looked gorgeous in an all-black dress that stopped a little below her knees. The small portion of her legs that were showing was toned and flawless. I mean, not a mark or hair in place. Her smooth, butterscotch skin was easy to envision resting on top of my shoulders. My eyes left her legs, slowly rising up her black dress that was snug against her hips, flat belly, and melon-sized breasts. The slight dip, well V-shape on the dress's neckline, showed a small amount of her cleavage. Still, it was enough to have me lusting over her.

Since being at my house for the past four days, Aúrea mostly wore clothes that hid her figure. Even the night I took her out on the town, she wore slacks. They did very little to expose her curves. When she was growing up, her body was the shit, but now, she was a grown woman, and it showed.

"Are you almost ready?" she asked, anxiously biting her bottom lip.

Damn, how I wanted to take that same lip into my mouth and suck on it.

"Almost. You good?" I turned all the way to face her, and I could see the hesitancy in her eyes. Aúrea's hazel eyes under long, thin lashes met mine. Her butterscotch complexion looked flushed, and I knew she was embarrassed or nervous, possibly both.

"No. I thought I was ready to do this. Now, I'm not so sure."

"It's cool to feel that way. I'ma be at your side the whole time."

"Thank you."

Slowly, I approached her, placing a hand on each of her shoulders. I pulled her into my chest, kissing the top of her head. She stepped back some after I did that but not enough to break our embrace. She looked up at me as I looked down at her.

"You've changed, but I still see a glimpse of the old you," she spoke softly.

It felt good to hear those words from her. If she noticed a change in me, then maybe she would trust that I could do all that I promised to do now. If she saw even a small part of the me she used to know, she would know that I still cared, still had a love for her. Then she would chill some and let me care for her like I always had wanted to do.

"That's good to know you see it. Maybe now, you'll stop trippin'." I smiled at her before winking.

"Maybe," she shrugged, and we both let out a quick laugh.

"You know you can do this, right? You came all this way to do this, and if there's one thing I know about you and have always admired about you, it's that you can get done whatever you put your mind to."

"This is different, though."

"Not really. It's only another obstacle to tackle and a bit longer of a hike to the top. You can do it, though."

"Thank you."

"You don't have to keep thanking me, Aúrea." It felt good, and I was probably blushing and shit. Though I meant what I said, she didn't have to keep thanking me. Shit, I should be thanking her for being here and letting me back in after all this time.

"I know, but if you only knew what I dealt with when I left, you'd understand why I appreciate all of this as much as I do."

"I've been ready to listen." Since she returned, there was so much I wanted to know. I wanted to know where she had been, what she was doing, how life was for her, and she had yet to speak on it.

"Now isn't the time." She shook her head and stepped back from me, and instantly, I felt empty. I needed her close. I didn't know how much until she put more distance between us.

"All right," I agreed, not wanting to make her uncomfortable.

"I'll meet you downstairs." She left my room, and I sat there staring at the door for a moment, confused as hell. Heading back to my dresser, I made sure my tie was straight, sprayed on my Gucci cologne, and headed out. It was time to get this chapter over with.

We sat in the back of the church, and when it was time to view the body, Aúrea surprisingly stood without hesitation. She walked the entire way with her head held high as I trailed closely beside her with my hand on the small of her back. My feet began to feel heavy the closer we got to his casket. I couldn't believe I was doing this. I knew people murdered and showed up to funerals like it was nothing. I wasn't that type of nigga, though. Had I known this was going to be the case, I probably would have burned his ass. Aúrea made it to the casket, and I stood back. Her body shielded his face, and I was grateful for it because I didn't want to see his ass.

"You violated me every chance you got, and now, you're going to burn in hell," she sobbed.

It wasn't loud enough for the entire room to hear . . . just me and maybe the first two people in the front row, for sure. What she said was clear as day. She didn't linger after that. She stormed off, and I rushed behind her. I didn't want to look at Von, but my damn eyes betrayed me, and I caught a glimpse of his ass before quickly turning my head and catching up to Aúrea. Seeing the side of his face, I knew the mortician did a good job on him.

"Aúrea," I called out to her, and I thought she would keep running. She didn't. She stopped, allowing me to catch up.

I placed my hands on her shoulders and turned her to face me. Tears were streaming down her face. Her bottom lip quivered. Her hands, her entire body, were shaking. Pulling her into me, I held her as tightly and closely as humanly possible.

"I hate him, Prentice. I know this is the wrong time to be full of hatred, but I am. I truly hate him," she cried. And I mean, hard. Those small shakes had become full-on tremors.

"It's okay, A." Kissing the top of her head, I rubbed her back and wasn't letting her go until she calmed down and removed herself from my grasp. It wasn't until people started filing out of the church that she interrupted our embrace. But fuck these people. I was gonna hold her until the sun went down, in this very spot if it was what she required.

"I wanna go to the burial." She took a step back while wiping her tear-stained face.

"You sure about that?"

"Positive. Seeing him in there wasn't enough." She nodded her head in the church's direction. "I have to see him be put into the ground. When he's there, I'm laying down all my burdens he caused in there with him. I'm letting them go forever."

"Okay," I agreed, ushering her to my car.

We followed behind the long row of cars to the burial ground, which only took about ten minutes. We sat watching everyone exit their vehicles and getting to the designated area before getting out of my car and standing behind the crowd. I held Aúrea's hand the entire time. I was not paying attention to what was being said, only watching my surroundings and making sure she was holding it together. Other than the tears that continued to fall from her eyes, she was doing fine.

I heard *Amen* and looked up to see the crowd dispersing. How I missed the ending of the speech, I didn't know, but I did.

"You ready?" I asked her, feeling her body stiffen. Looking down at her with furrowed brows, I tried to figure out what her problem was.

"Aúrea," I called out to her, only to be ignored. I stared at her intently, trying to figure out what had her so frozen.

"Oh, wow, Aúrea. How are you?" some woman asked that I didn't recognize. She shouldn't have been familiar to me since I only knew Aúrea's foster parents. Anyone outside of them would mean nothing to me.

"H-hi," Aúrea stuttered. She had finally found her words, I guess.

"How have you been, sweetheart? Wow, it's so good to see you. Von and Patricia were worried sick about you." She approached Aúrea with open arms.

"Thanks, but no thanks, ma'am. She's not here for all that," I cut in, stepping in front of Aúrea. I'm sure whoever this lady was had no clue of the hell she went through living with Von and Patricia. I wasn't going to allow people to come up to her like she should be sad because some damn saints raised her.

"Well, excuse me. Aúrea, it was good to see you, baby."

She rolled her eyes at me as she walked away. Two more people came up and spoke to her before Aúrea's and my eyes landed on her foster mother at the same time. I don't know how we . . . well . . . I missed her before. The saddest person in the area shouldn't have blended in with the crowd.

"Aúrea, are you okay?" I asked again. Those seemed to be the only words in my vocabulary today. This was a lot for her. I know it was. I guess asking the same question would eventually resonate within her, and she would be okay.

"Prentice, please, give me a moment."

"All right." I threw my hands up in surrender. She was gon' be straight. I was sure of it now. The fire in her tone proved it.

# 18

## *Aúrea*

When Prentice and I left his house this morning, I felt empty. I told him I was okay and ready for today, but I wasn't. I barely slept the night before, tossing and turning all night, going back and forth about whether I was doing the right thing. I even texted Rebecca. Well, I sent her an iMessage using Prentice's Wi-Fi because I still didn't have a working cell phone. Anyway, messaging her made me feel a little more prepared. Again, I wasn't as prepared as I would have liked to be. But having Prentice by my side was refreshing. I almost pushed him away after the incident with his girlfriend, who isn't his "girlfriend." If she is or isn't, at this point, I don't care. He confessed to her that I came first in his life, in front of me, and that spoke volumes. That was all I needed. Adrian would have never done something like that, and I gave his ass so much of me.

While we were in the church, I was able to keep my emotions tucked in. Prentice held my hand the whole time, giving me strength. When I got up to the casket, my heart thumped hard in my chest. What I expected to see and what I saw were two different things. Von had aged and not for the best. Or, it could have been the job the funeral home did on him. He didn't look the same.

Not like the man I remembered. This man looked old and worn down like he'd lived a stressful life. Like he was in his eighties and not his late forties. He used to favor the man who played Troy in *Waiting to Exhale* but definitely not anymore.

I couldn't help but wonder if guilt from what he'd done to me caught up with him. As I stared at him, I felt tears begin to well up in my eyes, and my anger pulled to the surface. I hadn't expected to say anything up there, only look at him, tell him how I felt, what he took from me . . . silently. Internally. My emotions wouldn't allow things to happen that way, so when I spoke to him about how I felt, I didn't care who heard. Apparently, not many people heard because there weren't any loud gasps in the room like there usually is when someone dropped something heavy like how I'd done. When I ran out after speaking, I felt some of the burden lifted from my shoulders. It felt good. I knew I wasn't done, which was why when Prentice asked if I was ready, I told him no because I needed to see Von's ass put into the ground. Now we were here, watching his body being lowered.

After watching roses being thrown onto Von's casket and the crowd starting to disperse, I should have been ready to leave. For some reason, my feet wouldn't cooperate, and I stood in place as if I were being held down by cement at the ankles. Random people were coming up to me, saying how wonderful it was to see me and that they were sorry for my loss. Not one person asked why I left. When my old caseworker, who happened to be a friend of Patricia and Von's, came up and spoke to me, I almost lost it. Prentice sensed it, and he sent her ass on her merry way. He kept asking if I was okay, and I knew he only wanted to help, but it wasn't helping at all.

I needed a moment and told him, so I walked ahead of him a few steps and stared at the woman who was supposed to protect me yet raised me together with her pedophile-ass husband. Seeing Patricia in a wheelchair and with an oxygen tank did something to me, though. It hurt me. There was no reason for me to feel any remorse for her, but I did. My eyes were stuck on her so long that she must've felt me watching because when she turned her head to look at me, her eyes widened as big as golf balls.

She grabbed the hand of the woman holding the back of her wheelchair, getting her attention before weakly pointing in my direction. She was at least four feet away from me, and I could still make out the shakiness of her hands as she struggled to lift her arm high enough to point at me. I began crying again, and through blurred eyes, I saw the woman walking toward me. I wanted to run because I knew Patricia sent her over, and there was nothing to be said. Prentice had to have been watching because, by the time the woman had made her way in front of me, he was right behind me with his hand on the small of my back, letting me know he was there.

"Aúrea," she spoke with a smile on her face and remorse in her tone, "it's so good to see you, baby girl. Do you remember me? I'm Patrice, your aunt. Patricia's sister."

She extended her arms to hug me, walking closer to me, and I stepped back right into Prentice. Patrice looked exactly the same from the last time I saw her, just a little older. She had aged well compared to her sister and Von. I remember Patricia looking just as pretty as Patrice. Both women used to look like the actresses Kim Fields and her younger sister, Alexis, Patrice being a replica of Alexis.

"Nah, she don't need no hug from you," Prentice told her, pulling me behind him.

*Damn, this man. He just keeps surprising me.*

"Oh, sorry. It's . . . We haven't seen her. We weren't sure if she was alive. I'm sorry if I scared you," she spoke, doing her best to look around Prentice to explain herself to me.

Wiping my tears, I took a deep breath and moved from behind Prentice to the side of him, prompting him to turn and look at me with a puzzled expression.

"I'm okay. I can do this," I told him, staring into his beautiful brown orbs. I *could* do this. Patrice obviously had no idea about the hell I endured living with her sister and brother-in-law, and that wasn't her fault. What was weird to me, however, was how she said they were worried about me. How could all of them have cared so much when I left, when not one of them cared enough to find out what the hell was going on with me when I *was* there? I mean, Von surely wasn't going to tell on himself. Patricia could have tried harder. No one on God's green earth could convince me Patricia did not have some idea that her husband had been raping and molesting me.

"Listen, Aúrea, I'm not trying to scare you or pressure you into anything. I'm sure you have good reasons for why you left." She paused, and I watched as her chest rose and fell. She looked over her shoulder at Patricia, who slowly nodded, and then she turned back to me.

"My sister is sick, and she doesn't have much time left from what the doctors have been telling us. She and Von always hoped that you would come back so they could make some things right with you. Now, I'm not sure what those things are because neither ever told me. I was only told that if you ever came back and either or both of them

had passed on when you did, I was supposed to direct
you to their lawyer. Even though my sister is still alive,
she wants you to meet with her and the family attorney in
two days. Are you willing to do that?"

Her eyes were pleading with me to agree while my
mind was going a mile a minute, trying to figure out if
that was something I wanted to do. Whatever Von and
Patricia wanted to make right, did I even care enough
now for them even to try? Well, Von was gone now, and
I wasn't even sure I needed an apology from Patricia any
longer. I wasn't sure if I even needed that apology now.

"Listen, I know it's a lot to ask, especially on a day like
today. So I'll give you the time and place, and if you can
or want to show up, that would be great. If not, then she
will understand. If you need more time, you can always
call the attorney and set up the meeting later. I just cannot
guarantee that Patricia will be there at a later date." She
went into her black bag and removed a business card,
handing it to me.

"The meeting will be in two days at 2:00 p.m. at the
address on the card. Patricia and I will be there that day.
We hope to see you." She stepped closer to me again,
leaned forward as if she was going to hug me, thought
about it, and backed up quickly, offering a smile instead.
I nodded my head and watched as she walked off toward
my former foster mother, whose eyes were still on me
with tears falling from them. I offered her a tight-lipped
smile and wondered if, in two days, I would be at this law
office able to listen to whatever it was she needed to say
to me.

"I'm ready to go now." I turned to Prentice, who took
me by the hand and led me back to his car. "Thank you
for being here." I'd been doing that a lot . . . thanking him.

I was sure I sounded like a broken record by now. It was hard not to express my gratitude. He was doing so much for me, way more than he had to, and I appreciated it. I also realized that I would have to pull back from him some. I didn't want to become dependent on him. I stuck with Adrian as long as I had because of dependency, and the woman I was trying to become would not thrive in a situation where I had to once again depend on a man to live. Aúrea was going to find out who she was and what she wanted without a man.

"You want to go to the house or out to eat?" he asked me as he pulled the car from the curb.

"Do you mind ordering in? I would like to go to your house and lie down."

Today's events were enough for me. There was nothing more I wanted to do than message Rebecca and tell her how I did today and Facetime Nijah to tell her the same while getting a little girl talk out of the way. She knew I was staying with Prentice, and, of course, I expressed to her how fine and attentive he was. She loved hearing stories about how good he had been to me. She also continued to say that me jumping into a new relationship was not the best move, and I agreed. I was definitely attracted to him, and more than anything, I was enjoying having my friend back.

"That's cool," he agreed, and I shut my eyes as he drove the rest of the way to his house.

I thanked the Uber driver as I exited his car before slowly making my way to the bottom step of the tall, white building. Removing my phone from my pocket, I searched for available Wi-Fi connections and connected to a free network nearby. I needed to quickly reach Nijah or Rebecca if this meeting didn't go as planned. Well, as planned was the wrong thing to say as I had no idea what I should even expect. Just as I had done the night before Von's funeral, I tossed and turned all night, debating on whether I was going to show up. Both Rebecca and Nijah told me I should, but even their advice wasn't enough to convince me.

I had created a list of the pros and cons of coming today before deciding to come. The pros had outweighed the cons and the realization that I would probably always wonder what would have come from this meeting if I hadn't come, hearing what Patricia's final words to me would be. So here I was, nervous as hell, walking up to this building. Prentice left early this morning with a promise to be back before dark. I was glad he had gotten out of the house because it seemed like he had no life outside of me since I'd been there. Besides, this was one thing I wanted to do without him. The upside of me not having a fully functional phone was him not being able to call me and see where I was and what I was doing. He was overly protective. At times, I didn't mind it, and other times, he got on my nerves.

"Okay, Aúrea, you can do this," I encouraged myself as I opened the glass doors of the Goldstein and Troop Law Offices. Slowly, I walked across the tile floors until I reached the door numbered 110.

"Welcome to Goldstein and Troop. How may I help you?" the petite Caucasian receptionist inquired.

"My name is Aúrea Shepard, and I was told to be here for a 2:00 p.m. meeting with the lawyer and Patricia Brown." My nerves were getting the best of me, and I was sure the woman heard the shakiness in my tone. She nodded at me before picking up the phone and letting someone know that I was here.

"Have a seat. Someone will be right with you."

Doing as asked, I took a seat and looked around. This one area of the building was huge, having at least five additional rooms and two reception areas. I could tell that they were making money here and had made up my mind that I would begin searching for a job of some sort once I left. I hadn't had to touch the money I saved because Prentice was openly doing everything for me, well, feeding and housing me. I needed to get a new phone, some more clothes, and toiletries. I was starting to get low on all of them, primarily because I had expected to be gone right after the funeral. Now, I wasn't sure when I would be leaving because I wasn't ready to walk away from Prentice at the moment. I no longer wanted to depend on him either, so I needed to get a job.

"Aúrea?" Someone calling my name pulled me away from my thoughts. I turned toward the sound of the voice, and my eyes slowly rose up the black tailored suit of a very tall figure. When my eyes met him, I instantly noticed how attractive he was. He resembled the rapper T. I., only a chocolate version.

"Y-yes," I stammered. I don't know why I was so nervous. Maybe because he was a grown-ass man, exceptional, Black, and successful. I mean, not that this wasn't a norm or possibility for a Black man. I just . . . Shit, I don't know. This whole thing was new to me.

"Hi, I'm Travis, the attorney your mother—"

"*Foster* mother, and since I'm grown, she's neither. You can address her as Patricia to me." I didn't mean to snap at him, but the little trance his looks had me in was gone the moment he tried to acknowledge that woman as my mother. She surely wasn't that.

"My apologies. Patricia is in my office and would like to speak with you privately before we go over the other reason you're here, which would be my job to explain. Of course, the one-on-one is up to you. So would you be open to speaking with her first, or should we get down to business?"

Putting my thumbnail into my mouth, I nibbled on it, contemplating my answer. I wasn't sure how we were going to talk. She looked like she had a hard time holding her head up, let alone being able to hold a conversation with me. But getting her side of things was one of the reasons I was here. I knew this was my opportunity to let her know about the horrible job she'd done protecting me.

"Yes, I'll talk to her."

"Great, follow me." He waited for me to stand before leading the way down a long, carpeted walkway. We got to the end of that and made a left, showing me that there was far more to this part of the building than I saw when upfront. He knocked twice on the door before opening it.

Patrice was sitting next to Patricia, who was in her wheelchair at the end of a long cherrywood table.

"Aúrea, you made it," Patrice said with a broad smile on her face that threw me off. Why was she always so happy to see me?

Shrugging, I went and took the seat across from where they were sitting. Patrice wasn't at fault in any of this. Still, I couldn't be fake with her or act like she was always around and the best aunt in the world. She knew as I did that she and I could count on one hand the number of times we interacted.

"We're going to step out and allow you two to talk. When you're done, press the red button on the phone, and we'll come back in," Travis said.

I nodded at him, then looked down at the table as he and Patrice left. It seemed like forever had passed before Patricia finally started speaking, and I could hear why.

"Aú-Aú-Aúrea," she struggled to say my name, and my eyes immediately shot up to look at her. "I-I'm so-sor-sorry," she forced out. Her voice was raspy and low. It was only audible because we were in this empty room. I could also tell she was straining to speak louder than her voice could carry.

I took a deep breath before pushing back the chair and standing to walk closer to her to sit. I felt terrible watching her struggle to speak. When I read on social media that she was sick, I didn't think she would look like this. Patricia had been a nurse, someone who specialized in health care. Why was she like this? How could she have allowed herself to *get* like this?

"Thank you," she said, barely above a whisper. There was nothing forced in her tone with getting this out, which helped me conclude that she had been straining to speak loudly when I was away from her.

"What happened to you?" I know she apologized and had things she wanted to get off her chest, but I wanted to know why she was in a wheelchair and needed an oxygen tank first.

"I've always been sick. Not long after you left, things went downhill for me. I have an immune disorder. Don't worry about me, though. That's not why we're here." Each word she spoke was low and raspy.

"I never knew you were sick."

"How could you? I didn't pay enough attention to you, which meant you didn't have to pay much to me. Still, you were a good kid, Aúrea."

She wasn't lying about that. Though I somehow had a reputation around my high school, I wasn't doing half the shit people claimed I was, nor was I doing nearly all I could have, given she worked so much and hardly paid me any mind. I had the life most teenagers dreamed of, the freedom to do whatever the hell I wanted. Instead, I did my schoolwork, chilled with Janae and Prentice, and, unfortunately, got fucked by my foster father—her husband.

"Surprised you noticed." I sucked my teeth, feeling myself become annoyed. She could attest to me not causing any trouble, yet she hadn't known what Von was doing to me?

"I did. Well, it was either that, or you were great with not getting caught. Your school never called, you were always in by curfew, and you were so independent."

"I was independent because I had to be." My words stung. Her expression showed it.

"I fed and clothed you. By the time we got you, you were pretty much able to take care of yourself. I'm sorry that I didn't realize—"

"You didn't realize that I was still a child who still had a lot to learn? Who still needed a mother figure? Who was dealing with things against my will?" My eyes were welling with tears. I didn't want to cry, but I did not want to let her see me cry. It wasn't something I could stop, though.

"You're right," she admitted with tears falling from her eyes.

"You need some water?" I quickly pulled myself together at the coughing fit she fell into. She shook her head rapidly, holding her hand up to pause me from whatever she thought I was about to do, which was screaming for help.

# 19

## *Prentice*

I took a right on Emerson Rd. and pulled into the back lot of the pharmacy I was in charge of. Today, I was driving my 2019 Honda Accord because it was the most inconspicuous car I owned. All my other vehicles were foreign, minus my Tesla, and when I was out in the streets handling business, I wanted to look more like a 9-to-5 worker versus the rich, street nigga. Not that my other cars automatically signaled that, but I couldn't put it past the cops to assume it if they saw me driving through known hoods. I stepped out of my car, dusting the invisible lint from my black Levi jeans. As I headed to the back door, this was also where the employees parked, so there was nothing suspicious about what I was doing. I knocked three times, which was code to let them know the boss was there.

"Hey, Prentice," Griffen, the doctor and owner of the pharmacy, greeted me with a brotherly hug.

"What's up?" I nodded, stepping through and allowing him to shut the door behind me. I looked around the big shelf toward the front and saw a line. Business was always good at this location.

"Busy today?" I spoke knowingly. It was more of a compliment than a statement.

"Yes, both sides of the business are doing good today," he informed me, bringing a small smile to my face.

"That's what I like to hear," I told him, following behind him to his office. This area of business, well, what was going on in the front, was all him. The other side was all me.

"Me too. And since you can see we're busy in the front, you think you can hang tight for a couple of minutes while I help my employees? Ted's ass bailed on me today, so I'm the only lead pharmacist," he expressed, looking stressed as hell. Just seconds ago, he looked calm and happy about the money coming in. Then once he realized he had to go back to the front, his mood quickly changed.

"Yeah, just don't take too long. I got other moves to make." He had business to handle, and so did I. I would only give him so long.

"Five minutes tops. Let me show this girl how to operate this machine."

"All right," I agreed.

Usually, I wouldn't have waited. I would have told him that what I needed and had going on was far more important than what he needed to do upfront. However, my patience had become a lot better since Aúrea came back. She was slowly changing things about me, and I had no issue with it, especially if it would make her comfortable enough to stick around. I wasn't sure what she and I would do in the future as far as a relationship was concerned, but right now, having my friend back was enough. I knew eventually, I would be trying to take it there with her. I went to bed too many nights with my dick on brick just thinking about her and knowing she was in the next room, and I couldn't do anything with her.

"Thanks for waiting, Prentice. You know we're usually better organized around here," Griffen said, walking back into his office faster than I expected.

"It's all good."

"So, here's the money for the products picked up from me, including the amounts and log sheets for the people who picked up."

"What you mean people who picked up? There should be only one person picking up from you at all times." I sat up in my seat, mugging the hell out of Griffen.

"I-I . . . Here, look," he stuttered, sliding the paper in front of me. I looked down the list and saw Sonic's name and Nick's. Sitting back, I relaxed a little, remembering that Nick had to make a pickup once because Sonic had some shit with his moms.

"My bad, Griffen. That name was approved for that day only. Things are to remain how they've always been. One name for the product and always me for the money."

"I gotcha, man. Shit, you almost gave me a heart attack. Today is just one of those days, and if I fucked up . . ."

"But you didn't, so let's just finish so that you can get back to work."

"There will be another order coming in next week. By Friday, it'll all be ready for pickup."

"Cool." I stood and extended my hand to shake while taking the bag of money. I went out the same way I came in, placed the bag in my trunk underneath the rug where my spare tire was supposed to be, and headed for my next destination. I was supposed to get up with Mr. Lewis today to talk. We had these meetings once a month where we talked about business and grown-man shit. He took on the role of my mentor and father figure, and I appreciated him for it.

I headed south on Emerson Rd. before hooking a left on to Edison. I needed to take the money in my trunk to the safe house. I drove carefully, doing the speed limit and using my signal for every turn until I pulled up to a small corner store owned by Sonic and me. His grandmother ran the store, and no one knew we had anything to do with it. We called it the safe house because it was safe, and it housed our shit. I was grateful it wasn't too far from the pharmacy, so I could get in and out, putting the money into the safe only we knew about, then left with my favorite bag of chips, Cool Ranch Doritos.

As soon as I was back to my car, I pulled my phone from my pocket, ready to call Mr. Lewis, and noticed a notification from my Ring app on my phone. I blew out a frustrated breath because if Brittney's ass showed up starting some shit, it was going to be her ass. Opening the app, I waited patiently for the damn thing to catch up and give me a playback.

"No!" I shouted, sounding like a little bitch. I didn't care either.

When it connected, I saw Aúrea rushing out of my front door to an awaiting car. I can't lie. If I weren't as young and healthy as I knew I was, the tightening of my chest would have led me to believe that I was having a stroke or heart attack.

"Where you goin', A?" I questioned as if she could hear me while putting my car in drive and peeling off the sidewalk. It was good that I dropped the money off because signals and speed limits did not matter this time. Getting to my house fast was all I cared about. I was on the other side of town at least half an hour from my crib, but I made it there in record time. My car was barely in park when I hopped out and rushed to my door. I twisted the knob, which was locked. To me, that was a good sign. She was either back or cared enough not to leave my shit wide open. I opened the door, bursting inside.

"Aúrea," I called out to her, racing up the stairs toward the room she'd been staying in. She had made the bed, and there was no sign of her in the house. I hurried to the closet and was thankful to see her clothes still hanging. After two days of begging, I had convinced her to stop living out of her suitcase.

I left her room and sat at the bottom of the stairs, removing my phone from my pocket. I don't know why I hadn't thought about calling her before. I scrolled through my contacts until I reached her name.

"Ain't this some shit?" I chuckled, realizing the number saved was the number she had before she left. I had no way of contacting her, and it hadn't crossed my mind until now. We'd been spending every day together. She was always here, and I was easily accessible to her, so exchanging numbers didn't even cross my mind. Now that I thought about it, I hadn't seen her on the phone or with one, for that matter. Regardless, when she came back, *if* she came back, that would change.

"Damn, she doesn't have a fucking key," I remembered aloud, standing from the stairs and heading to the front door. I checked my phone, and the time read 3:00 p.m., which prompted me to see how long ago she left.

Opening up the Ring app, I saw that she had left about a quarter 'til two. I sat on the front step, twiddling my damn thumbs with my left leg shaking, trying to calm myself down. She had just come back into my life, and I already couldn't see myself without her. I wasn't going to be any good if Aúrea disappeared on me again. Not only that, but I was also going to be pissed if she did.

The sound of tires rolling across the pavement caught my attention, and I saw a little black Camry pulling up to my front gate. The back door opened, and I saw her step out. Relief washed over me like a ho who dodged an STD. I stood to my feet so fast, power walking to the end of my driveway.

"Man, you trippin'," I drawled, wiping my hand down my face while opening the gate for her.

"I had something to do, Prentice. I didn't know I had to run my every move by you." She sucked her teeth, marching ahead of me.

I stood there looking at her like she was crazy as hell.

"Nah, you don't. But when you left and decided I was not important enough to keep in contact with and had me wondering if you were dead or alive for the past five years, it would've been nice to give me a heads-up," I spoke to her back. She stopped. My words must've done something to her. I could see her shoulders rise and fall, letting me know she was taking deep breaths to calm down, I assumed.

When she turned to face me, my heart broke. Her eyes were puffy. Her cheeks flushed . . . All signs that she had been crying.

"A, I'm sorry. I just—"

She held up her hand, halting my words. I wasn't sure if it was also my feet she was trying to stop as I was making my way closer to her.

"I didn't mean to make you think I'd walk out on you without a word," she spoke in a broken tone. She was afraid to make eye contact with me.

*Fuck, I scared her.* My face scrunched in confusion before taking my right hand and rubbing it down my face.

"You don't have to apologize to me, Aúrea. That's my bad. I shouldn't have come at you like that." Slowly, I closed the distance between us and gently reached for her hand, half-expecting her to pull back but grateful that she didn't.

"Who upset you? Besides me?" I asked as her eyes slowly made their way to mine. When our eyes met, I gave her my signature sexy, brown-nigga grin and was glad she reciprocated, forcing out a small smile of her own. No doubt, I had pissed her off. However, her eyes and flushed face told me she was upset long before she got here.

"Who I gotta beat up?" I cupped her chin, forcing her to keep her eyes on me. Damn, her lips were sexy as hell, and when she nervously licked them, it took everything in me not to press mine against hers.

"I went to the lawyer's office and met with Patricia, her sister Patrice, and the attorney, Travis."

"So you decided to go?" I clarified because she had been on the fence about going when she received the invitation. Not only that, but it also kind of hurt me that she hadn't thought much of me to let me in on it.

"Yeah, I realized it was something I needed to do. *Alone,*" she emphasized that last part, and I won't lie, that shit stung. Slowly, I removed the hold I had on her chin, nodding my head in understanding.

"So why are you so upset? I know your foster mom is in a wheelchair and all . . . If she hurt you, I know a few ladies over 80 willing to get down for a few dollars."

"Nooo," she laughed, making me smile. She laughed hard too like I told the best joke in the world when I was serious as hell. Patricia could get it, if necessary. Aúrea should've seen by now that I wasn't playing about her.

"It's fine. Though the meeting didn't go as I expected, it wasn't as bad either. Can we go inside now and talk?"

"We can do that."

She turned before me and walked inside like she owned my shit, and I had no complaint about it. This was a view I could get used to, which reminded me that I would be getting her a key made. Hopefully, that gesture would show her how much I wanted her here. I locked the door behind us and smiled, seeing Chuck and Rocko all over her with their tails wagging while she giggled. They never took to Brittney like this, and she spent more time around them than Aúrea had.

"All right, y'all, get down. Go sit," she told them, and like obedient children, they listened. The shit blew my mind, mainly because I had no idea they would listen to her. I always told them to leave her alone or get down, or I kept them out of the way for the most part. She took a seat on the sofa, and I did the same, waiting for her to begin talking.

"Patricia and Von left me everything as well as made me the beneficiary of his life insurance policy. I'm not rich, but I'm not broke, either. I also found out that Patricia planned to tell me about my birth mother on my eighteenth birthday, but, of course, I ran away, so I missed out on that information." She released an uneasy chuckle. "Anyway, if it's okay with you, I'd like to stay a little longer until my money clears, and then I'll look for a place of my own."

"I don't want you to leave at all."

"Prentice."

Her tone didn't sound like she was irritated. It was like she was pleading with me to not argue with her—I would honor that . . . for now.

"All right." I threw my hands up in surrender. "How do you feel about it all? The stuff with your birth mother, especially."

In all the years I've known Aúrea, we never really spoke about the woman who birthed her. She seemed to accept that her birth mother wasn't around, so there was never a reason to discuss her.

"I don't know. I guess I may look into it. Patricia told me she wasn't sure if she was alive. So I haven't fully decided if it's something I should look into," she shrugged.

"Well, you know I'm here if you need me, right?" I raised my left brow, looking at her, urging her to give the right answer 'cause if she didn't know, my ass was doing something wrong.

"Of course, I do."

"Good, then can I ask you a question?"

"Sure."

"Why is it that you don't want to live here? Everything has been good since you've been here. What's the problem with staying? I know you got your own money and shit, now, but that doesn't mean you have to move out."

She looked at me, and I could see she was thinking about the answer she wanted to give me. I just hoped it was an honest one.

"I'm not trying to mess up the things you already had going on before I got here. You've already made many adjustments since I've been here, and I'm not trying to get in the way."

"You're not in the way, Aúrea. How can you be in the way if a nigga wants you here? Why are you beating around giving me the real reason you not trying to accept my offer?"

"You have a girlfriend, Prentice," she blurted out, and I couldn't help but laugh. I mean, I let out a hearty-ass laugh because that shit was hilarious. I don't know what I had to do to show her I was single as a dollar bill.

"I wasn't making a joke." She sucked her teeth.

"It sounded like it, Aúrea, especially because I already told you that Brittney *wasn't* my girlfriend. What reason do I have to lie to you? You know what? It's coo'. We can drop that for now. I can show you better than I can tell you."

"If you say so."

"I do say so. You know you scared the shit out of me, right?"

"You told me," she giggled.

"That supposed to be funny?"

"A little."

"So, what's the reason you're not trying to stay with me?"

"It's nothing against you, Prentice. Honestly. My entire time in L.A. was spent with me living with someone. Then I got caught up in some stuff when I knew better. I came home to say my goodbyes, and I had no intention of staying longer than doing that. But now that I'm considering staying, I need to make my own way, and I need you to respect that, please. I just want someone to let me take care of myself on my own, for once. I can do it."

As hard as it was for me to agree with what she was asking, I guess I had no choice. I could give her what she wanted for now, but I wouldn't make it easy for her to be so distant as I had when she left.

"So while you were gone, and I was trippin', I realized I don't have your phone number, and you don't have mine."

"I don't have a phone. Well, I have one, but it's not turned on. It only works on Wi-Fi."

"Is that by choice, or you can't get one?" I hoped I didn't sound like an asshole. I knew she just came into some money, and since I never expected her to pay for anything while with me, I wasn't sure if she had a nickel to her name.

"A little of both, honestly. Before I left, my phone was cut off, and I needed to figure out my next move before deciding to get a new phone."

"I want to get you a phone."

"Prentice, no."

"It's not up for debate, Aúrea. Tomorrow, we're going to get you a phone, all right?"

"Fine." She rolled her eyes, sitting back with her arms folded across her breasts.

"Choose any phone you want," I told Aúrea as we stepped into the Verizon store. I planned to get her a phone, adding her to my phone plan, but I decided against it, realizing that she didn't want me getting her a phone anyway. To make her feel better, I would get whatever phone she wanted and put it in her name.

"Hi, I'm Erica. Do you know what phone you and your sister are shopping for?" The customer service rep kept her eyes on me, and her attraction to me was evident, which was why she called herself throwing a dig at Aúrea. We damn sure did *not* look like we could be related.

"Whatever phone I get, yo' ass surely won't be selling it to me," Aúrea spoke up, standing in front of me.

"Uh, I-I'm sorry," the girl stuttered, and I shook my head.

"I bet. You called yourself throwing a shot to get at him, and, honey, you're not even his type," Aúrea told her before walking off to look at the phones. I wasn't crazy, so I carried my ass on behind her.

It didn't take her long to choose a phone, and I stood to the side while a different associate helped her set it up.

"Thank you, Prentice."

"You're welcome. Now, dial my phone so that we have each other's number."

"I don't know your number," she confessed, laughing while handing her phone to me. I dialed my number, allowing it to ring a few times before locking her new number in.

"Why didn't you save your number?" she asked me.

"Wanted to give you the option to lock me in under whatever name you wanted to lock me in as."

"What did you save me under?" she questioned with a raised brow.

I grinned before shrugging, and she rolled her eyes as we both let out a light chuckle. We made our way to my car, and as soon as she was seated, she got on her phone.

"Nah-Jii," she sang into the phone. "It's me. You know who this is, so quit playing. No one else better be calling you, Nah-Jii. That's reserved for me and me only," she said to whoever she was speaking with.

I turned the music on low so that it didn't disturb her conversation, just loud enough so that my eavesdropping wasn't obvious.

"Everything is going pretty good. Really? You want to come out here with me?" she asked like she couldn't believe what she was hearing.

"Yes, I would love that. When can you come? Okay, I'll see you then. I'll call you when I get to Prentice's house, and then we can discuss everything. Okay, love you too." She ended the call.

"You hungry?" I asked, now that I was sure she was done with her phone call.

"Sure."

My phone rang, and I noticed it was Brittney. At first, I wasn't going to answer because I didn't want to be bothered with her ass. But I decided now was a better time than any.

"What's up?" I answered.

"Now you answer?" she yelled into the phone, clearly irritated. I noticed Aúrea looking at me from the corner of my eye.

"What do you want, Brittney?" I spoke her name because I wanted Aúrea to be sure it was her on the phone.

"Are you really just going to throw away what we had?" she whined.

"And what did we have, Brit? Were we in a relationship? Are you or were you my girlfriend?"

Waiting for Brittney's answer, I cut my eyes at Aúrea to see if she was paying attention, and she was. She also looked a little jealous, which made me glad.

"No, but—"

"There are no buts, Brittney. You and I weren't, nor are we, in a relationship." I blew out a frustrated breath. "Listen, Brittney. It's time we go our separate ways. I won't call you anymore, and you don't have to call me, cool?" I asked, even though I knew she wasn't cool with the shit.

"No, I'm not okay with that because you're not trying to give us a real chance."

"I'm out of chances to give, Brit. Have a nice life. You're a good girl. You'll find someone who's right for you. It just ain't me, ma." I hung up the phone, not bothering to hear anything else she had to say. She couldn't change my mind, and going back and forth wasn't something I was about to do.

"Did you really have to handle her like she was yesterday's trash?" Aúrea questioned, breaking the silence. With my brows furrowed, I turned to look at her, confused.

"How did I handle her like that?"

"If you don't know, Prentice, then there's nothing for me to explain to you. Just know you could have been nicer."

"You believe me now?"

"Yes, I believe you, Prentice," she laughed.

"And now you're moving in with me?"

"Don't push it," she told me, turning to look back out of the window.

I would let her have that. One thing she didn't know about this new Prentice was when I put my mind to something, I wouldn't stop until I got it.

# 20

## *Aúrea*

So much had happened since I first met with Patricia at her lawyer's three weeks ago. Now, as I signed the last document in the batch of papers in front of me, I asked the notary, "Is this all that's left?"

"Yes, the house is officially sold." She smiled, taking the papers from me, stacking them neatly before putting them inside her brown briefcase. We were sitting at the dining room table of my new condo.

"Okay, thank you," I said as the two of us stood, and I walked her to the front door. Locking the door behind her, I turned around with my back against it and looked at my new home—*my* home. The walls were a light grey. The floors were grey tile, which looked like hardwood. My living room was spacious and right in front of the open kitchen. My kitchen is one of my favorite parts of the place outside of my bedroom. The cabinets were white marble, the backsplash grey and silver. I wasn't a big cooker; however, I knew I would be making many meals in here with me having this kitchen. All my appliances were stainless steel, courtesy of Prentice, who I begged not to purchase me anything, but, of course, he wouldn't listen. The only reason I quit fighting him on it was that it was my way of giving into something he wanted since I moved out of his place, and he didn't want me to leave.

A week after I left the law office, my check was ready. I deposited it in the bank and began the hunt for a place to live. I liked the area Prentice lived in, but from what I could tell, there were only houses in that neighborhood, and I wasn't quite ready for a house yet. To my surprise, there was an area for condominiums and townhomes around the corner from his home, and that's where I ended up.

I'd only been here a week, and already it was fully furnished. Prentice was here every day. He was truly amazing and surprisingly hadn't pressured me for anything outside of trying to make me live with him. A part of me began to wonder if he found me attractive. I mean, he always called me beautiful, yet he hadn't tried to kiss me, sleep with me—nothing romantic at all. That was one of the other reasons I decided to move out of his home. I was starting to feel more like a woman he felt needed saving than a woman he could see himself in a relationship with, and it was not sitting well with me. Not that I wanted to be in a relationship with him or anyone else for that matter; still, it did something to my self-esteem that he didn't even try to push up on me in any way.

Walking over to the dining room table, I picked up my copies of the paperwork and headed upstairs to my home office. My condo had three bedrooms, and I used one for an office and the other for a guestroom. My home office was decorated yellow and white. I know it wasn't the traditional route of colors for a home office, but I always wanted to feel alive when I walked inside the room. I wanted it to make me feel energetic and ready, and since the sun was yellow and indicated the start of a new day, I went with that color. I opened the file cabinet and placed the papers inside before removing a medium-sized, rectangular, brown box.

I took the box, walked over to my white, generic, marbled desk, and sat down. I opened the box, pulling the contents out. Inside were my birth certificate and a photo of my birth mother and me. Her name was Aundrea Shepard. The area that was to include my father's name was blank. His identity would forever be a mystery. I looked at my mother's photo and could tell she was young when she had me, maybe 16 or 17 years old. Still, she was gorgeous, and I favored her a lot. We were both the color of butterscotch, with slanted eyes, pouty lips, and a button nose, with thick, curly hair. Two weeks ago, I picked this box up from Patricia and Von's house, even taking a few items from my old room that I left behind. I was shocked to see they left my room exactly how I left it that day, even down to my messy bed. The room was dusty as hell, which told me no one had been in there since the day I left, I assumed.

Anyway, I got everything out of there, including this box, sold the home, and donated the large items to women's shelters and the Salvation Army. When I retrieved the box of my birth certificate and photo of my mom, I was pissed at Patricia all over again, as well as emotional. She had all this information about where I came from and didn't tell me. I got over the anger quickly, though, because at least now, I had the knowledge and the option to decide what I was going to do with it. At the moment, I was going to let sleeping dogs lie. If Patricia fostered me at my mother's request, she knew where I was, and she hadn't reached out, so why should I?

The loud ringing of my cell phone captured my attention, and I rushed out of the room toward it.

"Hello."

"So, are you picking me up from the airport or what?" Nijah practically yelled in my ear.

"No. I would love to, but I have to work. Can you Uber here? I'll pay for it." I felt horrible. I wouldn't be able to greet my best friend properly when she made it into town. I just started my new job, and I couldn't get the time off. Well, I probably could, but I didn't want to look like the employee who was already asking for favors.

"Sure. Am I coming to your job or what? Because how am I supposed to get in your home?"

"I'll leave the key so that you can let yourself inside. I have a flowerpot right outside of my door. It's also a key holder. I'll text you the code, and you'll be able to get in."

"Cool, well, my flight gets in around 8:00 p.m., so I'll see you when you get home," she said excitedly, and I can't lie. I was getting just as excited as her. We went from seeing each other every day to it being over a month since we last saw each other.

"Love you. See you later." I ended the call and started getting ready for work. I still had a few hours to spare, but I was so happy about all the good things happening for me now that I looked forward to going to work. I was working part time at a local café which stayed open 'til 1:00 a.m. Friday through Sunday. Tonight, I was working the seven to eleven shift. Working wasn't something I had to do, especially since I inherited some cash and sold the house and cars, gaining me more money. Still, I knew that money wouldn't last forever, and since I wasn't the type to just sit in the house all day and had experience as a waitress, the café worked for me.

"This isn't nobody but Prentice," I snickered while rolling my eyes at the sound of my doorbell. I headed downstairs, opening my front door to see him standing there looking sexy as hell. He wore a pair of distressed dark blue jeans that hung off his hips just a little, held in place by a Hermès belt. The navy-blue T-shirt he wore had the Hermès symbol on the left side, while on his feet, he wore a fresh pair of high-top navy Air Force Ones. Prentice always looked like money when he stepped out.

"What are you doing here, Prentice?" I asked as if I were bothered by his presence, even though that was far from the truth. I'd gone from seeing him and being around him every day when living with him, and I was having a hard time adjusting to the change. I *was* adjusting, though.

"Man, I can come over here as much as I want. If you stopped acting like a stranger and brought yo' ass around the corner to my spot, I wouldn't have to keep poppin' up over here."

He walked inside, brushing past me, and I swear I felt my nipples harden. Closing and locking the door, I took a seat across from him on my sofa.

"It's only been a week since I moved out; plus, you've been here every day since then."

"You got a problem with it?" His brows furrowed.

"Would it matter if I did?" With my arms folded across my chest, I gave him the same look.

"Nope."

"Of course, it wouldn't," I mocked, shaking my head.

"What have you planned today besides going to work?"

"Well, nothing outside of my friend Nijah coming into town."

"That's what's up, I guess."

"You guess?"

"Yeah, I mean, I was used to being your only company, and now, you have a friend other than me," he spoke as if he were sad.

"I didn't say you couldn't stop by just because she's here, Prentice."

"Oh, I know that. You couldn't keep me away even if you had a little boyfriend coming around."

"Whoa. Don't go that far. I'm not even interested in having a boyfriend right now." At least, I thought I wasn't. Maybe if it were him trying to be my boyfriend, I would consider a relationship.

"That's good to know. Look, I came over here because I wanted to take you out to celebrate. I know I gave you a hard time about moving out and shit, but I'm proud of you. You got your own spot, a job, and you really doing good for yourself. Most of all, I'm happy that you're doing all of that here, with me close by. You could've dipped again, and you didn't. That means more to me than you'll ever know."

I looked at him and smiled. Prentice was amazing. The growth I saw in him every day since I got back made me appreciate our time apart. Had I stuck around, maybe he wouldn't have become this man. And the way he's made me feel every day since I've been around him would have been tragic not to experience him the way he is right now.

"When are we going to celebrate? I have to work, and then I'll have company."

"Right now. Go get dressed. You can even wear your work uniform, and I'll drop you off at work afterward."

"If you drop me off, how am I supposed to get home, Prentice?"

He gave me a look that said, "Quit fuckin' playing with me." I laughed before taking my ass upstairs to get dressed.

I had no idea where we were going, and I didn't want to wear my uniform out, so instead, I threw on a cute romper and brought my uniform along. I could change at work or wherever we were. Today, he was driving his Range Rover, and I swear it was my favorite of all his cars. He was currently letting me use his Tesla since I hadn't purchased a car of my own yet. That was one thing I wasn't in a rush to do. After driving his Tesla every day, there was no way I was looking forward to buying a car that I could afford, and that damn sure wasn't a Tesla or a Range Rover. My money could get me a used BMW, maybe, and it would be at least three years old. So I was going to keep using his car until he decided he wanted to take it back.

"Where are we going?" I asked, looking out of the window.

It still amazed me how our hometown had developed. Well, this side of town anyway. The hood hadn't been touched.

"Just ride."

Doing as he told me, I sat back in my seat and rode, listening to the music he played. Prentice's choice of music was always the same. He only rode to rap but only one rapper at a time. Today's rapper was Lil Wayne, and *The Carter III* was his album of choice. I didn't complain because this was one of my favorite Wayne albums as well.

When he pulled into the parking lot of our local zoo, I smiled. Not a place I expected him to bring me.

"You remember our first time here?" he asked.

"Yeah." I laughed at the memory. I had been standing with my back to the glass, and a tiger damn near broke the glass to get to me. Well, I'm exaggerating, of course.

The glass barely moved. Still, it was enough to scare the shit out of me, and I was done with the zoo after that.

"We not going by the tigers today, so you'll be cool." He exited the car, coming around to help me out, and I took his hand as he led me to the other side of the entrance, where we walked into a banquet hall.

"This is beautiful, Prentice," I complimented, looking at the nicely decorated table. "How did you know I would even agree to come out with you? You had all this set up for me?"

We moved closer to the table, and there was an array of food and fruits, and everything smelled great.

"Because I wasn't taking no for an answer. Letting you deny my invitation to live with me was the first and only no I'm taking from you." He pulled out my chair, waiting for me to sit before pushing me slowly closer to the table. I kept my eyes on him as he swaggered his way to the seat across from me.

"Thank you. This is very nice."

"Hey, you doing big things now, so I had to celebrate you in a big way."

"You're surely on the right track with this move."

"Glad you like it. So how do you feel about everything? You know, your place, working, being back here?"

"I feel like everything is finally good. I don't have any complaints," I told him honestly because I couldn't think of one thing to complain about when I was so grateful for all I had that I didn't have to have. When I came back here from L.A., I had hit rock bottom. When I left here for L.A., I had nothing. So I was more than appreciative of everything I had now.

"That's what's up," he said before removing the top from his and my plate. "You got this, or you want me to serve you?" he asked with a crooked grin.

"I can make my own plate *and* yours too." I didn't wait for a response as I used the serving spoon and placed the different items on both of our plates.

"Can I ask you something?" We had been silent for a few seconds, and I figured now was a better time than any to ask something I'd been dying to know.

"Anything. But you know that already." He looked me right in the eyes, and for a moment, I found myself afraid to speak. Why did I care anyway? Shit, who was I kidding? I cared because of how I felt about him, so I was going to ask my question.

"Since I've been here, the only girl I've seen you with . . . well, knew about, is Brittney, who wasn't your girlfriend, I guess. You're young, handsome, and single. What are you waiting for?"

"What do you mean, what am I waiting for?"

"Like, why are you single? Brittney was a pretty girl, and you've been with me a lot. I mean, I know you have to."

"Have to what? Want to have sex with someone?" he laughed.

I swear I felt my cheeks flush in embarrassment. I picked up my glass and took a sip. I didn't even want to continue this conversation now, pissed I stepped on a ledge like I wouldn't fall.

"My sex life I'm not going to discuss with you, only because there's this sexy-ass, butterscotch-complexioned girl with some thick, curly hair and a badass shape that makes me bite my bottom lip to keep my composure every time I see her. So, yeah, I'm waiting for her to be ready for a nigga like me, so she can be loved right."

I tell you, I felt my panties get soaked, like my water just broke. My heart pined as I did my best to keep still—

any idea I had about him not wanting me as anything more than a friend was dead wrong.

Dead.

Fucking.

Wrong.

However, now that I knew that, I didn't know what to do with the information. I did realize that I wasn't ready to act on it just yet.

"Okay. That was TMI," I whispered, when, in actuality, I was happy as hell that he said what he did. "Is there a restroom around here?" I needed to go and handle this puddle in my panties, mainly . . . removing them from my body.

"Back there," he pointed, and I popped up so quick that you would've thought someone lit a match under my ass. I hightailed it to the bathroom and removed my panties, placing them in my pocket. I would've thrown them away if we weren't in a public place.

"Pull yourself together, Aúrea," I told myself, taking deep breaths while looking in the mirror. My cheeks were a rosy color, giving away how flustered I was. Holding the edges of the sink with both hands, I continued to take deep breaths to calm my nerves. This man really had me on one.

"Okay, you got this," I told myself, exiting the bathroom. I wasn't all the way together, but I didn't want him to think I snuck off to take a shit in the middle of our lunch, so I went back to the table.

"You good?" he questioned, and I could've sworn he winked at me like he knew what I was doing in the bathroom.

"I'm fine."

"What do you plan to do next? You got you a place, a part-time job, so is there anything else you plan to do?"

Thankful he changed the subject, I smiled, feeling refreshed. This was something we could definitely talk about.

"Yes, I'm going to go back to school. I still want to be an actress. I'm just going to go a different route this time. Next week, I'm going to enroll at the community college majoring in theater."

"Damn, that's dope." His broad smile was infectious, making me smile as well. It felt good to see he was genuinely happy with my plans.

"Thanks. You know, I don't think we've ever discussed what it is you do. You have a huge house, a whole lot of expensive cars, and—"

"I have a couple of ways I make money, one we won't discuss. I have a consulting business, and I'm a silent partner in my mom's place and a restaurant."

Nodding to let him know I understood, there was nothing else he needed to say. One way he made money was legal, the other, illegal. We made small talk and finished as much of the food that we could before taking a quick stroll through the zoo, avoiding the tigers altogether. By the time we were done, I had an hour to get to work. Prentice dropped me off and promised to be back to pick me up. So I went to work, hoping that 11:00 p.m. came quick.

Prentice wanted to walk me upstairs to my door, and no matter how much I protested, he wasn't having it. When we walked inside, Nijah was relaxing on my sofa with her feet underneath her butt and my dark grey throw over her legs, watching TV. Either we opened the door super quietly, or she was so into the show that she hadn't noticed us coming in. Deliberately, I slammed the door and laughed when she damn near jumped out of her skin.

"Aúrea!" she sang when her eyes landed on me. She leaped from the sofa and rushed over to me, wrapping her arms around my neck. We held each other, jumping up and down like Celie and Nettie did on *The Color Purple*.

"I missed you," she exclaimed, still holding on to me for dear life, while I giggled uncontrollably. I missed her too and didn't realize how much until now. Nijah was my breath of fresh air.

"Damn, I wish I had been greeted like *that*." Prentice's voice broke our embrace.

"Shit," Nijah yelped, removing herself from me. She had been so happy to see me that she didn't notice him. And because I was so excited to see her, he had been forgotten about that quick.

When her eyes met Prentice's, she took off back to the sofa. It was then that I noticed the small-ass boy shorts she had on. She picked the throw blanket up and wrapped it around her waist before walking back over to us.

"I'm sorry. I'm Nijah, Aúrea's big sister from another mister." She extended her right hand toward him, holding the blanket with her left.

The way she introduced herself to him brought a smile to my face as I realized she was the female version of Prentice. Crazy. It was something that I was just now aware of. Being around him all this time, seeing how protective he was of me, was almost the same kinda way Nahji was. They weren't exactly the same type of crazy when it came to me, but I knew without a doubt they both loved me.

"I'm Prentice. Nice to meet you." He shook her hand.

"Thanks for looking out for her. I mean, I know you knew her first and all, but this girl is my heart. I'm glad she has someone like you looking after her."

"She's my heart too, so no thanks needed."

Nijah cut her eyes to me, and I hurriedly shifted mine to the floor, flattered and embarrassed at the same damn time.

"Good to know." She was grinning her ass off as I elbowed her. She wasn't slick, and though she wasn't flirting with him, she was absolutely calling herself playing matchmaker. All it took was seeing how sincere Prentice was when it came to me, and she was silently marrying me off to him.

"Aúrea, I'll see you tomorrow, all right?" He turned his attention to me.

"Still?" There wasn't a reason for me to be shocked that he planned to come by tomorrow. He visited every day. I should've known having company wasn't going to change that.

"What? You thought 'cause your people was here something was about to change?" He grabbed me by the waist, pulling me into him, kissing the top of my head.

"Guess not," I whispered. Damn, this boy was getting me hotter and hotter and bothered by the day. He released me, and I'd be damned if my heart didn't sink at the separation.

"Lock the door," he ordered as he opened my front door.

"I will." I placed my hand on the knob, holding it as he stepped outside.

"I'll see you tomorrow," he reminded me. "Bye, Nahji," he teased, smiling before we all laughed, and I shut the door, locking it.

"Giiirrrlll," Nijah sang, smiling so big that if her cheeks burst, that would be no surprise.

"I know what you're thinking, and your ass needs to relax."

"Look, I know what I said about finding yourself and all of that, but that man right there? You can go against every damn thing I told you. I know a good man when I see one, honey."

"You do, huh?"

"Damn right. Let's not forget *I'm* the one who advised you *not* to get with Adrian's ass, and who was right? You or me?" She used her index finger to point between us.

Rolling my eyes toward the ceiling, she spoke again before I could even say something smart.

"You can roll them eyes all you want to. You know I'm right. *Anyway,* since you want to act like you didn't want to drag his ass up those stairs and ride him 'til tomorrow—"

"Change the subject, Nahji."

"Okay, okay." She threw her hands up in mock surrender, doing a horrible job of suppressing the smile she so desperately wanted to show.

"What were you doing since I've been gone?"

"Talking to yo' ass every day, Aúrea, and working. You know that."

"Did you go by Ms. Jackie's and let her know I was okay?"

"Sure did, and she said Adrian came by looking for you. Hell, I've caught him sitting outside of my apartment a few times looking for you."

"He didn't say anything to you, did he?" Just knowing Adrian's crazy ass had been stalking Nijah's house and going to the café to look for me put my nerves on edge. I don't know why I thought he would let me go by now. I should have been an afterthought. "Why didn't you tell me, Nahji?"

"Because all you would've done was worry, and I didn't want you doing that. Adrian's ass doesn't scare me. I already told you that. Besides, his dumb ass would be under the jail if he tried anything."

"What do you mean?"

"Look." She handed me her phone, and I looked at the multiple messages she had from him. There were screenshots of him threatening not only her but also me as well.

"I'm sorry, Nahji." My heart broke, and guilt took over. He wouldn't have been harassing her if it weren't for me.

"Girl, you know better than to apologize for that sorry-ass nigga. You have no control over him acting like a bitch. Once again, his threats *do not scare me.* Neither does his punk ass. Plus, he doesn't know you're out here, so you don't even have to see his ugly ass again."

"Okay, but you know he isn't ugly."

"He acts like a bitch, so he's ugly. A person can be fine on the outside, but if their insides are ugly, that shit will eventually show on the surface, and Adrian's ways make him hideous."

"You're right, I guess. I stopped liking his ass after the second time he slapped me."

"The *second* time?" she looked at me like I were crazy.

"Yeah. He didn't slap me hard enough the first time, I guess." It wasn't meant to be funny; still, both of us burst into laughter.

"I'm thrilled you're here. You gonna stay for a while?"

"I don't know. Probably until I begin to feel like a third wheel. That damn Prentice is about to make you his woman soon, child. *Real* soon, and it doesn't look like any of your efforts to fight it will work."

"We are just friends."

"Yeah, keep telling yourself that," she teased. "I know your friend-boo is going to be coming around. Please make sure my time here is not spent in your home. It's really nice, but I'm trying to go out and see the town."

"I got you, I promise."

# 21

## *Prentice*

Standing at Aúrea's door with a bouquet of roses, I held my hand up, fist balled, ready to knock, only I hesitated. Why in the hell was I so nervous? It wasn't like we hadn't gone out on numerous occasions. Keeping it real with myself, I knew this time was going to be different. Before the night was over, she would know how a nigga really felt about her, and I just hoped that she was open to receiving what I was trying to give, which was full access to my heart. She been had the shit, yet, with the way things were going, she needed a reminder and reassurance that I wanted her to have my shit and give me hers in return.

Taking a deep breath, I sucked up the shit and knocked on the door. Knocking on her door made me feel lame as hell. There was no reason I didn't have a key. She needed to fix that.

"Hey, she'll be down in a minute," Nijah spoke, letting me inside. She was still out here, and since Aúrea enjoyed having her around, it was fine with me as well. Long as I got my time in with A, there was nothing for me to complain about.

"Awe, those flowers are beautiful," Nijah complimented, and a nigga felt his cheeks heat up.

"These ain't nothing," I shrugged, trying to get my cool back.

"So, where you and little sis goin' for y'all date?"

"It's not a date," I quickly corrected. My voice had gone up a notch too, which had me sounding nervous as fuck.

*Damn.*

"It sure looks like a date."

"It ain't, though. Me and Aúrea have our own thang. We just hang out."

I don't know who I was trying to convince, myself or Nijah. Honestly, I would have loved to call this our first official date, but she continued to make it known that a relationship or even dating wasn't something she was concerned about now. So forcing this outing to be a date wouldn't work in my favor, I was sure.

"Okay." She shrugged and went and took a seat on the sofa. She sat down, tucking her feet underneath her butt. No lie, Nijah was drop-dead gorgeous, and if I met her in another lifetime, shooting my shot wouldn't even be a second thought. I'd probably be on one knee with a ring in front of her. She had a smooth, caramel complexion. Thick in all the right places, about a D-cup bra size. If I had to compare her to someone, she looked like a shorter, darker, thicker version of the singer Mya, except she wore her hair shoulder-length straight with some kind of red tips at the bottom.

"Okay, I'm ready," Aúrea spoke, stepping into the front room, looking breathtaking. She wore a pair of black shorts with some boots that went high up her legs and a pink and black shirt that hung off her shoulders. Her usual curly hair was straight with a part on the side, reminding me of the style the late Aaliyah used to wear.

If Aúrea didn't want me or any other dudes lusting after her, she was damn sure making it hard, looking the way she was looking. I shifted a bit, hoping neither she nor Nijah noticed me adjusting my dick.

"All right, let's go." I tried to sound unmoved like I wasn't tripping, and like tonight was a regular night like any other, but if Aúrea didn't know, I was fronting. Nijah's ass sure did. The mischievous smirk on her face gave it away.

Holding the door open, I waited till Aúrea got in front of me.

"You sure you're gonna be okay?" she asked over her shoulder to Nijah.

"Girl, yes, bye."

When she said that, I wasted no time pulling Aúrea farther out the door and shutting it behind us, knowing that Aúrea would probably cancel on me if she didn't receive the right answer.

"You look beautiful."

Aúrea smiled at my compliment as she got into the car. We were in my Tesla tonight. She'd been driving it, but I missed being behind the wheel of the vehicle, so tonight, *I* was driving.

"Where are we going?"

"Just ride."

She sucked her teeth before sitting back and doing what I asked. Since I hoped to use tonight to lay my feelings on the table, a public place with a large crowd wasn't going to work, so I paid to rent out the entire restaurant. It wasn't really fancy, just a Japanese spot across town. When we walked inside, I immediately noticed how Aúrea's eyes widened in surprise.

"You like it?" I asked, smiling knowingly when she looked at me.

"There's no one here."

"We're here. That's how it's supposed to be. Tonight only, anyway," I shrugged, taking her hand and leading her over to the small sitting area. Shortly, a chef came out and began setting up. When he lit the fire over some onions, Aúrea's ass just about jumped out of the seat and her skin.

"It's not funny, Prentice. I wasn't expecting that," she fussed.

My ass was laughing hard as hell too.

"My bad, my bad." Wiping my hand over my mouth, I forced myself to stop laughing.

"You've never been to a spot like this?" Now, my curiosity had taken over, wondering what kind of life she really had out in L.A., where she hadn't even been to a place as simple as a teppanyaki restaurant.

"No."

"Glad to know I brought you here first."

"So, what's the special occasion?"

"Since when does it have to be a special occasion for us to hang out?"

"It doesn't, you're right," she mumbled.

"Aúrea." My tone was intended to get her to look at me, not frighten her, which obviously it had because she jumped. This was the most I'd seen her so jumpy since the day she came back, and I wondered why. Right now, the only conclusion I could come to was her new houseguest. Nijah seemed cool and all, but I didn't know her. She also didn't know me, and if she were the reason for this little shift in Aúrea, she'd get a first-class view of the bottom of the Pacific.

"Yes?"

"What's wrong with you? Did I do something wrong?"

"No. No, I have a lot on my mind."

"You ready for your houseguest to go and don't know how to tell her? If that's it, you know I'm a pro at sending females on they way."

"Not at all. So you bet not try to send her off." She waved her finger at me.

Speaking as gently as possible while I reached across the table to take her hands, I requested, "Then tell me what's up with you. I can tell something is bothering you. I need to know something, preferably the truth, though, A, 'cause whatever is bothering you is written all over your face."

She accepted the invitation, taking my hands, looking me in the eyes, and smiling.

"Can we just talk about it later? Let's enjoy dinner first, please?"

Nodding, I released her hands.

The cook finished our food, and we ate mostly in silence. Occasionally, I'd ask some corny-ass question, but for the most part, we were both in our own world. So far, shit wasn't going how I planned for tonight, and Aúrea's mood wasn't the most inviting for the kind of intimate conversation I wanted to have.

"Are we going straight to my place when we leave here?" she asked.

"That's up to you."

"Well, I promised to tell you what's been up with me when we leave here, but my place isn't where I wanna have the conversation, though."

"All right, I have a place in mind we can go."

"Okay." She gave me a closed smile as I stood up, walking over to her, extending my hand to help her up. We exited, and I brought her into my car before getting in and driving off.

Soft music played in the background. Since Aúrea had been driving my car, her phone connected automatically, and she had some soft-ass playlist going.

"Who is this singing?" This song was pretty dope, the lyrics anyway. I wasn't too much into R&B unless it was baby-making joints, so for this to catch my ear said something.

"Oh, it's Jhené Aiko."

Nodding, I turned the radio up a little more. The vibe was good and relaxing, even though on one of the songs, baby girl was talking shit.

"Wow, I haven't been here in forever." Aúrea laughed when she noticed where I parked the car.

"Me either," I told her honestly.

We were parked at Chill Cliff, as the teenagers liked to call it now. Shit, we did too, growing up. It was a spot way outside of town that overlooked the city and the water. It was dark out, so only the establishments that were open and a few streetlights lit up the city. The view was dope, though.

"The view of the city is beautiful. Always has been, I guess. Just can appreciate it more now that I'm older," she confessed, looking straight ahead.

I removed my seat belt, then pushed the seat back as far as it would go, and turned to face her as best as I could.

My Tesla was a nice-sized car and roomy, but I was a tall dude, so getting completely comfortable wasn't an option. This would work, though.

"Did tonight seem like a date?"

She turned and looked at me, seemingly confused by my question.

"I mean, I guess it could've been considered that or just two friends hanging out."

"What if—?"

"L.A. was everything but roses for me, Prentice," she spoke, cutting me off. She paused, I guess, to see if I was going to start talking again or shit, I'm not sure. So I pressed my lips together, waiting for her to finish.

"My first year in L.A. I was homeless. Even though shortly after getting there, I met Nijah, who took me in. I still hadn't had my own place, so to me, I was homeless with a place to stay." She paused again, taking a deep breath.

"When I got comfortable with her, I started looking into acting and landed a commercial. That was honestly the happiest time of my life, well, since I got there."

I wondered if it was the commercial I saw since she spoke openly right now, but I wasn't going to interrupt to ask. I'd find out later.

"I thought I was the shit after that and went on more auditions for parts I didn't get. Still, my determination didn't waver, so I kept trying. One day, I was at an audition for a modeling gig for a magazine ad, or maybe it was a commercial. Anyway, there was this guy who intrigued me."

My fist balled and opened. My mood shifted almost instantly when she said that. Hearing about her feeling another nigga wasn't something I was feeling nor wanted to hear.

"So, he approached me and told me he had these connections and was an agent. He dressed the part and had a few gorgeous women with him, so there was no reason to think he was lying."

She looked away, wiped her eyes, then looked back at me. I was doing my best not to show the anger slowly brewing, not just because I was a bit jealous of her speaking of another nigga, but also because Stevie Wonder could see this wasn't a good recap of what she dealt with in L.A.

"I fell for what he told me and eventually fell for him. By the time I realized he wasn't going to help make me a star, I was already stuck and in love.

"Everything was good. I moved in with him against Nijah's wishes, of course. Then it all went bad. First, he was verbally abusive. Then he cheated a lot. Well, he always cheated. He just stopped caring to hide it once he knew I wasn't going to leave him. After that, he started hitting me and forcing me to do—" She stopped, shaking her head as if she were trying to erase a horrible memory, and I felt my blood boil.

"Where this nigga at, Aúrea, and what's his name?" I'd heard enough. Her admitting that he put his hands on her left nothing else for her to tell me, except what I needed to go and handle his ass.

"Prentice, no. I left, and he's way in L.A.—"

"Just take me to the nigga, Aúrea, or give me his information."

"Why?"

She sat back, folding her arms across her chest in defiance, and all I could do was chuckle. This shit wasn't up for debate. I had no problem answering her question, though.

"So I can handle him. You can't tell me no shit like that and not expect me to want to go and see dude," I seethed.

"You wanted me to be honest with you about my life out there, so that's what I was doing. I didn't do it because I wanted you to put your life and freedom on the line for me. I don't need saving," she yelled as tears fell from her eyes.

It hurt to see her cry. But my anger was more prominent than her hurt feelings. My pride and love for her wouldn't allow me to know another nigga had violated her and me not move on it. The promise I kept to myself to nip shit in the bud quickly when it came to her and anyone causing her harm was more critical than her begging me to leave the shit alone or any later consequences I may face.

"I'm not giving you that information, Prentice, so let it go."

There was finality in her tone. Had I been the Prentice she knew five years ago, that may have meant something. The man who I am now let what she said roll right off my shoulders.

"He's going to get handled, Aúrea." The finality in my tone matched hers, possibly exceeded it because she couldn't keep me from going to L.A. to get his ass.

"Who are you?" She looked at me as if she were searching for the answer.

"I'm still Prentice Mayor."

"No, you're not the same."

"I'm not, Aúrea. The Prentice you knew five years ago before you left couldn't protect you. The one in front of you can. Ask Von's bitch ass." My emotions were all over the place, and once the words left my mouth, I wanted to punch the shit out of myself.

*Fuck.*

"You didn't?"

Not able to look at her, I turned my head, looking out the front window. Lying to her wasn't an option, and confirming my little slipup wasn't one either. The less she knew, the less she could tell if ever the shit came up in a court of law.

"Prentice, you don't have to protect me. Never did. That's why I left you. You had so much going for you, and my only plan was to chase a dream and get away from my abusive foster father."

"You made a choice for me that wasn't cool to me; yet, you thought it was best. Don't condemn me for doing the same on your behalf." My eyes were back on her.

"Okay," she conceded, catching me off guard.

"I sell weed and pills." Drugs didn't carry as much time as murder, so I figured telling her that would take her mind off my dumb-ass confession.

"Prentice."

"It's not something I'm gonna do forever, A."

She sat up in her seat, damn near climbing over to me, taking my face into her hands.

"You're my best friend. I just got you back in my life, and I don't want to lose you behind revenge or your current occupation."

I felt my eyes moving rapidly, following the movement of hers. Oddly, we were both searching for something within the eyes of the other.

"I'm good, A, on both ends. The shit I'm doin' already has a deadline, and a trip to L.A. ain't on my schedule anytime soon, so you don't have to trip." Slowly, I removed my face from her hands. Her friend-zoning my ass for what seemed like the hundredth time cut me kinda deep. Tonight absolutely wasn't going as planned. Her being my woman anytime soon also didn't look like it would happen soon.

She sat back in her seat, staring out the window as I started up the car.

"We're leaving?"

"Yeah, it's late, and I have to go help my mom in the morning." I told half of the truth.

"I ruined our date, huh?" She released an uneasy chuckle.

"Not at all. It wasn't a date, and I got exactly what I needed from you tonight. You opened up to me and finally told me what life was like for you over the last few years. Not that I like what I heard, but I can understand you better and why you prefer the single life."

"It's not that I prefer the single life. I don't want to ruin our friendship, and I also need to continue working on me."

Smiling, I didn't even feel the need to reply. I hadn't said anything about a relationship with me. So that meant I needed to prove I could be her man *and* best friend.

# 22

## *Aúrea*

I had never been a big Monday person. Today, I looked forward to it. It was the first day of classes, and I was overly excited. So excited that Nijah practically put me out of my own house because my anxiousness was getting on her last nerve. She was still staying with me and had been at my place going on two weeks. I knew when she got ready to leave, I would be heartbroken.

From Superman: Have a good first day of school.

I smiled, reading the text message from Prentice. I found the nickname fitting, given all he tried and wanted to do for me. Even me giving him a hard time, he still made me a priority. Regardless of whether I wanted him to be, he was my superman.

Since the night I told him almost everything about my time in L.A., including my relationship with Adrian, things between us started to get a little weird. Well, mainly on my part because I tried avoiding him, too embarrassed to face him after indirectly saying I didn't want a relationship with him. Even though that wasn't the truth because I wasn't sure what I wanted, then admitting to sticking with a guy who kicked my ass made me feel dumber than I had been for sticking around. Had I revealed all that I'd done for Adrian, I was sure he'd want to kill him and look at me differently. What also ate at my conscience was his confession of hurting Von. Not that I was mad at him for it. Von got what he deserved. I was angry that he put his life and freedom on the line to avenge something that happened to me years ago.

To Superman: Thank You.

I replied to him, then threw my backpack over my shoulder. For some reason, my mind drifted to the last time I tricked off in the club. I guess it was the guilt of not telling Prentice, feeling embarrassed, or both.

Quickly, I wiped the tears that fell from my eyes as I shook off the memory. My attempted rape was the only thing Adrian seemed to sympathize with me about, at least I thought so. But maybe it wasn't sympathy. It was his way of reminding me how he had saved me. His acting as if he cared was only his way to make me remember that I owed him.

"Okay, Aúrea, it's okay. Leave the past in the past," I spoke, forcing myself to suppress the memory.

Today was supposed to be a good day. It was going to be a good day, and I would leave the past in the past. I opened the school's app on my phone, locating the campus map to find my class. After discovering it, I rushed to the other side of campus. The walk was cool. Now that I knew which building my class was in, I'd be parking much closer. The class was held in the campus theater room.

"Welcome to Theater 101. I am Professor Mack. Nice to meet you all."

I took my seat right as the teacher introduced himself. He was a tall and scrawny white man with glasses. Though he looked a little nerdy, there was also some character to him. He looked like he could switch up his look in a heartbeat if he had to. Guess that's why he was the teacher. The stage lights were shining, and he spoke with a mic. The room was huge, and I doubted his voice would carry way to the back by the entrance.

After we went around the room introducing ourselves, he split us up in pairs to do monologues. There was an even number of males and females, so that's how we were paired. Boy, girl, boy, girl.

We stood in a circle on the stage.

My partner was this white kid who was cute in a young *'N Sync* Justin Timberlake kind of way. We went over our lines and were applauded. And it felt good. Just like that, I was back in my element.

"And your name is . . .?"

My ears perked up at the sound of a raspy yet sexy voice. Slowly, my head moved, and my eyes landed on the chocolate cutie across from me.

*Damn, how did I miss him?* I wondered. He wasn't cute. Homeboy was fine. I had been floating from the feeling of acting out. My lines had to have been the reason I missed out on seeing him. My eyes were damn sure glued to him now. He wasn't Prentice by far but still fine in his own right. He had to feel me watching him because he looked in my direction and winked before I shyly turned away.

Professor Mack directed a few more monologues before dismissing the class. I couldn't wait for Wednesday as I looked forward to coming back.

"Excuse me." A light tap on my shoulder halted my steps and forced me to turn around. I had barely made it to the middle of campus when I was stopped.

"He-hey," I spoke, shocked to see the dark-skinned cutie from my class.

"I'm Damian. We just got out of class together."

"I know. I'm Aúrea," I smiled.

"Pretty name for a pretty woman."

"Thank you."

"So, if I'm too straightforward, you can let me know. I was wondering if you didn't have another class, could I treat you to lunch?" He smiled, and damn if it wasn't beautiful. There was something about a chocolate man with straight white teeth.

"Uh, I . . . uh . . ."

"It's just lunch. I mean, unless you've eaten already. If so, we could do dinner later." He put his hands in the pockets of his navy-blue Abercrombie joggers and shrugged his shoulders up innocently, grinning like he knew I couldn't deny him.

"Where would we go for lunch?" A quick meal wouldn't hurt, and all I was doing was having food with a classmate. Besides, it felt good having a guy other than Prentice swoon after me, and it had been way too long since I'd been intimate . . . not saying Damian was about to get my goods, though. But it was a possibility if he played his cards right and we got to know each other.

"There's a little diner right across from campus. We can walk there."

"Okay. I'm new here, so do you mind leading the way?"

"Not at all."

Damian reached his hand out to me, and I frowned.

"I'll carry your bag. It's a little soon for the holding hands part, ain't it?" he laughed.

"Oh, shoot. I'm sorry." Quickly, I removed my back-pack from my left shoulder and gave it to him, feeling dumb as hell. One thing my ass knew how to jump to lately was conclusions.

"It's cool. Come on." He smiled, easing the tension.

As we walked, I slipped my hand into his, catching him by surprise. He looked at me with raised brows, and I smiled.

"How many classes are you taking?"

"Just one for now. I'm trying to get back into the swing of things, so taking this short-term class is my way of doing so. Eventually, I'll enroll full time."

"That's dope. Here's the place right here."

We walked into a place called JJ's Diner, and the smell of barbecue hit my nose as soon as the door opened.

"Something smells so good."

"Everything here is pretty good. My favorite is the tri-tip sandwich. That's what you smell. They smoke it out back for hours."

"I may try it." We sat down, looking around, and I opened my menu. The place was nice, decorated in orange, purple, and white, the same colors as the school mascot. There was only a couple of waitresses, which was why we seated ourselves, and the menus were waiting at the table.

"It's always my go-to. If you want, you can try some of mine and choose something else for yourself."

"That's sweet of you." My cheeks heated up. *Damn, I'm blushing.*

"So, this what we doing, A?" Slowly, I turned my head to look behind me because I just knew I had to be tripping. Sure enough, when my eyes landed on Prentice looking like a tall glass of ice water on a hot-ass day, I knew I wasn't tripping. His hair was freshly lined, face smooth and moisturized like he sweated cocoa butter, and bushy eyebrows intact over his brown eyes underneath his lashes that I would pay to have on my face. He was dressed casually yet expensive as always in a black Fendi T-shirt, blue jeans, and black-and-white retro 13 Jordans. I think they were . . . Yep, I had just taken all of him in that fast because there was no way to look at Prentice and not observe all of him before going back to his face. A full view of Prentice was never disappointing.

"What are you doing here?" Confused was an understatement. There hadn't been any communication between us that told me he would show up here today. I wouldn't have agreed to it if there were. He was still to be avoided outside of texts and calls right now.

"Came to check on you since today's a big day for you and shit. But I see you rather be entertaining some lame." He sucked his teeth.

"Who the fuck—" Damian spoke up, and before things could go all the way left between these two, I stood.

"Damian, I'm sorry. Can I take a rain check?" My eyes pleaded with him as I lifted my backpack from the seat.

"The fuck you can," Prentice protested.

"Sure, see you on Wednesday," Damian smirked. I can't lie. It was cute and kind of a turn-on that he didn't let Prentice's antics scare him.

Instead of saying anything further to him, I pushed past Prentice, storming out of the diner.

"Tell me how you claim you not trying to date and don't want a relationship, but I catch you on a date with a nigga?"

"First off, why are you coming at me like I lied to you or something? Second, it wasn't a date. I just met him today in class, and he asked to take me to lunch."

"Sounds like a damn date to me." Now, *he* was pissing me off. How dare he speak to me like he owned me? This was the shit I dealt with being with Adrian, and since I was single as a damn dollar bill, Prentice damn sure wouldn't speak to me like this.

"You need to lower your voice and find a better way to speak to me." My words were slow and deliberate. He needed to feel every word.

"Nah, you not 'bout to turn this around on me. You not supposed to be out with no dudes, Aúrea."

"Says who?" With my hands on my hips, I challenged his ass.

"Me, dammit."

"And *who* are you?"

"Aúrea, you the one who keep saying you not looking for a man or relationship. Yet you on a date and shit."

"It's not a date. And if it were, so what?"

"I'm tryin' to protect yo' ass," he spoke, and I swear it felt like air left my body, and exhaustion took over.

"Prentice, I don't need protection. I'm not the same girl I was five years ago, and even she could handle some stuff on her own. I'm not your responsibility, and I *thought* I made that clear." I used my right hand to massage my temple while my eyes remained on him. This was a stressful situation that was so unnecessary.

"Maybe not, but I love you too much not to step in. I'm going to always step in because of my love for you."

"I love you too, Prentice, but you don't see me trying to control your life." I wasn't trying to sound like a bitch or ungrateful. I just wanted him to understand that he couldn't just continue to make rules for me.

"That's what you think? Yeah, yo' last nigga really fucked you up because clearly, you don't know the difference between somebody looking out and control. But it's cool, Aúrea. I'm out."

Without another word, he turned around, leaving me standing there, looking stupid. And for the first time with his back turned to me, watching him walk away, I knew I would have to be a fool to let him.

# 23

## *Prentice*

Aúrea really had me fucked up this time, and not only did she have me fucked up, but I also had myself fucked up too. I wasn't this dude. A nigga had grown up, changed, and she had me damn near running behind her like the 18-year-old I used to be. That stopped now. That shit stopped today. She'd been through some shit, and I knew that. Had she not been so damn closed off like she didn't even know a nigga, I would've known the full extent sooner and could've nipped a lot of stuff in the bud sooner. Still, that didn't give her the right to play me like she'd been doing. For her to have told me she wasn't looking to date was understandable, but it was evidently a lie.

On top of that, she calls herself looking at me like *I'm* the one with two heads. She told my ass one thing, yet did another instead of just being real with me. Ain't that some shit? She kept saying dating and shit weren't what she wanted. Then I catch her on a date with some college dude. Truthfully, that shit was like a punch to my stomach. Maybe she just didn't want to date the dude who was into street shit over the safe-ass college boy. Not that I didn't get it. I just didn't understand it. If that's what she wanted, though, so be it. She ain't have to worry about me no more. Leaving her standing there, I hopped into my Range and blasted Notorious B.I.G.'s "Get Money." Yeah, Lil' Kim had a verse on here talking 'bout fuck niggas. After B.I.G.'s verse, I was turning the shit down because I wasn't feeling no woman's empowerment-type shit right now.

Doing at least sixty in a forty, I got home in record time. When I got out of my car, Aúrea sped in right behind me in my Tesla. She wasn't trying to fuck with a nigga exclusively but was still driving my car. At this point, I was hoping she was bringing my shit back. She barely put my shit in park, then hopped out, rushing toward me.

"Prentice," she yelled.

I sucked my teeth before turning my back to her. Her eyes and tone were evident that she knew she fucked up with me, and no lie, the shit moved me, but not enough to stop me from making my way to my front door and placing my key in the lock. I had just about shut the door before Aúrea caught it.

"*Really,* Prentice?" She looked at me, chest rising and falling with her arms folded across her breasts and brows furrowed.

Looking at her, I chuckled before turning my back on her once again. She had the nerve to be pissed.

"Stop turning your back on me." She forced her way in front of me. She stood there, and that was cool.

I looked everywhere *but* at her. Avoiding eye contact with her wasn't hard due to towering over her with my height.

Her tone was full of emotion, and there was no doubt she was on the verge of crying. That wasn't my intention to make her cry. Slowly, I lowered my head to look into her eyes. They were moist.

"What, Aúrea? You made yourself clear already. I'm good. I ain't looking to be your savior, protector—none of that shit. A nigga do love you, but I'm good." I stepped back, putting distance between us so that she could get a good look into my eyes to see I wasn't playing.

"That's not what I want, Prentice. I mean, I want you to know that I don't need saving, but I also don't want you just to say forget me and leave me alone and not love me." Her eyes pleaded with mine. Her actions were confusing the hell out of me.

Wiping my hand down my head, I took a deep breath and peered into her eyes.

"Then tell me what it is you want, A."

I didn't feel like I needed to be any more specific with my question. She wasn't dumb. She knew that one question could be answered a million ways, yet I only cared about one.

"I want y-y-you," she said nervously, which wasn't good enough for me. With a raised brow, I looked at her, needing her to sound a bit surer.

"I want you, Prentice." This time, her tone spoke volumes—held confidence. What I needed now was for her to show me.

I took a few steps, closing the space between us. Latching my fingers in the belt loops of her jeans, I was pulling her body toward mine with ease, placing my hands on her waist. My lips were on hers, gently at first, but I was a bit more aggressive when I didn't sense any hesitation, mashing them together. I took my tongue, using it to part her lips, when she surprised my ass by opening her mouth, willingly inviting me in. The minty remnants of a piece of gum had lingered on, and I hungrily sucked on her tongue until the flavor had become my own.

"Mmm," she moaned softly, eyes fluttering into the back of her head.

Aúrea tossed her arms around my neck as she continued moaning in my mouth, causing my dick to spring forward. It was yearning to be set free, and the way we were making out, it wouldn't be too much longer.

Without hesitation, I moved my hands from her small waist, lifting her by the ass as her legs reflexively wrapped around me. I walked her to the sofa, taking a seat as she continued clinging to my body. Aúrea was kissing a nigga like she'd never see me again, and that shit felt good. It was confirmation that she'd been fronting all this time. Slowly, I peeled my lips from hers, making contact with her eyes.

"If we do this, there's no turning back, and you're mine . . . exclusively. Stop me now if that's not what you want."

Aúrea kept her eyes on mine as I waited, almost impatiently, for a reply. She was nibbling on her bottom lip, thinking about what she wanted to say. Ultimately, she didn't say a word.

She removed her shirt, giving me a full eye view of her black lace bra where her breasts lightly spilled over from at the top.

"This answer your question?" she asked me, a smirk playing at the corner of her lips.

I nodded before once again attacking her lips. She placed her hands on my face as I helped her out of her jeans. The snug fit had her having to practically shake her way out, which had her on her feet so she could do so more quickly. Once they were at her ankles, she kicked them off, not giving a damn where they went. Aúrea prepared to resume her seat on my lap when my lustful stare had her covering herself. All I saw was perfection as she stood before me in her black lingerie, and I wanted her to know it. My hands went to remove hers as I kissed along her flat stomach. I couldn't even fully appreciate taking in every inch of her body before she was stopping me by again, cradling my face in her hands.

"I'm not the only one removing clothes around here, am I?" she asked, her tongue running across her bottom lip.

My dick practically sprang free, and she saw it too from the way it was bulging. As she'd done moments ago, I was stripping out of my clothing, tossing them wherever. She giggled at my eagerness as I swooped her in my arms bridal style. For a moment, we just stared at each other before our lips reconnected. I carried her to my room, laying her across the bed. Instead of going forward, I was stopping myself, much to her disappointment. She'd been doing so much back and forth, so I had to be sure this was what she wanted. I couldn't handle her ass leaving again, but I'd rather her be upfront and not lead a nigga on.

"There's no turning back now."

"Good." The huskiness in her tone was sexy as hell as I slowly made my way between her thighs. As much as my dick wanted to feel her, my taste buds needed to be satisfied first . . .

I removed her panties before taking her thighs into the cuffs of my arms, pulling her into me.

"Ahh," she moaned as her back arched from the bed.

I had latched on to her clit, sucking before taking my tongue to lick from every inch of her fleshy folds.

"Mmm," escaped my mouth as my tongue slowly spread her pussy lips.

Her sweet nectar immediately greeted me and had my ass tripping. This was some shit I'd wanted to do when we were younger, but there was so much that stopped it from happening. If I knew then she tasted like paradise, I don't think I would've let her go. This shit right here was going to be a part of my daily routine, like getting the recommended intake of eight glasses of water.

"Prentice . . . I-I'm gonna come," she moaned.

Damn, I hissed. Definitely a record for me—one I wouldn't complain about, either.

Aúrea's hand pressing on the top of my head held me in place as she came. Her legs shook violently in my arms as she tried catching her breath, but I wasn't letting up.

"I c-ca-can't," she protested, still trying to remove the latch my mouth had on her clit.

"Just one more. Come for me one more time," I mumbled in between sucks.

"Prentice, I caaaannn't." Her confession, apparently, hadn't been true as her legs began shaking again.

Feeling satisfied, I removed my mouth from her, then sat up, taking off my boxers.

"Oh, shit," she whispered, her eyes just about bucking from their sockets.

"What's wrong?"

"I don't remember it being so big."

I grinned at the comment as she began blushing. I'd told her ass I wasn't that same boy she'd left behind. I was clearly going to have to show her. Leaning down, pressing my lips into hers, and sticking my tongue into her mouth, I used my free hand to remove a condom from the drawer of my nightstand. Pulling back, I ripped the wrapper with my teeth, took out the condom, and rolled it on.

Aúrea opened her legs wider for me without instruction. I inched the tip of my dick closer, knocking at her entrance, barely able to get the head in as she sucked in some air.

"You okay?" Slowly, I continued to press into her opening.

"Uh-huh," she moaned out. It was like music to my ears.

*Good,* I thought. I pushed all of me inside her while biting her neck as she cried out, digging her nails in my back. Aúrea was wet as hell, but she was also extremely tight. With all of me inside, I paused. She probably thought I was giving her a few moments to adjust to me when I was simply basking in the feeling. We felt fucking good together, and she knew it too. Aúrea began to move, slow winding her hips, promoting my own movements. Slowly, I moved in and out of her, and it seemed she got wetter with each stroke. I was doing my best to be gentle, but the way she was gripping my dick had me struggling like a motherfucker.

"Damn, baby," I groaned. I held my face in the crook of her neck while biting down on my bottom lip hard enough to draw blood, hoping the pain helped ease the pleasure my manhood was receiving because what I wasn't trying to do was come prematurely. Not again like the last time I was with her. I pulled out, shutting my eyes tightly and taking a second to gather myself before slamming back into her. She gasped out, convulsions capturing her body. I slammed into her again . . . and again . . . and again, as she cried out.

"Ahh . . ." Aúrea's walls tightened around me, and I felt her raining down my shaft.

"Just one more time. Come for me one more time." Kissing down her neck, I released her right breast from her bra, taking her nipple into my mouth, allowing my tongue to flick over it lightly.

"Prentice, I can't."

Her plea sounded like a challenge to me, so I pushed into her slow and rough like I was trying to connect my dick to her stomach. Like I was trying to intertwine our souls into one. I was thrusting in her hard, giving her everything I had. Our skin slapping together and the pleasured moans escaping us were all that could be heard as she did what she said she couldn't do. She was coming, shuddering so damn hard that it had me filling up the condom.

"Damn, Aúrea." I kissed her lips, then her temple, before slowly sliding out of her, lying on my back, and pulling her on top of me.

"No more running from me, A. It's you and me from this point forward."

"Okay," she readily agreed, making me feel good as fuck.

"No more little dates either. I don't care if it's yo' damn professor. If I can't be there, then the shit isn't important enough for you to be, either."

"Okay," she laughed this time.

"You're mine now."

"I'm yours." The smile on her face made me feel good. She kissed me, then removed herself from my grasp, making her way to my bathroom. My dick just about rose again watching her ass jiggle.

"You need to discard that, right?"

Nodding, I sat up, throwing my legs off the bed. Removing the condom, I threw it into the trash in my room.

"Yeah, so we can go another round."

"You know you can give me at least ten whole minutes to recover."

"You may as well tell Nijah that you're staying with me tonight."

Shaking her head with a broad smile on her face, Aúrea used the towel she had to gently wipe me off before taking the trash can with the condom and the towel out of my room.

Within seconds, she was back, being pulled into my lap.

"Ten minutes have passed—"

The blaring of my house phone halted the rest of my words. Tapping Aúrea on the butt, I eased her from my lap. If my house phone was ringing, that meant something needed my immediate attention. Walking over to my nightstand, I removed the phone from its cradle.

"Hello?"

"Prentice." My mom's shaky voice hit me like a ton of bricks. It was evident that she'd been crying, and my mind went to Prima. If something happened to my little sister . . .

"What's wrong, Ma?" My mood had changed, and Aúrea, rushing to my side, let me know she sensed it.

"Gerald. H-he . . . We got into a fight."

"That nigga hit you?" I seethed. He'd be dead before the sun rose if he put his hands on my mother.

"No, no, he didn't hit me. He just . . ." She breathed heavily, pausing, and knowing my mother as I did, she was contemplating whether to tell me what that fuck boy had done. It was too late, though. She shouldn't have called if she didn't want me to know.

"What did he do?" Holding the phone, I walked into my closet, grabbing some boxers, sweats, and a T-shirt, getting them all on damn near in one swift motion.

"He cleared out your sister's bank account," she said sadly, and there was also some embarrassment in her tone. She had every right to feel like that too. Who wouldn't be embarrassed about a mothafucka stealing from their own child?

"How you know it was him, Mom?" There was no doubt she wouldn't pin this on him if it weren't true. Getting more details would determine the level of an ass whopping he was getting. He damn sure was getting one.

"When I went to make the payment on my store, I asked the bank rep to deposit money into Prima's account, then give me the balance, and all she had was the hundred dollars that I'd just deposited. When I asked what the hell happened, she told me he removed the money."

"Why the hell was he on Prima's account anyway, Ma?"

"I only added him recently. He said he wanted to put money in there for her, and then we started talking about if something happened to me, he needed to be able to take care of her—"

"I'll be there in a minute," I cut her off. She didn't need to explain anything else. At the end of the day, his ass manipulated her, then stole from his daughter—my sister—and shit, me too because, of course, the majority of the money in Prima's account came from me. I could and would replace the funds. Come tomorrow, it would be, and then some, so that wasn't the problem. The problem was Gerald's ass violated. He must've taken me for a bitch to think he could get away with it.

"Prentice, what's going on?" Aúrea asked with a worried expression on her face.

"Promise me you'll be here when I get back." Cupping her face in my hands, I kissed her lips, awaiting her answer. She'd better give the right one, or after handling Gerald's bitch ass, I'd be dragging her back here from wherever she was at.

"Tell me what's going on," she demanded.

"My mom's boyfriend did some fuck shit, so I'm goin' to holler at him."

"Prentice." She spoke my name like she knew I was about to do some crazy shit.

"Chill out. He's my sister's daddy. He gets to live." I winked at her, and she rolled her eyes.

"I'll be here," she promised, and that made a nigga feel good.

Rushing out of the house, I hopped into my Honda. Nah, I wasn't going to kill Gerald, but he was getting his ass whooped.

Knowing how the predictable punk worked, I drove to the bar he was known to frequent. Sure enough, his car was parked out front.

Stepping inside, it took me a second to spot him in the smoke-filled room. It was dim, except for the light coming in through the stained-glass windows. There wasn't a huge crowd, yet the small layout and how the patrons were scattered about made the room look fuller than it probably was. When my eyes landed on Gerald, he was nursing a cup of some brown shit. Most likely, some Hennessy. I stalked quickly over to his ass, pulling the extra seat out before sitting.

"Prentice, what you doing here? It's a little too late for us to try bonding and shit."

"You stole from my sister?"

"That's my daughter. What's hers is mine, and vice versa. No way I can steal from my own child," he slurred.

With my thumb, I wiped the bridge of my nose, trying to relax. If I didn't, Gerald's ass was gonna touch every wall in this establishment, and I wanted to move a little smarter than that.

"All right, well, then, you stole from me, and you and I both know I'm not having that shit. That money in Prima's account, *I* put it there, and you can either give it back in cash or pay by taking this ass beating. Matter of fact, you still gon' have to see me."

"Possession is eight-tenths of the law, and what's Prima's is mine, so no one stole from you or owe you shit. Besides, once this investment goes through, you can have the little money back and then some. You won't be talking that broke shit when this flip goes through." He smiled like the damn Cheshire cat. Dumb ass didn't even know possession was nine-tenths of the law, reason one his dumb ass shouldn't have been stealing.

"Come holler at me outside, Gerald." It wasn't a request. Plus, I was done talking to his ass.

"I still got drank in my cup."

"All right." Slowly, I stood, and before his ass could form another sentence, the glass he'd been sipping from was removed from his hand and came crashing down on the top of his head.

"Ouch, man." He held the top of his head before looking down at his fingers. His eyes widened at the sight of blood on his fingertips. Yanking him by the collar of his dingy black shirt, I practically dragged his ass outside.

"I'm going to call the police," someone shouted.

"Do it." If that shit was supposed to scare me and stop this ass whopping Gerald was about to get, then they thought wrong. Pushing the door open with Gerald's head, I let him go as he stumbled to gather himself instead of tripping over the curb.

"Get yo' bitch ass up." Standing over him with my fists balled, I mushed him upside the head.

"Yo' mama not gon' have this shit," he called himself informing me while trying to stand. Once he was on his feet, I sent his ass flying right back down with a quick left to the chin.

"If yo' bitch ass keep my sister's money, you better not show yo' mothafuckin' face again." I stole on his ass once more before getting into my car.

No police sirens sounded, so I assumed I was in the clear as I made my way to my mother's house.

"Oh, so now you use your key?" she questioned with her hands on her hips.

"Take his name off of Prima's account, Ma."

"Boy, I did that already," she spoke as if I should've known that. Shit, she shouldn't have had him on it in the first place.

"If he doesn't give back the money, he can't come around here no more." I looked her in the eyes. She needed to see this wasn't a game.

"Shit," I mumbled, opening and closing my left hand. Gerald's chin against my knuckles wasn't a good combination.

"He's still Prima's father, and what happened to your hand?" She came close to me, taking my hand in hers, examining the swelling.

"Prima's father got a damn rock for a chin," I chuckled.

"Boy," she hissed, turning and leaving me standing there for a few seconds. She came back with a bag of frozen vegetables for my hand.

"I appreciate you looking out for us, but the last thing I need is for you to get into any legal trouble, Prentice. What if he calls the police?"

"His ass better not. If he does, oh well. Punk ass shouldn't have taken my sister's money."

"Prentice, still, he's not worth your freedom."

She tried reasoning with me, but it was too late. He got his ass whooped, and if the cops were going to be called, then so be it. Truthfully, in the back of my mind, I did worry a bit. If he'd steal from his own daughter, snitching on me was going to be simple as Prima reciting her ABCs.

"I'll be fine, Ma. And the money will be back in Prima's account tomorrow too, regardless of whether he gives it back. Make sure you call me if he shows up here."

"Prenticesss," Prima sang, running into the room.

As always, my arms were open wide for my baby sis. It was crazy that her own father could steal from her. She was such a precious jewel, so it baffled me that he didn't want the absolute best for her.

"What's up, pretty girl?" I asked, kissing her cheek before placing her back on to her feet.

"Ummm, there was this new toy . . ." she grinned.

"And you want big brother to get it for you?" I smiled knowingly.

"Yes, can we go?"

"Yes, not today, though, okay?" The pout on her cute face made me feel bad about turning her down. However, I needed to get back to Aúrea and finish nursing my hand. After whopping Gerald's ass, going to a kiddie store was the last thing I was trying to do. Slipping back inside of Aúrea was more of what I wanted—what I needed right now.

"Ookay," she whined, making my mother and me laugh.

"Okay, Ma, remember what I said. I'll be back through soon." I kissed Prima's cheek once more before doing the same to my mother.

"All right. Be safe and cross the street if you see Gerald again."

"He better cross first." I winked at my mom before closing her door behind me. I meant that shit too. If he knew what was best for him, he'd do the right thing and steer clear of me.

# 24

## *Aúrea*

"I almost thought you were giving me the lease to your condo," Nijah teased as we took our seats.

"You have not been at my house that many days by yourself." Rolling my eyes, I took the mimosa from the nail tech.

"Tuh. Like hell."

"*Two* days, Nahji." I sucked my teeth as if I were offended, even though I wasn't. I experienced a tad bit of guilt because I went MIA on her for two days. Of course, she knew where I was. Still, it didn't make it right to leave her at my house when she came all this way to be with me. So today was my way of making up for it. Everything we did today would be my treat, starting with this mini-pamper session at the nail salon.

"You know I'm not upset with you, and all will be forgiven, especially if you give details. I mean, I know it was good . . . kept yo' ass gone for two days, so it better had been. *And* you were walking funny," Nijah laughed.

Shaking my head, I felt my lips unintentionally spread. Just the thought of Prentice made me smile. It was something I couldn't help. Well, since the day he made love to me.

Prentice did things to my body that I didn't think he was capable of. Shit, my body did things underneath him and on top of him that I didn't know *it* was capable of.

"Well, Prentice and I are official now." Shyly shrugging, my eyes met hers waiting to see her reaction.

"I knew that, duh."

"What do you want to know, Nahji?" My tone was so condescending, which I did purposely. There was no doubt that I would give her details about Prentice and me. Not *too* much detail, but she would get *some* info.

"You seriously playing with me right now?" she paused, turning toward the nail tech. "Can you please refill my drink because my little sister here is testing me?"

"You are so dramatic."

"Nah, you play too much. Had me sitting in the house for days, and the moment something exciting happens, you wanna hold out. It ain't like I'm asking his dick and shoe size or what angle he hit from. Those are things I do *not* want to know."

Shaking my head, I pointed to the hot pink nail polish chosen for my toes before turning my head back in Nijah's direction.

"So, Monday was my first day of class, and I met this fine-ass guy named Damian in my drama class. Ooh, he may be perfect for you." Damian was *definitely* Nijah's type.

"So, he's single?" she perked up.

"Yes. So anyway, after class, he approached me and asked to take me to lunch, so I said—"

"Wait? Ho, you did *not* just try to pass me a dude who's interested in *you*." She popped me on the hand, making me laugh. It wasn't me trying to be shady, and Damian was strictly my classmate and nothing more. Wouldn't be anything more. Granted, he could've been. Nonetheless, he wasn't.

"No, Nahji. He's my classmate only. Do you want me to finish my story or not?"

"Continue, ho. Get the matchmaker shit out of your head too. Any Damian I meet on the street, even if it's back in L.A., is getting turned down," she seethed.

"Whatever. Well, we walked to this diner not far from campus. We were seated only about three minutes, and then Prentice walked in."

"Oh, shit!" Her eyes enlarged as she sat up in her seat, inching closer to me like she knew the next thing I said was going to be *really* good.

Her reaction shouldn't have been comical to me because Prentice bringing his ass into that diner was everything opposite of funny.

"Yup. He flipped out on me. Accused me of being on a date, which I wasn't. Just about beat Damian's ass before cursing me out and storming off, leaving me standing in front of the diner looking crazy."

"Then how the hell did you two end up, you know, how y'all ended up?"

"Because I hightailed it to the parking lot, jumped into his car, and did damn near eighty to catch up to him. Honestly, Nahji, it took all of two seconds to realize that if he were really done with me, I'd be miserable."

"Told yo' ass you was feeling him on a level way stronger than friendship as you *tried* to claim."

"No, well . . . A friendship was all that I wanted from him. Yes, he is my first true love. He's also my best friend, and after being in that horrible-ass relationship with Adrian for so long, fear kept me from thinking Prentice and I could be anything good. Like, obviously,

I don't know how to be a girlfriend. I even messed up the relationship I had with him five years ago. So it was easier to keep him friend-zoned." Oddly, as good as being with Prentice felt, everything I just said still made perfect sense. Being a girlfriend wasn't a simple task for me, and because I still loved him, I didn't want to screw it up.

"Well, looks like *that* plan failed," she snickered.

"Big time."

"This won't end badly, Aúrea. He's crazy about you, and you finally know what you want and need from a man. It's okay to be scared. Just don't allow your fear to sabotage something that can be wonderful. Especially since he got your ass over here glowing like a damn glow stick—*and* walking bowlegged."

"Shut up."

That was the only comeback I could come up with because she didn't lie. I was glowing, and sex with Prentice had knocked my knees every way but straight. Just thinking about how he slid his tongue from the bottom of my pussy to the top, paying close attention to my clit, made me shudder. Then how his mushroom head unlocked the opening of my pussy before the length and girth of him came all the way in, stretching me wide, yet finding a perfect fit . . . It left no doubt in my mind that I was made for him.

"All right now, Aúrea, come back to earth," she teased.

"You just have to be extra."

"Hey, being regular is far from fun."

She had a point, so there would be no protest from me about it. Living a little was something that I was going to do more, mainly because all of the things holding me back were no longer obstacles in my way. There was no

Adrian and no Von. Only space and opportunity to live how I wanted.

"All done," the nail tech announced. Both Nijah and I inspected our toes, making sure they were to our liking, which they were, before I paid and left a hefty tip.

"Can we go get something to eat? I'm hungry," Nijah whined.

"You are such a brat, and to think, *I'm* supposed to be the *little* sister."

"You still are the little sister, but today is on you, though, so I'm taking full advantage."

"Obviously."

"Hey, what about that place right there? There's a small crowd, so they must be good." Nijah pointed across the street from the nail shop where we stood. The place wasn't directly across the street, but we were in the perfect place to see it and the crowd.

"Oh my," escaped from my lips in a whisper, just not low enough for Bionic Ears Nijah to not hear me.

"Is there something wrong with that place?"

"No, not at all. It's a complete replica of the place Prentice and I had our final meal together."

"Huh?"

"When we ran away from home, we ended up behind a restaurant. The owner fed us and gave Prentice $300 for the two of us, even though he disagreed with us running. It's crazy because that place was hours away from here. But this looks exactly like it."

"Well, this is the perfect time to take a trip down memory lane . . . Was the food he fed y'all good? You said it was your last eating place."

"It was some of the best food I'd had."

"Then that solves it. Let's go." Nijah practically dragged me across the street toward the restaurant.

"That was five years ago. There's no guarantee he owns this place." Fear began to take over. What if he owned the restaurant? What if he remembered me? The last time he saw me was not pleasant, not to mention I acted like a little thot. Although my life was together now, it still wasn't what it was supposed to be, or maybe it was, and God had only laughed at my plans.

"Only one way to find out." She continued to drag me.

We made it and waited behind about two couples before we were seated. The place changed a lot, with upgrades to the furniture, from what I could tell. The renaissance vibe was still there, as well as the photos.

"This place is nice. Does it look the same?"

"Pretty much. Different tables, chairs, and that area over there." I pointed toward the kitchen, where there was now a bar area across from it. "Oh, and it was darker."

"Excuse me." At the sound of a male's voice, both Nijah and I looked up.

When my eyes met the figure before us, my nerves began to run amuck. They altered between fear and embarrassment, which was crazy because neither should be emotions I felt. Then he smiled at me. And strangely, all anxiety, fear, and embarrassment washed away. Calmness instead came over me. The same calm I experienced five years ago that told me he could be trusted.

"M-Mis-Mr. Lewis," nervously I verified.

"Beautiful Aúrea." He extended his arms, and without hesitation, I stood to embrace him. "Wow, look at you. All grown up," he complimented me.

"Thank you. You changed the place up a bit." Stepping back from the embrace lightly, I swung my hands around to emphasize the changes.

"Yeah, just a little bit . . . You mind?" he asked, pulling a chair from a nearby table to take a seat.

"Not at all. This is your place."

The sound of the clearing of one's throat captured Mr. Lewis's and my attention, and when my eyes met Nijah's, they rolled right in the back of my head before a light snicker released from my throat.

"Mr. Lewis, this is my best friend, Nijah. She's visiting from Los Angeles."

"Nice to meet you, Nijah." He shook her hand, offering her the same warm smile he'd given me not long ago.

"Nice to meet you. I heard the food here is amazing."

"Oh, so you remembered?" Mr. Lewis chuckled, directing his attention back to me.

"No way could I forget," I admitted while extending my leg to kick Nijah's hungry ass underneath the table. She had no filter at the worst times, I swear.

"Give me a second to go put in an order for you ladies. Then I will be back to speak with you, Aúrea. Don't worry about the bill either." Mr. Lewis winked before getting up and heading toward the back.

"You just have no home training sometimes." Sucking my teeth, I looked at Nijah.

"I have plenty of home training. My ass is just hungry, and before you two traveled down memory lane, I just wanted to make sure a hot plate was going to be in front of me sooner than later." She shrugged. "Now, why didn't you tell me Mr. Lewis was a handsome, older man? He could undoubtedly be Zaddy." Now her ass was laughing.

"Ewe. You have to be joking because the only vibe I get from him is a father figure or grandpa. No, he's not that old. Still, seeing him in any sexual light is disgusting."

"That's 'cause he saved yo' ass. Had today been the first time you two met like he and I, you would see the same potential in him that I do."

As much as I wanted to laugh, I couldn't. Shaking my head was more fitting because I knew Nijah's ass was serious.

"Okay, we are going to change the subject. I'm not sure what he's going to bring us to eat, but it'll be good, I'm sure."

"Is it crazy that he remembers you?"

"Not really. I pretty much look the same; just a bit thicker, and my hair is longer . . . Hey, what do you think if I give him back the three hundred he gave us?"

"I would tell you to keep it. Besides, Prentice already paid me back," Mr. Lewis spoke, taking the seat he'd left. Though it was pretty noisy inside the restaurant, he had heard me clearly.

"Prentice?" I felt my face scrunch, displaying the confusion I felt at Mr. Lewis's admission.

"Yes, shortly after I met you guys, he came back and worked it off. Then the two of us have been . . . What do you young folks call it?" He paused, and I could see the wheels turning in his head. Since I wasn't sure what he was trying to say, I didn't suggest any words. Just waited for him to continue. "Rocking. Yeah, that's it. We've been rocking ever since."

Both Nijah and I fell into a hearty laugh at Mr. Lewis trying to sound hip.

"That's not the word? 'Cause I know I didn't just tell a joke."

"No, no, Mr. Lewis. That *is* the word. You caught us off guard, that's all . . . So Prentice has been working here?"

"Yes, and he has become a partner of mine in a sense. I love that kid like a son."

His admission made me smile. It also made me wonder why Prentice hadn't mentioned Mr. Lewis or any of this to me. I'd been home long enough for him to say something. He did mention a restaurant. He didn't say it was Mr. Lewis's or that he moved the man closer to our hometown. I wonder if he still had his original place.

"Wait, how long have you been back? Have you not seen him? Honestly would've expected you to be here with him."

"Hey, Mr. Lewis, I'm good company too." Nijah cut in just as a waitress brought our plates, putting them in front of us.

He chuckled before looking at her. "I don't doubt that, young lady. It's just that those two were attached at the hip when I met them. Even a blind man could see that the distance between them wouldn't last long."

"Oh, it didn't. They back attached at the hip," Nijah informed him matter-of-factly, and I kicked her ass underneath the table again.

"Oh really? I'm kicking his ass," he said, turning back to me.

"Me too," I chuckled.

"So, how long have you been back?" he asked me.

"A little over a month now."

"Are you back for good?"

"I am."

"Good. You know, I saw you on that T.J. Maxx commercial," he informed me, and my ass smiled so hard, he damn near saw all my teeth and cavities if I had any. It was flattering, to say the least.

"Yes, she was so pretty. I can't wait to see her on the big screen," Nijah chimed in with her mouth half full, genuinely happy for me. This was one of the many reasons I loved her so much. At any given time, she was riding for me.

"Still gonna pursue acting?" he asked with a raised brow.

"Kind of. Right now, I'm taking a class on theater at the community college."

"That's great. I always knew things would work out for you."

"You did?" That was a surprise to me because I always felt like he told Prentice something bad about me. Yes, my mind had been made up when I decided to leave Prentice behind that day. There was still something lingering in the back of my mind that told me Mr. Lewis had some form of influence on how things shifted when we left his restaurant.

"I did. Of course, I wasn't blind to there being something you were running from. And I had made a couple of prejudgments that weren't entirely accurate. There was still something there letting me know that whatever you were going through would change for the better if you grew and allowed it to. Seeing you now shows that's exactly what happened."

"It took a lot of work, but I am thankful to be at the place I'm in now," I told him honestly.

"Prentice has grown a lot too."

"Mr. Lewis, I know you got this bro code and all, but how many girls have Prentice brought here?" Nijah asked, causing me to shake my head at her ass once again.

If I got paid for every time I shook my head at some Nijah nonsense, I'd be rich as hell. However, this question I wasn't going to knock her for. I mean, if Mr. Lewis answered with a big number, surely I'd be jealous and upset.

"Yeah, and I abide by the bro code . . . If you must know, though, this place has only been reserved for Aúrea."

"Mcaning?" she quizzed.

"She's the only girl allowed here with him." He winked at me, and we laughed.

To say Mr. Lewis was lying would be a stretch because there was no way to prove it. It did feel good, though, that he cared enough to protect my feelings regardless of the truth. And Prentice's because he would get his ass cussed out.

"This food is amazing," Nijah complimented, changing the subject. There was no doubt in my mind every female needed a friend like her in their life.

"Glad you like it. You know you're welcome to eat here anytime."

"Oh, thank you. I'm going to take you up on that offer so much you may want to take it back later."

"Give me a few moments, ladies." He stood and left the room to handle whatever.

"Well, from what I see, Mr. Lewis has a soft spot for you and Prentice. Whatever he saw in you two those years ago obviously stuck with him."

"Maybe." Shrugging my shoulders was also my way of hoping to shrug off the feeling of doubt that came over me. This small reunion with Mr. Lewis wasn't going bad at all. Yet, it began to make me wonder.

I'd been back home for about a month, and he spoke so highly of Prentice and their relationship, so he should have known I was back. The only thing coming to mind right now about why he didn't know I returned was because he said something to Prentice about me that would make him feel ashamed to bring me up. The excuse that he had been with me and hardly left my side since I moved back could suffice in reasoning why this was Mr. Lewis's first-time hearing about my arrival in town. Something in my gut told me that wasn't the case, though.

"I'm back, ladies. You have room for dessert?"

"We do," Nijah spoke swiftly. My friend had a good appetite, and had it not been for the ass she was carrying, it would be a wonder where everything she consumed went.

"Hey, Mr. Lewis, can I ask you a question?"

"Sure." He took a seat, giving me his undivided attention.

"I'll be back. Going to the restroom," Nijah announced. And I was greatly appreciative of her absence at this moment.

"Do you think I'm good enough for Prentice?" The question was left field, and though his opinion shouldn't have mattered, it did. Hearing that he and Prentice had become close on top of Prentice's mother never being a fan of mine, I guess I just cared to know one elder who felt that we were meant to be.

"I think that you and Prentice have something that is meant for you to share this lifetime. In other words, it's possible that you two are meant to be. However, only the two of you know that. You are never supposed to be with someone based on an approved perception. You base your relationship on the feelings that you provide each other. If you feel that he's the man you're supposed to be with, then that's who you be with. From my eyes, I can see a strong connection that pulls you two together. Continue to embrace that. Besides, if Prentice is as crazy about you now as he was back then, you got a good man on your hands."

"I sure hope so." Nijah came right in time to give her two cents, as usual.

"Thank you, Mr. Lewis . . . for everything."

"Anytime. I'm going to go box up the dessert for you two and Prentice."

"Thank you," Nijah and I said in unison as he got up.

"You think Mr. Lewis got a girlfriend? I didn't see a ring on his finger."

"Maybe we should go to the sex store when we leave here."

"Oooh? Why? You 'bout to try some freaky, nasty shit with Prentice tonight? Yes, sis, keep him wanting more," she snapped.

"No, for *yo'* ass. Because you gotta need some type of stimulation if you steady over here feenin' for Mr. Lewis."

"Oh, I packed my handy dandy eggplant with me, ho. Plus, I've never needed help getting a man. You see me." She smacked her lips just as Mr. Lewis came back.

"All right, ladies, here you go, and Aúrea." He turned to me.

"Yes?"

"Don't be a stranger."

"I won't."

"*We* won't," Nijah corrected, pulling a light laugh from Mr. Lewis and me.

We took the boxes of dessert from him and left the restaurant. This visit went better than expected. What I gathered more than anything was that Prentice and my past were what connected our future. I was crazy about that man, and there was no reason to continue to try to deny it.

# 25

## *Prentice*

As late as it was when the sandman had caught up to me, it was a surprise that my internal alarm clock was on point—waking me up before the sound of my alarm going off. Who was I kidding? Sleeping in, well, at least until my alarm had gone off, had become a regularity over the last couple of weeks. What changed this morning had changed my sleeping pattern. There was no doubt about it. Waking up out of my sleep was more than likely caused by the lack of warmth that I felt on the opposite side of the bed. Rolling over, I extended my arm to the space that Aúrea normally occupied. Releasing a low groan, I knew this was not a feeling I wanted anymore. Having her here was just as addictive as a heroin addict needing their second hit. And if she weren't back tonight, making my way to her place to carry her ass back would be at the top of my priority list.

The only reason she was able to leave without me tripping last night was that she whined about feeling guilty since for days, she had been staying with me, leaving her friend who was visiting from Los Angeles. Nijah was cool as hell, but she was interfering with the live-in pussy and companionship that I'd gotten used to. Quiet as she tried to keep it, Aúrea was feeling some kind of way because of how close we had gotten. Even after staying with me most of the time, driving my car, and giving me pussy on the daily except for when her cycle came, she still was trying to avoid being my official girl. To me, that's what we were . . . in a whole-ass relationship. She was mine, and I was hers. Neither of us was fucking or seeing anyone else. We were practically living together, all the shit people in relationships do. Still, getting her to say that things between us were official proved harder than I thought, which was why the dude she was messing with in L.A. was still going to get his. Leaving her to handle him was going to be an easy separation because of the rewarding result.

Flipping from my stomach to my back, I picked up my cell, resting on its charger on my nightstand. There were no missed calls nor texts.

"A'ight," I scoffed. There weren't many people I expected to hear from on this line, yet the two who should have hit a nigga up to make sure I was straight hadn't. My mom and Aúrea. It was cool, though.

To Wifey: Have a good day.

I shot the text to Aúrea, then finally made my way out of bed.

There were a few things on my agenda for the day, which would only start after brushing my teeth and washing my ass. Street business and my legit business needed to be tended to today, so it was only right to dress the part. Being the kind of man who could do both and look good while doing it, I opted for a pair of Ralph Lauren khaki pants and navy polo with the blue and white 13s. Once I decided on my 'fit, I took care of my hygiene and exited the house.

Because my house was on the other side of town in one of the areas better known to house the wealthy, it took me a minute to make it to the old neighborhood. When I pulled up, the first car I noticed was Sonic's, which was not surprising at all. Instead of getting out to shoot the shit, I pulled behind his car and waited for him to come to me.

"You off house arrest?" he asked as he sat in the passenger seat.

"Fuck you talking about?" Sucking my teeth, I turned my body to face him fully. The mug on my face wasn't inviting either.

"Yo' ass has been MIA not even on the business tip, 'cause that's always handled. However, you done canceled two kickback nights, and oddly, I haven't even met sis." He had this perplexed-ass look on his face which only lasted about half a minute before he burst into laughter. The frown adorning my face was so intense I felt the dip in my brow.

"You sensitive-ass nigga," he teased.

"Nah, you just need to focus on talking about shit you know about. Like this money and not where my dick been."

"Nigga, ain't nobody said shit about yo' dick. Don't play with me like that." His demeanor quickly shifted, proving I struck a nerve.

His smile had vanished, and there was damn near smoke coming from his ears. He needed a swift reminder that I too could get on the bullshit he was on.

"If you worried about why I ain't been hanging with yo' ass, then you worried about where my dick been."

"We may as well change the subject now because shit gon' get further left. You playing too much."

Chuckling, I extended my fist over to him for a pound. That was my way of calling a truce. That would have happened regardless. Sonic was my boy, and we didn't beef over just anything. Granted, if he disrespected Aúrea, that would be the end of our friendship.

"You'll meet her soon. Her homegirl too, if she doesn't shoot back to L.A."

"Shit, make the introduction ASAP 'cause if her friend cute, she won't be thinking about a plane ticket, but a new lease."

"Then the introduction gon' wait 'til homegirl shake, 'cause—"

"Bro, you hating?" he cut me off, making me laugh. Hell, I was laughing so hard you would've thought Chris Tucker told the joke.

"I got you, bro. But look, let's talk business real quick because I got another stop to make before getting to my spot."

"You need me to follow you?" His question didn't surprise me. He was always ready to ride with me if needed.

"Nah, this a simple trip. Pick up a bag, drop a bag."

"I feel it. What I have has already been dropped off, and the count was straight."

I nodded to let him know all was well. My phone vibrated before I could say anything else. I removed it from the cup holder where it had been and smiled at the text from Aúrea, letting me know she would be hitting me up when she finished class.

"It's time for your lovesick ass to go, huh?" Sonic chimed.

"Not 'cause of what you think. I already told you that there was a couple more moves I needed to make. Won't even lie to you, though. If my girl needed me right now, I'd dip."

When the words left my mouth, I didn't regret them because they were honest. However, I sounded like a lovesick teenager, and if Sonic decided to clown me, I couldn't even be mad.

"I don't doubt it. Make sure you make time to put me on with her homegirl . . . then again, maybe not. My player's card hasn't expired yet. Shit still got a good five-year-run at least."

"Yeah, a'ight." He said that shit now, but if he met Nijah, he'd be ready to risk a whole lot of shit.

Sonic extended his hand this time, and we dapped up once more before he exited my car. My next destination was to Mr. Lewis's restaurant to drop off money for a small renovation needed in the kitchen area. It wasn't even because of the small stake I had in the restaurant. It was necessary since one of the cooks fucked up and damn near burned the appliances.

The ride to the restaurant was quick because I did no playing getting there. My final destination was my office, and getting there on time to meet my client was a must.

"Prentice." Mr. Lewis's voice hit my ear as soon as I stepped through the door.

"'Sup, old man?" I greeted him as he embraced me with a hug.

"You know you ain't shit for not telling me Aúrea was back in town. Bringing money for the kitchen don't mean yo' ass is in the clear."

Being the straightforward person he was, he got right to the point and was serious as hell. He had a right to be. Letting Aúrea's return slip my mind was kind of messed up. However, he knew better than anyone that I ran a very thin line with logical thinking when it came to her.

"It really slipped my mind, old man." I tried playing it cool when really, I wasn't trying to hear him cuss my ass out.

"You a damn lie. You done been through here more than a few times since she's been back," he called me out on my shit.

"You right, somewhat. You know I'ma make it right, though."

"I ain't trying to hear that shit. How're things going between y'all, though? The short version."

"Shit, I know what I want, and she does too. She's scared for some reason, so we just taking it day by day, I guess."

Mr. Lewis wasn't Sonic, so keeping it real with him about Aúrea and my situation was as easy as putting my right and left legs into jeans. The old Prentice would have been afraid of being honest with him. The years of him being the present father figure I needed pulled me out of that shit quickly.

"I'm going to tell you like I told her. There's a magnetic force between you two, and since she's come back, you've already picked up where you left off. You're looking out for her, proving just how important she is to you. Life hasn't been easy for her. You know that more than anyone, so give her the time she needs . . . Eventually, she'll be your wife." Chuckling, he patted my back.

"All right, old man. I gotta go."

"It was all good until I brought up marriage." He laughed heartily while I shook my head.

"Nah, I really got shit to do." Which was partially the truth. There was no doubt in my mind that Aúrea and I could take those vows. My future didn't even seem like one without her in it. Still, the only thing I was ready for right now was a relationship—marriage and all that could come later.

"Thanks, son," he said, taking the envelope full of cash. His calling me son was his way of letting me know that what we had just engaged in was friendly banter. It was also his way of letting me know what has been evident since the day I met him, which was he had my back. He could've cussed me out from this way to Sunday, and there would still be no doubt in my mind concerning how he felt about me. I dapped him up one last time, then dipped.

My seat hadn't had time to warm before my cell rang. Seeing Aúrea's name flash across the screen brought a smile to my face. My ass really had it bad.

"What's up, beautiful?" The smile on my face was surely heard in my tone.

"Um, nothing much. I wanted to know if you had time to meet up with me?" She sounded like she was unsure, and that shit made my stomach turn a bit. Her reservations about me were nerve-racking.

"Something wrong?" The joy and easiness that was in my tone had turned to panic.

"No, Prentice," she snickered. "I want to come to see you and talk . . . about . . . us."

"Pull up. I'm at my consulting office. I'm about to shoot you my location."

"Okay." She perked up, and my dick jumped. Knowing she wanted to talk to me about us had me feeling good. Yeah, the conversation could be one that wouldn't make me too happy, but her saying, "us," kept me hopeful. If the relationship weren't what she wanted, she would've used a different choice of words, I was sure of it. I was also sure of the moment she told me she was officially mine, that we were breaking this desk of mine in.

Since it would take some time for her to get to me from her college campus, I decided to take care of what I drove all this way for. My client needed a spreadsheet, which would present him with ideas for opening businesses and the different income brackets. Investing was another of my specialties, so he would also be getting information on the best ways to invest his money to make it grow. As much money as I made in the streets, this was my favorite hustle. Helping people, using my knowledge from both books and the streets to make them and me more money, was rewarding.

"Mr. Mayor, you have a guest by the name of Ms. Aúrea here to see you," my assistant Leslie spoke, peeping her head in my office door. Apparently, the smile on my face was contagious because Leslie was smiling too. Surely, she didn't know what she was smiling about.

"That's fine. Let her back, and you can take the rest of the day off."

"You sure? You're supposed to have a—"

"I'm positive, Leslie. You have the rest of the day off, with pay."

"Okay, see you later." She rushed her happy ass out, and there was no dispute from me. The quicker she got out of here, the better.

"Your assistant rushed out of here like she had the winning lottery ticket," Aúrea teased, stepping into my office.

Standing from my desk, I met her halfway, immediately pulling her into my arms and kissing her lips.

"You missed me?" she giggled in between kisses.

"You know I did. I hope you and Nijah got y'all girl time outta the way because you coming home tonight."

"Home?" she questioned as if I said something wrong.

"Yeah, home," I reiterated.

When she backed away from me, my heart felt like it dropped to my balls. Though my instincts told me to pull her back into me, I decided not to. She came to speak to me, so I would let her control the narrative.

Somewhat.

"So what's up?" My left brow raised as my eyes met hers.

"Um, I was thinking about all the time we've been spending together, and I wanted to tell you face-to-face that . . ."

The rapid beating of my heart could be heard through both my ears, almost deafening all the other sounds around me. I wasn't this dude anymore, the guy who feared shit, who was hung up on a woman like I couldn't get another. For Aúrea, I was, though. Shit was embarrassing and mind-boggling.

"Prentice, did you hear me?" She took my hands into hers, bringing me back from my thoughts.

"Nah, my bad. What did you say?"

"So now that I'm ready to be your girlfriend, you don't hear it?" She pursed up her lips, tilted her head to the side, and looked at me sideways.

"Oh, we official now?" My smile was so big, the corners of my mouth had to be about an inch from my ears.

Shit, if she thought Leslie acted like she just won the lottery, my joy was like the first Black president getting elected into office.

"That's what I said unless you want to change—"

Before she could let that dumb shit slip from her mouth, my lips were on hers, kissing her as if we wouldn't be able to kiss again for years.

"Mmm," she moaned into my mouth . . . The invitation I needed to take things further. Lifting her by her ass, I carried her over to my desk, where I sat her down.

"You wore this short-ass skirt to school?" I noted, rubbing my hands feverishly over her exposed thighs.

"Only because I knew I was coming to see you," she spoke breathlessly, placing her lips back on mine.

Aúrea's lips and tongue tasted like strawberry Starburst. I worked my hands all the way up her thighs until my fingertips reached the hem of her underwear. That was as far as I'd gotten before she was lifting her ass off my desk to assist with the removal of her panties.

As hard as my dick was, there was no way to avoid the craving for her juices. So down I went, pulling her a little closer to the edge, hoisting her legs in the crooks of my arms.

"Ahh." Aúrea's moan was loud enough to shake the walls. That was one of the things I loved about our intimacy. She was never quiet. She always voiced how good I made her feel . . . loudly.

Wanting to bring her to her peak quickly so that the tension building from my balls to the tip of my dick could be relieved, I quickly flicked my tongue across her clit. Then I pulled it into my mouth, sucking with just enough pressure to make her quiver.

"Prentice, I'm com . . . coming."

"Let it go." Mumbling my order seemed to be all she needed as her legs began to shake, and I could taste her sweetness on my tongue.

"Mmm," Aúrea moaned again as I stood and dropped my pants, completely freeing myself. In one quick thrust, I slid into her slippery folds and held myself there. Her pussy was something to brag about, which was why I was a damn plum fool behind her ass.

Slowly, I began to slide in and out of her, looking down at her juices coating my shit, and that had me ready to bust just knowing she got that wet for me.

"Prentice, you feel so good."

"Shit, you feel good too. Come for me one more time, A. I'm ready to bust."

I was trying to hold it, but the excitement of us becoming official and the way she was spilling onto and hugging my dick, the usual lengthy sex we had was not a possibility right now.

"Yes," she agreed. As I sped up and used my thumb to put pressure on her clit, I wanted this second nut from her to be a bigger one, and what I wanted I got because she came so hard she pushed me out of her. Not missing a beat, I placed myself back inside of her, stroking a few more times before pulling out and nutting onto the chair clients sat in. It would be replaced today.

"I'm going to go to the restroom and get paper towels," she said, pulling her skirt down.

"My private restroom is right there," I motioned toward the door at the far-right end of my office.

"Okay."

"You can handle that." She extended her paper towel-filled hand toward me while she motioned toward my nut that was drying on the chair.

"I'm throwing that mothafucka out. Don't trip." Taking the wet towels from her hand, I used them to wipe my hands before setting the paper towels on top of the mess I made on the chair.

"Soo, what's next?" Aúrea asked me with a bright smile on her face and her hands at her sides as she shrugged her shoulders slightly. It was funny that she was trying to put on this shy, innocent act when her legs were just spread wide as hell for me, without issue.

"Shit, you gon' be at the house when I get there, with my dinner ready," I joked. Well, almost. If she'd provide all that for me, there was no way I'd turn it down.

"Getting ahead of yourself now, aren't you?" She was still smiling, but the shy girl act was gone.

"Nah, ya man just putting in my request."

"I need you to know something," she spoke seriously, catching me off guard.

"Anything."

"When I was with my ex, he was demanding, abusive, both physically and verbally, which you already know. I understand that you are joking, and even though I'm putting up a brave front, it's hard for me not to feel a bit afraid. I need you to be a little more conscious of what you say and how just until . . ."

Her words trailed off, and I knew she was trying to say until she "healed," and it pissed me off. Dude was *definitely* going to meet Von in hell. We had gotten comfortable with each other again, me more than her, and I felt like shit because my being comfortable made me forget what she'd been through.

Pulling her into me as gently as possible, I placed my right hand on the right side of her face before pecking her lips softly.

"I apologize. I never want you to think I'm disregarding what you've been through and how you feel. Having you back in my life has been one of the best things to happen to me in a while, and I won't front, a nigga got a bit excited." The crooked grin on my face that most women found attractive, hopefully, brought her comfort.

"I know you're aware that I won't hurt you, but I'm going to reiterate that shit anyway. I'd hurt myself before hurting you, and I'm bodying anyone who tries to hurt you. You know that, right?" My eyes bore into hers as she smiled slightly and nodded.

"Good. Now, I'm going to try to chill some with the things I say that could trigger messed-up emotions for you, but if I slip, don't be afraid to tell me that I've made you uncomfortable and always remember, it's never because I'm out to hurt you, but because yo' heart and yo' pussy got a nigga sprung." We both smiled at that statement.

"I know." She leaned in and kissed me this time before stepping back.

"So, I need to get to my place and chill with Nahji for a bit. Then I'll meet you at your house. How much longer will you be here?"

"Shit, about another hour or so. When Nijah supposed to leave . . . I mean, is she staying? Shit." No matter how I worded the question, it sounded terrible. Luckily, it didn't offend Aúrea because she just laughed.

"That sounded so wrong, and you know you're not my only friend, right? Plus, I don't want you to be my only friend." She laughed. "Anyway, she is debating on staying out here for good, which I'm very happy about, and if she stays, she will be at my place, and I will be at yours."

"Ours," I corrected her.

"Ours," she repeated, beaming.

"Come on. I'm going to walk you to the car and finish up here so I can get home, and we can exercise again."

"Prentice, I'm not moving out of my place just yet. We talked about me living on my own and taking care of myself, remember?"

"I do, but I thought I gave you enough time with all that." I grinned. It was worth a shot. I knew when Aúrea's mind was made up, there wasn't much I could do to change it. I would still try, though, and even if she didn't move in with me, I still wanted her to consider my place hers and that she could come and go as she pleased. Would having her there daily be better than the latter? No doubt, but I was going to try to honor her wishes.

"You do not have all of your marbles, I'm convinced," she laughed.

"Maybe not, but my offer still stands, and my casa is su casa, regardless of whether you move in."

There was nothing to say to that, as she hadn't actually told a lie. When it came to her, maybe I was a few marbles short. Taking her by the hand and leading the way to my car, I felt like a new man.

"Prentice Mayor?"

Aúrea and I barely exited the door of my office before police officers met us. Out of instinct, I pushed Aúrea behind me, stepping in front of her as a shield.

"What's up?" It was hard as hell to play cool when my stomach was in knots. There was a lot I'd done today and, shit, every day, and though my hands didn't touch any of the illegal products I dealt with, in the court of law, my ass would still be found guilty. My mind raced, trying to figure out why these mothafuckas were at my place of business, specifically looking for me. Yeah, this was my shit, but it was all legit.

"Prentice, what's going on?" Aúrea spoke softly as she took my forearm, squeezing it tightly. All that did was let me know she was scared for my ass, which pissed me off.

"So you are Mr. Mayor?" the officer questioned again. He was about my height, maybe a little shorter, about an inch or so under my six feet. His nationality may have been Hispanic, yet many features made him look Caucasian as well, the blond hair on his head being one.

"I said, what's up? Why are you here?" The officer needed to get to the point.

"We have a warrant for your arrest." His words hit my ears like a ton of bricks, and I damn near shit my pants.

"A warrant? For what?" My voice went up an octave. My palms suddenly felt like they were sitting in a puddle. This wasn't my first time coming into contact with the cops. However, the times I had, it was on some petty shit. If they were here because of my weed and pill business, I'd be sitting in a cell way too long. Shit, a day was going to be too long.

"Because your ass assaulted me." The sound of Gerald's punk-ass voice was music to my ears. Nah, seeing him didn't bring me any joy, but if he were the reason for the cops being here, it was a punishment I could handle because the time would be short.

"You called the cops on me, G?" I looked his ass up and down.

"Who is that, Prentice?" Aúrea was now standing beside me.

"My mom's punk-ass boyfriend."

"You need to come with us, sir," the cop interrupted.

"Why? I didn't touch his punk ass."

"Yes, you did. I have the medical records to prove it." He held up a piece of paper that didn't mean shit to me 'cause I didn't care. Had his ass been put in the hospital from the ass beating I gave him, and he made it out, then maybe he didn't get beat badly enough.

"You can clear that up at the station. You have the right to remain silent . . ." The officer's words trailed off as the feel of his partner's hands on mine removed my attention from his words. His ass moved fast too because, within seconds, my hands were cuffed behind my back.

"Noo, no, don't take him." Aúrea was full of panic as she tried pulling me away from the officers.

"Babe, it's okay. I'll be out soon. Go to the house, get my mom's info, and call her. She'll know how to contact my lawyer. I'll be out quick, I promise." Seeing the fear and panic on her face as the tears welled in her eyes made me feel like shit. This was the last thing she needed to witness me going through. Thankfully, this was a simple arrest . . . simple compared to what it could have been.

"Are you going to be okay?" she asked, tears finally falling.

"Babe, yes. Just do what I said. Keys to the house are in my office. Go do what I said so that I can get out and come home to you, all right?"

"Okay," she agreed, kissing my lips, not caring about the cops as they forced me into the backseat of the car.

She stood there, watching as they drove off with my ass.

# 26

## *Aúrea*

Watching Prentice being carried away in a police car crushed me. How did a day that started so well end like this? When I came to my senses and told Prentice I was ready to be his girlfriend officially, we made love like we were supposed to, and it was supposed to be happening again, at his . . . well, *our* house and in his . . . *our* bed. Yes, being his girlfriend and being on some what's-yours-is-mine type of thing would take some getting used to, except in this case because my heart was in the back of that police car with him.

Taking a deep breath, I rushed back into his office and removed his keys from his desk. My nerves were on edge, and it took me about five minutes to figure out how to lock his office. Once I did that, I planted my ass in the driver's seat of his Tesla. Saying fuck the speed limit, I made it to his home in record time. As always, Rocko and Chuck greeted me at the door. I patted their heads and rushed to his home office, looking for whatever information on Tasha he had. His mother hadn't even crossed my mind, and to be honest, she was way at the bottom of my list of people to see. However, as I've always done for Prentice, I'd tolerate her ass. I just hoped she knew that I wasn't a teenager anymore, and if necessary, she'd get her ass kicked or cussed out, whichever came first. Prentice would have to forgive me.

"What am I looking for?" I grumbled. He totally sent me in here blind.

I took deep breaths to calm my nerves. Then my eyes slowly scanned the well-decorated office. The mahogany bookshelf housed nothing but books, at least that's what it looked like.

"Duh," I spoke, blowing out a harsh breath as the place to look came to mind. Prentice kept a list of numbers near the phone in his bedroom. Taking a note from track star Natasha Hastings's book, I sprinted out of the office and into Prentice's bedroom. I snatched up the book, and right near his mother's name read, "*In Case of Emergency*." I flipped to my name to see what it said and near it was the word "*Wifey*." Smiling while ripping his mother's information out of the notepad, I rushed out the door.

Pulling up to a nice home just as big as Prentice's, I double-checked the address noted on the paper against the address put into my GPS, and according to both, I was in the right place. Exiting my car with a purpose, it took me just a few steps to reach the wooden door and ring the bell.

"Who is it?" someone yelled from the other side of the door. The thick wood wasn't even enough to make me mistake the voice. This was Tasha's home.

"Aúrea." My voice sounded strong, even though fear rushed through my veins.

There was a brief moment of silence before I heard the sound of locks being unlatched. The door opened, and my mouth liked to have fallen on the floor. Tasha had always been a pretty woman, gorgeous even. She just had a shitty attitude, which made her ugly. Staring at her now, five years later, I realized that time had been good to her. She didn't look like she aged at all. Her honey complexion was flawless, with not a mark or wrinkle in sight. Her hair was in a short pixie cut with burgundy highlights. Tasha stood in front of me, looking like she could pass for Halle Berry's twin.

"Aúrea, Prentice doesn't live here. How did you know where I live?" Her face showed confusion and not disgust as I thought it would, even though her tone didn't sound too welcoming either.

"I know . . . I came here because, because . . . the police arrested him."

"What do you mean he was arrested? Get in here." She practically pulled me into her home, which was unexpected since I stood in her doorway this long.

"What did you do?" she asked, and I frowned. This shouldn't have surprised me. *This* was the Tasha *I* knew, the one who thought anything terrible that happened to her son was *my* fault.

"I didn't do anything. Your boyfriend did," I told her matter-of-factly.

"My boyfriend?" The puzzled look on her face was there for about two seconds until it turned to a look of guilt.

"Yes, *your boyfriend*. He showed up at Prentice's job with the cops, who arrested him. Before they took him, he told me to tell you and for you to call his lawyer."

Watching her closely, I saw her chest heave. She was either panicking or trying to calm her nerves.

"You can have a seat." She nodded toward a nice-looking grey sectional as she removed her cell from her back pocket.

"Monty," she spoke into the phone.

Taking her up on the offer, I went and sat down while doing my best to hear the conversation.

"Prentice was arrested . . . hold on." She removed the phone from her ear and turned to me.

"How long ago was he arrested?" she asked me.

"Um, about an hour now," I informed her.

"He was arrested about an hour ago . . . An assault charge . . . Monty, go get my baby, no matter the cost. You know we have it . . . Okay, thank you." She ended the call.

I sat there waiting for her to say something else to me. Instead, she began pacing the floor, and for the first time, I saw that we had something big in common—our love for Prentice. Seeing her frantic made me realize that my pain was nothing compared to what she probably felt. She was his mother, the woman who brought him into the world. No way did my pain measure up to hers.

"Gerald," she yelled into the phone, pulling me from my sympathizing thoughts, "did you *really* have my child arrested?" she screamed. "Why would you do that?" she asked, and I wish I could hear his answer. That was the million-dollar question that I'd pay a billion dollars to get the answer to.

"You deserved it. You stole from his sister—your *daughter*. You better go to that police station and tell them you made a mistake."

Although I could only hear Tasha, she was doing a damn good job from the looks of things, in my opinion. She was setting his ass straight, and it felt good to hear.

"Listen to me, you dumb ass. I could have probably forgiven you for taking the money, but if you don't do whatever you need to do to get my son out of jail, I will *never* forgive your ass, and you won't see my daughter another day of your life if you don't end that shit . . . It's *not* a damn threat, Gerald."

Prentice did have a younger sister, and Tasha bringing her up made me curious about where she was. All the yelling her mother was doing right now, if she were here, she would have made herself known by now.

"What will it take for you to go down there and tell them you lied?" she asked, finally removing the base from her tone. She now sounded like she was begging, pleading, with him.

"You seriously don't want anything to do with your daughter?" her voice cracked, her face full of emotion.

"Fine. You got that. Just do what you need to do for my son. I'll call you when the lawyer draws up the paperwork." She tossed her phone onto the chair across from me, making me jump a little.

"Between the lawyer and Gerald's punk ass, my son should be out soon," she spoke, plopping down on the love seat.

"Okay," was the only thing I could think to say.

"His bitch ass wants to give up his parental rights," she voiced. I was sure she wasn't speaking to me, and if I gathered what she'd just said correctly, her baby daddy was a whole bitch. To want to give up his daughter was a real ho move.

She didn't bother saying anything else. I watched her staring off into space as we both sat there. I wanted to leave. Yet, I wasn't in a rush to do so because she was my only connection to Prentice. Since she knew and spoke to his lawyer, she held all the information. The lawyer would call her with the updates first. He wouldn't call me at all.

"When did you get back?" Tasha broke the silence between us. Her question was not farfetched, given the five years which separated the last time she and I saw each other. Besides, it came at the right time because as much as I wanted to hear the information, just sitting in her home, staring at the walls would be awkward as hell.

"A couple of months ago. I returned for my foster . . . Von's funeral."

Her eyes widened at my admission.

"How are you?" That question caught me off guard. This woman had changed.

"I'll be better when Prentice is out of jail." Sure, her question was regarding Von. I doubted she was ready for that answer, though.

"So will I. However, my question was concerning your foster parents."

Looking at her, I debated in my head whether to be honest with her. Two outcomes could come from my truth. She could believe me, or she couldn't. The only issue I was having currently was, how much would it bother me if she didn't believe me?

"I didn't go to the funeral because I cared about Von. I went to tell him to kiss my ass." I was straightforward. The internal battle I was having with whether to tell her was no more as I figured honesty was the best policy. Not only that, but I also wanted her to feel like shit for how she treated me all those years back. The shock from my response was written all over her face, and rather than let her heal from what I just disclosed, I decided it was better to keep speaking since the wound was already opened.

"Von raped me weekly for five years . . . *That's* why I ran away."

The gasp from her throat rang in my ears.

"Did my son know?"

"He did."

"Damn," she whispered before her head fell into the palm of her hands. She was getting a lot put on her plate today.

"Why didn't you guys come to me?" she asked, and I chuckled, but not because it was funny. The laugh escaped my mouth without any effort from me at all. That was just my natural reaction to her question because she and I both knew she was the least approachable person during those days.

"You weren't a fan of mine back then. And with all the gossip going on about me, would you have believed me?"

"I believe you now," she stated.

"Thank you." Shrugging was another natural reaction. I mean, her believing me now was great. I just wished that she had been the kind of adult I needed back then.

"My son missed you while you were gone."

"I missed him too."

"So, are you two back . . . well, are you and my son—"

"We decided today to give being a couple a shot," I cut her off.

"Well, if it's okay with you, I'd like for us to start over."

My eyes met hers, and there was so much sincerity inside of hers that even if I wanted to, denying her that would be so fucked up of me. Plus, my loving Prentice meant loving his mother, as well.

"I'd like that" flowed smoothly from my mouth, although my heart couldn't decipher if I were being honest. Maybe I was, and fear kept me from seeing it. The smile she gave me was warm and genuine.

"Well, all we can do now is wait. Monty is a damn good lawyer, so my son will be home sooner than later.

Plus, Gerald's punk ass said he'd take back the accusation, so he'll be home soon."

"Can I leave you my number to call me with any updates?"

"Sure, but you're also welcome to stay. Monty should be at the precinct by now, finding out what he has to do to get Prentice out."

"Thank you, but I have to feed his dogs . . . and my friend is visiting from Los Angeles where I moved from, so I need to go check on her. She's staying at my place."

"Oh. Okay, well, sure. Give me your number, and as soon as I hear something, I'll call you." She extended her arm with her phone in hand and passed it to me.

After inputting my number, I stood ready to leave. Being here made me more emotional, and it was only a matter of time before I broke down. Breaking down here was out of the question.

"Mommy, I'm hungry." The soft voice of a child came from my right, and there was a little girl, the same complexion as Prentice, standing in a uniform, khaki skirt, and navy polo, rubbing her eyes.

"Prima, come here, baby." Tasha stood, arms wide open, meeting the pretty, curly-haired girl halfway.

"This is Prima, Aúrea. She's my baby girl, Prentice's little sister." Tasha made the introduction as Prima just lay on her mother's chest.

"Nice to meet you, Prima."

"You too," her soft voice brought a smile to my face. She finally made eye contact with me, and she was gorgeous. Long, black lashes, thick, perfectly arched eyebrows, a button nose . . . She was a walking beauty, and for a moment, I imagined having a daughter by Prentice as beautiful as she.

"Well, I'm going to get her dinner. You make sure to take care of yourself. Prentice is strong. He will be fine and home sooner than later. He's not going to want you sitting home stressing."

*Easier said than done.* "I know. Please don't forget to contact me when you hear anything."

My hand was finally on the doorknob.

"I won't," she promised.

Knowing Tasha would update me on Prentice eased some of the weight off my shoulders. Still, until he was out of jail and in my arms, emptiness would consume me. My heart was with him.

# 27

## *Prentice*

The smell of piss and mothballs entered my nose, causing my stomach to turn. The hard steel underneath me was slowly making my ass and legs fall asleep. With my back against the dirty wall, my eyes scanned the small room. The walls, which I assumed started as white, were filthy grey with handprints and possibly dried shit on them. The ceiling had tissue stuck to it, with pieces that fell sporadically on the concrete floor. I scoffed, thinking that either this room was always occupied or no one cared enough to clean it. There was an old, white man across from me with long grey hair and an even longer grey beard. His clothes were worn and filthy, letting me know that they had thrown my ass in here with a homeless man. He was sleeping on the floor in the corner furthest from me when there was an empty bench right where he was. When he rolled over, I was presented with a whiff of his odor, making me gag. As soon as the stench hit my nose, it not only brought tears to my eyes but also brought back the memory of the dumpster Aúrea and I slept near when we ran away.

"Damn," I mumbled, thinking about the look on her face when those punk-ass cops threw me in the back of the police car and drove me away. The heartache she felt was written all over her face, and Gerald's bitch ass better pray I don't see him again because he was going to pay for this shit. The difference between his first ass whooping and this next one would be me not making the same mistake of thinking he wouldn't snitch. So if he had even a tad bit of intelligence, he'd stay far away from me.

The sound of footsteps heading my way led me to sit up, turning my body slightly so that my back wasn't toward the homeless dude but also not toward the bars. This holding cell was small as hell but would be used to my advantage if need be. Since being thrown back here, the only person I'd come in contact with was the sleeping, homeless man. This tier wasn't empty, and niggas were shouting and cussing like it would get them out of here, knowing damn well it wouldn't.

"Mayor, Counsel."

Hearing my name with the word "counsel" behind it sounded like music to my ears. I'd been here a few hours and was thankful Aúrea could reach my mom, who had quickly reached out to Monty. Though I hadn't gotten in trouble in a while and had been able to stay off the cops' radar with my illegal dealings, I kept a lawyer on hand, never missing a payment on the retainer fee . . . just in case. Monty was one of the best defense attorneys in the county. He wasn't cheap, but today would prove him worth it as long as he got my ass up out of here.

Standing, I waited for the guard, who looked like he just graduated from college, to open the gate. Once he did, I stepped out of there, hoping I wouldn't be re-turning.

"Can I ask you something?" the guard asked me.

"What's up?" I decided to entertain whatever question he wanted to ask because of how young he looked. As I said, he looked like he hadn't graduated too long ago.

"You are in here for fighting, but you don't look like you would even associate with the guy who pressed charges on you."

"That's 'cause he not the kind of nigga I associate myself with," I shrugged.

"I figured that," he said, stopping at the door at the end of the hall and opening it for me.

I stepped inside, and my eyes immediately met Monty sitting at the table looking through some papers. There was nothing for me to say to the young guard because the small talk we had was pointless anyway. Especially since he wasn't saying shit to help me get out. What he thought surely was not going to post bail for me. I looked over my shoulder, providing him a look that said he could get lost, and he recoiled a bit before shutting the door. Shaking my head, I stared at Monty for another second before speaking.

"Monty, what's up?" I spoke, bringing his attention from the papers to me. Whatever he was reading better be in favor of getting my ass up out of here. He stood, extending his hand for mine. I liked Monty because he looked me in the eyes when he spoke and when he greeted me with a shake.

"Prentice, I got here as soon as I could after your mother called," Monty informed me before taking a seat. I was sure that every cop in this building felt intimidated when he walked his expensive ass in here. The other thing I liked was his intimidating appearance. He walked like he could fuck up anyone who challenged him. Monty was an older cat whose ethnicity was Indian and Asian. He had taken his height and complexion from the Indian side, while his facial features and sharp mind showed signs of his other side.

"So what's the word? Am I getting out of here?"

"You'll be out as soon as you go before the judge. Unfortunately, that won't be until first thing in the morning. The judge's presiding—"

"That's some bullshit. How niggas be bailing out on the same day?" I scoffed, really puzzled as fuck.

"Your charges are the reason you're not able to bail out tonight. However, tomorrow, you will be out. I ran into your accuser, an, uh, Gerald Campbell, who said he would drop the charges. He can't do that without speaking to a judge."

"My mom must have gone off on his bitch ass."

"Not sure, but with him saying that you did not attack him, they will have no reason to hold you. You'll pay a small fine for wasted time and then be set free."

"Why his bitch ass can't pay the fine? I wouldn't even be here if it weren't for him." I sucked my teeth, becoming more irritated with this crooked-ass system.

"He should have to. However, once he takes back the charges, I'm going to ask that he be held accountable for filing a false police report. For that, he'll get jail time or pay a fine."

"Nah, you don't have to do that. I don't want to seem like I turned rat on his ass."

"That's not what it'll look like at all. Besides, you don't want to make the judge feel like he was threatened to renege, rather than to do so on his own recognizance."

"Do what you gotta do then, man." I blew out an exasperated breath.

"Have you gotten your first phone call yet? You should have been able to call me," he informed me.

"Hell, nah, I didn't." I gave Aúrea instructions to take care of everything for me, so my phone call had slipped my mind because I trusted her to do precisely what she'd done.

"Well, they still owe it to you. So you can call your mother and let her know you're okay. I still plan to call her and tell her everything as well. I'm sure she'll want to be here to pick you up once you're released in the morning."

"Yes, call her. Tell her do not tell anyone I'm getting out, including my girl."

"Will do." He began placing his things back into his briefcase. "I'm going to tell the guard now to give you that call before I exit the building. I've been waiting for a reason to sue their asses, so if they deny your call, it'll give me a reason," he spoke, making me chuckle.

He tapped on the door, alerting whoever sat on the other side that we were done. As soon as they opened the door, he demanded I get my phone call, making sure the guard walked me to it before he left. Since he was going to call my mom, I decided to call Aúrea. I knew she was going crazy, worrying about me. I hoped that she had gone to her place with Nijah because I didn't want her alone.

"Hello," she answered breathlessly on the first ring.

"Babe." Her voice brought me peace, and I hoped that my tone conveyed that.

"Prentice, are you okay? Are you coming home? Do I need to come to get you?" The questions left her mouth so quickly she almost sounded as if she were speaking another language.

"I'm good, Aúrea. How are you?"

"Worried about you. I want you home, like now," she whined, and that shit warmed and broke my heart at the same time.

"I'll be home soon, babe. Just stay strong and keep it tight for me." I chuckled, hoping to lighten the mood.

"If it's not tonight, it ain't soon enough, and you don't gotta worry about me keeping it tight." She sucked her teeth.

"Babe, I have to go. I'll call you again soon, okay?"

"You still haven't told me anything, Prentice," she fussed.

"Babe, I won't be in here long, all right? Just stay at your crib, and when I'm out, I'm going to take you home."

"Okay," she sighed.

I know I was wrong for not relaying to her what Monty had told me, but there was a reason for that. When they released me in the morning, I'd go check in with my mom, then make my way to handle something before going home to her.

Speaking of my mother, I hoped whatever ill feelings she harbored for Aúrea were gone because if they weren't, she had to figure out a way to get over that shit. This time around, I wasn't letting Aúrea go anywhere, even for her.


Just as Monty said, I was released and paid a small $500 fine while Gerald's ass got hit with a $2,000 fine that I was sure he'd pay with the money he stole from Prima. Served his ass right. After my mom paid the fine, I got the paperwork clearing me of everything. Monty made their ass give me paperwork showing that the arrest would not be on my record. I got in the car with my mother, directing her to take me home with her.

"How are you feeling?" Mom asked as she drove us back to her house.

"Good, besides the fact, I want to fuck Prima's sperm donor up." Usually, cussing in front of my mother was something I tried avoiding, but this whole situation had me fucked up, though.

"Well, you won't have to worry about him anymore. Unfortunately, Prima won't either." My mother's tone expressed her anguish, and each time she had that type of tone, it was because of Gerald's punk ass.

"Why not?"

"He agreed to drop the charges on you if I agreed to get the paperwork drawn up for his rights to Prima to be removed," she informed me.

"What the hell? *That's* what you had to do to get me out? Ma, I could've stayed in there, or shit, Monty would have gotten me out just like he did."

"Yeah, but Gerald taking back his statement helped get you out quicker. Besides, it wasn't me who asked for his rights to be given up. It was him, and if he doesn't want to be a part of his daughter's life, who am I to force him?"

"She's better off without his ass anyway. Prima will never feel unloved, unwanted, or end up feeling like she missed out on a father because I'll be there for her every step of the way," I promised, meaning every word. Had I known Gerald didn't give a fuck about my sister as a father should have, I would've killed his ass when I had the chance. Shit sucked that my sister would grow up without her father as I did. Sad to say, this would be something my mom would have to live with, knowing she chose two washed-up, sorry-ass baby daddies.

"You're right. When were you going to tell me Aúrea was back?"

"After she and I figured out what we were doing."

"From what she tells me, you two are an item now."

"We are, and I hope that you will finally accept her 'cause I love her."

"I was wrong about her. I apologized, and she and I have agreed to start over."

"Good." My insides were on fire with joy. It had me feeling like the young boy who always made my mother proud.

"And why are you coming home with me?"

"To shower, and because I have something to do before making my way home to Aúrea."

"Prentice, you better not be going after Gerald."

"I'm not. I promise." I meant it too. Gerald wasn't worth another second of my time unless his absence began to hurt Prima. Then we'd have a problem again.

"All right," she quickly replied.

Though I wanted to chill with my mom a bit longer, there was something I needed to do. So after showering and cleaning jail from my body, I hurried to the spot where I would always meet Nick and Sonic. Just as I expected, they were there before me.

"What's up? I thought we were gonna have to come break you out that ho," Sonic spoke, dapping me up.

"Had they tried to throw the book at ya' boy, that's what y'all better had done."

"Without hesitation, my nigga," Nick spoke up, giving me pound as well.

"So who is this nigga we gotta go get at?" Sonic asked, getting straight to the point.

I intended to handle Adrian, Aúrea's ex, myself, but this little jail shit made me think twice about it. It had taken a lot of digging, but a few days ago, I finally found the information I needed to get at dude, no thanks to Aúrea.

"Dude is in L.A.?"

"This 'bout sis?" Sonic questioned knowingly. He still hadn't been properly introduced to my girl, and he wasn't cussing my ass out about what he knew I was getting ready to ask him.

"Yeah. Dude was foul and needs to be handled."

"Say no more. We'll call you when it's done."

"Thank you." My eyes shifted between the two as I dapped them up. After giving them the information I had and Adrian's description, I left to be with my girl. There was no doubt they'd handle things accordingly because if they didn't, it would surely come back to bite me in the ass.

# 28

## *Aúrea*

After hanging up with Prentice the night before, I stayed awake as long as I could, waiting for him to walk . . . well, knock on my front door, only to fall asleep and wake up disappointed because he was not there. Nijah was doing her best to lift my spirits. She was doing the most to lift me up, and no matter her effort, it just wasn't happening. It wouldn't happen until my man was home. His mother called me shortly after he and I hung up, telling me nothing that helped the situation, only further frustrating me. By the time sleep came to visit me, it was a little after 3:00 a.m., which was short-lived because Nijah was shaking me awake.

"What do you have planned today?"

"Sleeping," I groaned, pulling my pillow over my head, hoping she took the hint to leave me alone.

"That's what you're *not* about to do. I refuse to let you wallow away. He told you he was getting out, right? So get your ass up and quit acting like he just got life in prison . . . Wait, that was the wrong thing to say," she backpedaled.

"No shit. And I don't feel like getting up. I'm going to stay in this bed until Prentice comes to get me out. Besides, it's still early. I just fell asleep two hours ago."

"It's ten in the morning, Aúrea. You mean to tell me you were up until 8:00 a.m.?" She sounded so disappointed.

"No, at 3:00 a.m. Wait, it's ten?" That had me removing the pillow from my head, frantically sitting up, reaching for my cell that somehow made it from beside me to the foot of my bed. There were no missed calls or text messages. The disappointment had to have been etched on my face because, within seconds, Nijah wrapped her arms around me.

"It's okay, baby sis," she soothed, rubbing my back as I cried.

I don't even think my heart felt this broken, nor did I cry this much when I left him five years ago. Knowing he was in jail presented a different kind of pain, and I just wanted it to go away.

"Why is he not out yet?" Sobbing the question did nothing but add to the doubts I had about his release.

"His lawyer will get him out. Look, get dressed, let's go to breakfast, check on those big-ass dogs of his that you two love so much, and by the time we've finished all of that—"

"He still may not be home," I cut her off.

"And he may call while we're out and about. If you sit here all day doing nothing, the day will drag, making you feel worse than you do. It's best to get up, get out, and get busy. Please, or I'm getting in this bed and crying all day with you. We both know you don't want that."

"Fine—only because you're right. Listening to you cry is the last thing I want."

She laughed, releasing me from her arms.

It took me about thirty minutes to handle my hygiene and get dressed before Nijah and I were out of the house. We first made sure that Rocko and Chuck were straight, which took almost twenty minutes to do because convincing Nijah to come inside with me and pet them took most of our time. She was afraid of them, and I did not want her to be, especially since she would have to visit me here often. The dogs had taken to me so well that they listened to my commands as if I were Prentice. Since I wasn't Prentice, though, Nijah had every right to be afraid. The dogs showed me love, and I had to be crazy to think that was enough. But I had enough pull to bring a stranger around them. Plus, Nijah's ass was shaking so much one would think she was inside a freezer naked. Showing fear to two big-ass dogs was the wrong thing to do. But my boys held it down and made me look good by being kind to her ass. After the meet and greet was completed and I was positive Rocko and Chuck were okay, Nijah convinced me to go with her to the mall. We shopped and ate, and every ten minutes, I checked my phone, only to be disappointed and feel stupid since my ringer was up as high as it would go. When we left the house, it had been around noon, and once we made it back, it was going on seven in the evening—prompting me to believe that tonight would be another night without Prentice.

"We have popcorn, mini Mr. Goodbars, Lays plain, and Hershey's with almonds, mimosas, and chicken wings. Our stomachs will hate us in a few hours." Nijah smiled, walking into the living room with a tray full of snacks. I immediately took the glass containing the mimosa and drained it in two gulps.

"Okay, tonight is a get-wasted kinda night," she snickered, taking a seat next to me. "What are we watching?"

"Horror," we said at the same time before cackling. Scary movies were our thing, especially when one of us was going through something. We found it better to be afraid out of our minds of monsters than to cry over a sappy romance when tears were already too familiar and running from our eyes like leaky faucets.

It took less than five minutes to find a scary movie on some streaming site that Nijah swore by. By the time we reached our third movie, my stomach was aching, and we both fell asleep.

"Nijah, put me down before we both fall, crazy ass," I grumbled, my eyes still closed. I felt my body being lifted from the sofa.

"Damn, I feel like Nijah?"

My eyes popped open, and if it weren't for his secure grip on my body, the jerking I'd done would have landed my ass right onto the floor.

"Prentice," I screamed, wrapping my arms tightly around his neck and kissing his face.

"Oh, so now you know me?"

"I was half-asleep, babe," was my justification before kissing him again. He carried me up the stairs, exciting me because I knew my bedroom would be the destination.

"Yeah, I'ma let you have that. But if I find out you and Nijah been bumping coochies, we gon' have a problem. Sis might come up missing," he joked, holding me tightly once again as I tried leaping out of his arms.

"Okay, that wasn't funny," I fussed, serious as hell.

"Mistaking me for a woman with breasts wasn't either, but I didn't drop you like I should have."

"You really trying to have me mad at you your first night home?" I raised my brow in question.

"You're beautiful." His smile was so broad and gorgeous that my clit jumped.

"When did you get out?" Changing the subject was the best thing to do, and getting the answer to my question was more important than going back and forth about something neither of us took seriously anyway.

"Just now. I came straight here," he spoke, placing me on my feet. Walking over to my nightstand, I flicked on the lamp that stood there.

"That would be believable had you had the same clothes on from the day you were arrested." My observation was on point because, for a brief second, his eyes widened in shock before they altered into a grin.

"Damn, you pay attention to your man, huh?"

"Of course. Now, when did you get home?"

"I went home, checked on the dogs, showered, and came here right after. The house was my first stop anyway because I needed to make sure your stubborn ass wasn't there alone waiting for me."

"You know you scared me half to death, right?"

"It wasn't my intention at all. You know that."

"I do. Doesn't mean you didn't scare me, though."

"You accept my apology?"

"Is that what this is?"

"Yes, I'm sorry to put you through that, A."

"Prentice, tonight opened my eyes on so many levels. I don't want to lose you. Just the thought of thinking you weren't coming back to me scared me shitless. It also made me realize just how much I love you." Being honest with him was important to me. Having him understand just how deep my feelings were for him was important. It was also my way of pleading with him to no longer do anything that could jeopardize his freedom and this relationship of ours that I was not willing to let go of anytime soon.

"You love me, huh?"

*Damn, why does he have to be so sexy?*

"That's what I just said." Placing my hands on my hips, I dared his ass to say something out of line. Maybe if he did, then it would be the sign I needed on whether we were actually supposed to be together.

"I love you too," he said in the most melodic, passionate tone I'd ever heard from him. Or maybe he said it in a masculine way, and that's just how my ears received it. Either way, his admission felt amazing. Him pulling me into him by my waist and placing his lips on mine felt terrific too.

"You know I'd do anything for you. Seeing the look on your face as they put me in that cop car is a look I never want to see again. You don't have to worry about me doing anything to be put in that situation again," he promised me. I knew from the look in his eyes he meant it. The rapid thumping of my heart proved it as well.

"Does that include quitting the job that could land you behind bars?" Was it right for me to ask that he quit doing what he had been doing to make his money? Probably not. And was it selfish of me to ask? Perhaps so. Overall, was my heart in the right place, as I asked? Absolutely.

"It does."

*Did I just hear him right?*

"You heard me right," he verified, letting me know the confusion was written on my face.

"How could you say okay so fast?"

"Because you asked me." His left hand graced the left side of my face as our eyes intertwined.

"I'm not trying to run your life. I just don't want to lose you."

"Believe it or not, you can't make me do anything. The goal was never to be hustling like that forever. Me getting locked up, though briefly and though not for what it could have been, opened my eyes a bit wider as well. You, my mom, and my little sister are my world. To continue putting myself in anything that can remove me from y'all would make me the dumbest nigga alive, and we both know I'm far from that. I'm quitting. Not tonight 'cause it don't work like that. Very soon, though. You riding with me 'til I throw in the towel?"

"Even after."

"I love you, mayne." Taking me by the ass, he lifted me, and with ease, as they always had done, my legs found their way around him, tightly.

Our lips connected as we kissed feverishly. My tongue colliding with his sent jolts of pleasure through my body. Prentice provided me a level of pleasure that was indescribable, and it was addicting.

His lips traveled from my lips to my neck, where he sucked hard, lovingly, undoubtedly leaving passion marks that would be worn like a badge of honor. As he lay me on my bed, my legs loosened from around him as he lifted and removed his shirt, pants, and boxers in one swift motion. I blinked, it seemed, and he stood before me in his naked glory with the perfect body. Had I not been exposed to his masterpiece of a body on numerous occasions, I would've blamed his light stint in the clinker for his chiseled perfection.

He interrupted my admiration when he took my hands, helping me sit up and remove my tank, then my shorts, leaving me naked just as he was. His intense gaze was almost intimidating. I say almost because I was more so turned on by it.

"Keep them legs open," he ordered, slapping my thighs. As if his hands were hot, my legs snapped opened.

I did not close them on purpose; it was out of reflex. It was due to the pounding of my clit that needed a little alleviation that only the closing of my legs could provide until he took over again.

Slowly, he made his way between my legs, and as always, his mouth found its way to my clit before his dick did. Pleasing me with his mouth almost always came first. My back arched off the bed, nearly high enough to look like I was the main character in one of the *Exorcist* movies. Prentice alternating between flicking and sucking was sending me into overdrive, and as the heat rose from the tip of my toes to my pelvis, I knew my peak was near.

"Baby, I-I'm coming." The words somehow found their way out of my throat.

"Fill my mouth with it then," he mumbled, my clit still in his mouth. The vibrations from him speaking, then going back to sucking did the trick because I came hard as hell. My legs shook. My entire bottom convulsed.

"Stop," I yelled at him, pushing his head from between my legs while clasping my thighs against his face at the same time. My clit was too sensitive for him to be still kissing it, and though pleasure would follow if he continued, I needed a breather.

"Don't be pushing my head." He came up, pressing his lips on mine, letting me taste my juices as he slid inside of me.

"Damn, A, you did keep it tight for yo' boy, huh?"

If he expected me to answer him while sliding inside of me so calculated, he had to be out of his mind. Besides, that could not have been a question. Of course, I'd stay tight for him. The only way my shit wouldn't be as tight is if it were *he* who tore my walls down.

"Ahh."

"You gon' come for me again?"

"Mmm."

"Nah, use your words, A."

"Yes. Yes. I will-I am, I'm—coming." I was sure to have awakened the people across the street as I announced my orgasm so loud.

"Good shit." He pressed his lips back on mine, and after about three more pumps, he was releasing inside of me.

"You two nasty mothafuckas should warn me next time so that I can sleep with headphones." Nijah's voice boomed from the other side of my door, making Prentice and I fall into a fit of laughter. This was the kind of joy I never wanted to let go of.

# 29

## *Prentice*

Today was a day to celebrate. It was the beginning of the first day of my new life, and I couldn't be happier about it. Shit was good. Real good. And today's celebration was proof of it. The last two months, I had been working my ass off to get out of the game, making more paper than I ever had in such a short amount of time, putting myself in a position to exit the game gracefully. The plan I put into motion to carve out my future was perfectly executed. Now was the time to celebrate, and I was more than ready to do so.

I passed my small empire over to Sonic, took my cut of the money, which was a smooth million, and vowed never to look back. I had just finished spraying my Dior cologne as I stood in my bedroom, looking myself over in the full-length mirror. Fresh to death was how me and my attire could be described. The navy-blue Tom Ford suit I purchased was tailored to perfection, with a pair of navy Tom Ford dress shoes to match. My hair was cut and lined perfectly, and my curls were moisturized on top of my head.

"The car just pulled up."

Aúrea's beautiful voice and body entered the bedroom. She looked like perfection, with a navy dress that dipped low at her breasts and a long slit up her left leg, and her back was out. Her hair was straight and flowed down her back. As fine as she looked, I didn't want to share the sight of her with anyone else. Luckily, my party was invite-only, and those on the list knew not to violate by looking at my woman for too long. She was also lucky that I was even letting her come out of the house in that damn dress.

"I'm ready." Taking the few steps and stopping right in front of her, I kissed her lips.

"Mmm," she moaned, making my dick jump.

"I thought you just said the car was outside."

"It is."

"You must don't want to make it to that mothafucka moaning against my lips like that. It's nothing for me to hike that dress up over your waist."

"Well, that's not about to happen, so let's go," she giggled, taking me by the hand and leading me to the limo that waited for us outside of my house.

As we rode in the back, it took all of my willpower not to at least taste her. She knew I was feening for her as well because her ass made sure to sit on the opposite side of the car. That was a mistake, though, because giving me a perfect view of her only made me want her more. Right when I was ready to throw caution to the wind and say fuck it, the car stopped, and the driver was exiting. We had arrived at our destination.

"Time to celebrate, baby," she squealed as I exited the car first, then held my hand out for her to take.

"Yeah, just don't celebrate too much. When we get home, I'm doing everything to your body that I didn't get to do before we left, and then some."

"That's fine with me. I didn't plan to drink anyway."

"Yeah, all right." I spoke like I didn't believe her because I really didn't. Aúrea wasn't an alcoholic or nothing like that, but baby girl knew how to get lit when she wanted to. Her drink preference was always champagne, and there were going to be bottles of that shit throughout the room.

"Wanna bet?"

"Depends on what the prize is for the winner," I told her.

"Well, my prize from you would be a new car. Not sure what you'd want, but because I know I'm going to win, what you want doesn't even matter." She shrugged like she was so sure of herself. The certainty she was showing, though, had my ass second-guessing making a bet, so instead of even continuing the conversation, I changed the subject.

"Bet all these people happy we made it. Now, the party can get started."

"I'm not even going to call you out about what you just did. C'mon." We both laughed as we entered the building.

My guests were already on the dance floor, and the first two fools my eyes landed on were Sonic and Nijah. Surprisingly, they were keeping it P.G. The party planner I hired brought the room to life just like I wanted with the silver and blue decorations, and the DJ so far was playing the songs on the list I'd given him. Aúrea and I made our way around the room, saying what's up and thank you to people who showed up for me before stopping at the table my mother and Mr. Lewis was sitting at.

"Hey, Ma," I spoke, leaning down to kiss her cheek.

"Son, you look like a million bucks. My genes aren't to be fucked with," she slurred.

"Mr. Lewis, how much did she drink, and you just sat here and let her do it?" My eyes cut to him. My party had only started about thirty minutes ago, so my mom being already so tipsy was surprising.

"I ain't let her do nothing. Why you think she sitting her ass down?" he chastised me while still getting up to embrace me with a fatherly hug.

"You invited your father?" my mom slurred again.

"He here?" I checked because I hadn't run into him yet.

"Over there, with some girl that's damn near your age," my mom spat.

I looked over my shoulder, and sure enough, my dad was sitting at the table with a chocolate beauty, who was smiling all in his face.

"I did. He'll stay away from you, though, Ma."

"He better. Daughter-in-law, how are you?" My mom turned her attention to Aúrea, who chuckled before leaning down to hug her.

"I'm good. Hi, Mr. Lewis." Aúrea greeted him with a hug as well.

"Girl, be happy I raised my son and not that man over there," my mom said to her.

"All right, Ma, we gotta go speak to the other guests." Turning to Mr. Lewis, I said, "Look after her, please."

"You don't even have to ask."

Taking Aúrea by the hand, we made our way to the dance floor and had only been dancing a few moments before we had Sonic and Nijah on one side of us and my father and his date on the other.

"Son, when did you get here?" he asked, stepping away from his date to hug me.

"Been here for a little bit. Glad you could make it," I told him.

"Wow, honey, he looks just like you," my dad's date observed, causing me to scoff a bit. Yeah, I favored my pops, but that was about it, and I didn't think that was enough to brag about.

"Dad, this is my girlfriend, Aúrea. Aúrea, this is my dad."

"Nice to meet you," Aúrea spoke as he kissed her cheek. Now, had he not been in here with a chick around A's and my age, it would have seemed like a harmless kiss to me. Since he was, that shit didn't sit well with me, so I broke up the short embrace so quickly that Aúrea probably wasn't even sure his lips touched her skin.

After chilling, eating, and dancing a little longer, it was time for me to make a toast, and though my party was jumping, I was ready to get home and make love to my woman.

"Can I get everyone's attention?" I asked, speaking into the mic the DJ provided me.

I waited a few seconds for everyone's eyes to be on me and appreciated their attention. To me, that showed they cared, not just about me but what I had to say as well.

"I just wanted to thank you all for coming and celebrating with me tonight. I know most of y'all know what this party symbolizes for me, and for those of you who do not, just know you are a part of a significant milestone in my life. Two months ago, I vowed to change some shit up for the better and was able to do it, not effortlessly, but with purpose, and I have this woman right here to thank for that." I leaned over and kissed Aúrea's cheek, and *awes* flowed throughout the room. Aúrea's face flushed, showing her blush, and my damn cheeks felt hot, indicating I too was blushing. I'd take that, though. Showing how much I loved my woman was never shameful.

"Once again, I want to thank you all for coming out. Make sure you get home safely, and I'll see y'all soon. Salute."

"Salute," everyone said in unison.

"Let's go," I whispered in Aúrea's ear, making her giggle. She didn't protest, though, and I rubbed her booty the entire walk to the limo.

"Did you enjoy yourself?" she asked me in between the kisses I was placing on her lips as I backed her into the stairs. We weren't entirely in the house before I was on her.

"Yup, and once you provide me my happy ending, I will have really enjoyed my night." My hands were roaming her body as my dick throbbed in my pants.

"Relax a bit, babe. Can we get up the stairs first, at least?" She slowly eased out of my grasp.

"I'ma carry you up."

"No, you're not. You've had a little too much to drink and are not about to drop me on these stairs. Babe, just come on. Plus, I have a surprise for you."

"All right, man." I sucked my teeth. "And you know I wouldn't drop yo' ass either, no matter how much I drank."

"I know, Prentice." She sounded irritated as hell.

Without another word, I followed her up the stairs, constantly adjusting my dick in my pants. The tailored suit was all fine and dandy . . . until I was hard as hell.

"Wait right here," Aúrea said as she made her way into the master bathroom. We had barely walked through the bedroom door.

I watched her ass jiggle as she walked away, and I freed my member from my slacks, then sat on the bed.

"You not going to sleep, are you?" Aúrea's voice entered the room before she did.

"Now, you know I'm not going to sleep."

"Good, because you can't until you get my surprise." She sexily walked closer to me in nothing but a blue lace bra and panty set and a long black box in her hands. When she got closer to me, stopping in between my legs, she handed me the box.

"What's this?"

"Open it and see," she smiled.

I looked at her curiously with my right brow raised, wondering what the hell was in the box. I held it to my right ear and shook it. There was a little clatter, which told me nothing.

"Just open it." She rolled her eyes.

"A'ight."

Removing the wrapper from the box, I can't even front. A nigga was excited to be getting a gift from my girl. This was something she didn't have to do, so it meant that much more. Once the box was completely open, my eyes went from what was inside to Aúrea, who looked like she was holding her breath.

"Is this for real?" I questioned. I knew I had a few drinks, but I didn't feel drunk enough to be seeing doubles.

"It is," she admitted shyly. I looked down again, staring as if what were in my hand would change.

"Are you upset? I mean, I know it's soon, but this is—"

"You having my baby, so how can I *not* be happy?"

Happier than I'd ever been was really how I felt. Nah, we hadn't planned for her to get pregnant, but we also weren't doing anything to prevent it either. Tonight proved to be worth every sacrifice I made to get out of the drug game. Aúrea's pregnancy may not have been planned, but it was damn sure the right time, though.

"I love you," I told her, taking her by the face, gently bringing her lips to mine.

"I love you too," she spoke into my lips before pushing me back onto the bed and riding me until we both fell asleep.

# 30

## *Aúrea*

"*Aúrea, you and I should have had one more night together before you hit the road.*"

My heart thumped roughly in my chest as its sound pierced my ears. Still, it wasn't hard or fast enough to drown out his voice. A voice I'd know anywhere and could recognize in a room filled with a million voices if it came down to it. After all these years, he still looked the same. Had the same clothes on from when I saw him last. Why he was even standing in front of me right now was not only puzzling but scared me shitless, as well.

My eyes opened as far as they could go at the sight of him slowly moving toward me. Instinctively, I tried backing away, yet my feet would not move. It was like the part of my brain that registered movement to the body had paralyzed. The closer he got to me, the more fear began to take over, and the feeling of hot liquid rolling down my cheeks let me know that this wasn't a dream.

Then why the hell can't I move? I thought, internally willing myself to turn the hell around and get as far away from him as my legs would carry me.

"You knew I had something special to give you, and you just left before I could give it to you," he said snidely. The look on his face was one of amusement.

*"Get away from me." The words left my mouth, but to my ears, they sounded like mumbo jumbo. The words were not easy to make out at all. Honestly, I sounded like a Charlie Brown character.*

*What the fuck?*

*"Why? You used to enjoy when I touched your face softly like this." His hand caressed my face, but it felt like a thousand ants crawling all over me, causing me to shudder.*

*"See, you still like it. Do you still like this?" he asked before moving in closer and taking his long tongue, licking my face from the edge of my jaw to right underneath my eye.*

*My eyes shut tightly at the feel of his tongue on me, so tight that I hoped when I opened them again, he would be gone, or I'd be blind and could no longer see him.*

*"You always cried, just so that I could lick your tears away," he chuckled, removing his hand and hot breath from my face.*

*The rapid beating of my heart slowed, and a little easiness came over me. Something told me that he was gone. Maybe Prentice had come into view, making him retreat. My eyes popped open, only in disappointment, because he was still standing in front of me, just in a different location. We both were in a different place—my old bedroom.*

*"Okay, good. This is a dream." I sighed, feeling relief.*

*"That's what you think this is?" he chuckled.*

*"I know it is because you're dead." My spunk had come back, anger and attitude present.*

*"If this were a dream, tell me why you feel this?" he asked just as the feeling of his hands caressing my breasts overwhelmed me.*

"*Don't touch me,*" *I screamed once again, trying to back away, but I couldn't.*

"*Why not? It's not like you don't like it. It's not like you never liked it. How many times did you orgasm at the feel of my hands down there, playing with your little pink bud?*" *he asked cockily.*

"*Never,*" *I protested with hot tears running down my face, forming a small puddle on the bottom of my lip.*

"*Not being able to tell the truth has always been an issue of yours . . . tsk tsk tsk.*" *He waved his index finger at me as if he were reprimanding a child.*

"*I never lied to you. You raped me damn near every day for five years!*" *My chest heaved up and down. Steam rose from my body, and as loud as I yelled, it once again wasn't clear.*

*Von looked at me, laughing hard. I mean, his entire body shook as he laughed at me, clutching his stomach, showing every tooth in his mouth.*

"*It's not rape if you liked it. Watch. I'm going to prove it to you right now.*"

*Before I knew it, my body was being hoisted into the air and then thrown onto my bed, and immediately, Von was on top of me.*

"*Stop! Don't touch me! Get off me!*"

*His hand forced my legs open, and I felt his fingers enter me. How he'd done that so fast stumped me. Where the nightgown I had on only seconds ago went blew my damn mind.*

"*You know they say, pregnant pussy is the best pussy,*" *he spoke, licking the side of my face.*

"*Stop. You don't have to do this.*"

"*Yes, I do. You had me killed for nothing.*"

"It wasn't for nothing! You were never supposed to stick your old-ass dick in me," I cried—screamed—tried bucking around to get him off me, which failed.

"That baby you're carrying is going to end up just how you did," he cackled. "What made you think you were special enough to bring a kid into this world?" He laughed again. "That baby will end up meeting someone like me to make him or her feel good. Just as I'm about to do to you now." His breath on my ear felt like a light was being held at it. It wasn't until I felt him penetrating me that the heat near my ear left, and everything went black.

"Wake yo' ho ass up!" A deep voice and slap across my face jolted me awake.

"No no no," I cried, shaking my head.

"You thought you were going to get away from me?" he gritted, snatching me up by my hair.

"Ouch."

"You owe me, Rae, baby. Why would you leave a nigga, knowing how good I was to you?" The grip on my hair gave me an instant headache.

"Why are you doing this? Let me go, Adrian." My hands clawed at his, trying hard to remove them from the death grip on my head.

"Bitch, scratch me again, and I'm going to break your fucking neck," he yelled with so much force I knew he wasn't lying. I removed my hands from his, and my eyes shut tightly as I hoped it would alleviate some of the pressure.

"You took shit out of my house. Left before making me some money and came out here and got pregnant by another nigga." The grip on my hair loosened as he tossed me to the floor.

"A-Adrian, it wasn't like-like that." I tried pleading with him.

*"That's exactly what it was like, you ho-ass bitch. Did you tell that nigga how many times I prostituted yo' ho ass? Damn baby in yo' stomach probably not even his,"* he laughed.

*"It is,"* I boldly defended as my hands subconsciously went to my stomach. The feel of it shocked me, and when I looked down to see my belly, it was as big as a basketball.

*"The fuck?"* I mumbled. There was no way my belly should have been this big when I hadn't known but a hot second that I was pregnant.

*"You either come back with me and finish doing the only damn thing you're good at, which is selling your pussy, or I'm offing you, that nigga, and the damn baby after I gut the little mothafucka from your stomach,"* he seethed.

Everything about him right now was catching me off guard: his tone, his attire, his demeanor. Adrian stood before me looking like hell spit him up. He was still handsome, but anger and hatred poured out of him as his hand rose with a gun.

*"No, no, Adrian. Please don't do this."* I was sure my cries fell on deaf ears as he looked at me blankly.

Still on the ground, I backed away from him as quickly as possible, only to be blocked by a sleeping Prentice.

*"Prentice, get up. Run, baby."* I tried waking him, pushing, and screaming at him as Adrian drew closer to us.

*"You may as well let me kill you. All of you, because once he knows who you really are, he won't want you, and he damn sure won't want you as his baby mother."* Adrian's laugh rang through my ears, sounding like the evil villain he was.

*At one point, this man loved me. At least, I believed he did, and I'd have to try using that to my advantage to save my baby, Prentice, and me.*

*"Whatever you want me to do, Adrian, I will. Just please don't hurt us. You promised never to hurt me again." Tears rolled down my face as I tried pleading with him.*

*"Fuck you" was the last thing he said before his size eleven foot collided with my stomach.*

"Noo." My body jolted up as my scream penetrated my ears.

"Aúrea, baby, what's wrong?" Prentice's worried voice sounded like music to my ears as his arms wrapped around me and brought me relief. However, the nightmare I'd just awakened from felt so real that my body still shook from fear, and my tears were still flowing.

"I saw-saw them," I sobbed.

"Saw who, babe?" he asked, stroking my back softly.

"V-Von and A-Adrian."

"They're gone, A. They can't hurt you," he whispered.

"I know, but . . ." Before I could finish speaking, thoughts of what both Adrian and Von said about me came rushing to the forefront of my mind. This life Prentice promised me was one I didn't deserve because I wasn't meant to be loved. I was meant to be hurt, raped, beat, and most of all, not meant to be someone's mother. That reality broke me, and I sobbed hard and loudly in his arms.

"Baby, it's okay. I promise, they can't hurt you again." The certainty in his tone soothed me enough to calm the shakiness of my body.

"I-I need to tell you something," I whispered.

I didn't want to admit to him what I was about to, but I knew it was something that had to be done, especially with me being pregnant.

"You can tell me anything, and it won't change how I feel about you." He kissed my forehead.

"When living in L.A., I prostituted and stripped." Pushing the words out felt like I had just been punched in the stomach. I could only imagine what my words did to Prentice.

"Dude made you?" he asked, pulling back to look me in the eyes.

Nodding my head at him provided the answer.

"It's a good thing he's gone. Otherwise, I'd kill his ass."

"You keep saying he's gone. How do you know that?"

He just looked at me, and I knew the answer.

"Prentice."

"Don't worry about it. It won't lead back to you or me. I couldn't do nothing, knowing another nigga had violated you. Now that you told me what you just did, he got exactly what he deserved by what happened to him."

"What if I'm not a good mom?" That question was more important to me than dwelling on Adrian.

"You'll be the best mother. You love hard. You're dedicated, loyal, kind, beautiful. All the makings of a bomb-ass mother. Don't doubt that." He kissed me.

Taking a deep breath, I tried letting his words move from my ears to my heart, but I still had a hard time placing them there. The doubt I was feeling was a bit stronger.

"You still want me, even though I sold my body?"

"I still want you. That's never going to change, Aúrea. What you did was what you had to do; it's not who you are. Who you are is everything I need and want in my life and more . . . baggage and all. Now, just let me love you so much that everything you don't like about yourself is a distant memory, all right?"

"Okay." For the first time since waking up, I smiled.

"You know I got you, right?" He sexily licked his lips.

"I do." And I did.

"I love you, a'ight?" He smiled at me.

"I love you too." I smiled back, finally feeling at ease.

# Epilogue

## *Prentice*

*Aúrea was squeezing the shit out of my hand as her legs were propped in the stirrups of the hospital bed. I stood to the left of her with Nijah to her right as we waited for another contraction to hit so she could push.*

*"Nahji, give me your hand," Aúrea whined with her right hand slightly bent at the elbow and lifted in the air, awaiting Nijah to oblige her request.*

*"Hell no. I love you, Aúrea, but if I allow you to squeeze my hand once more, I'll need surgery to fix the bones you break and even to be able to spread my fingers apart."*

*"Why are y'all laughing?" Aúrea asked me and the nurses, who couldn't help the light chuckles that fell from our mouths. Her scowl shut us all up as another contraction hit, prompting her to squeeze the shit out of my hand.*

*"See, even Prentice's face shows discomfort. Aúrea, I swear you're about to give birth to the Incredible Hulk." Nijah sucked her teeth while shaking her head.*

*"I'm about to have you kicked out." Aúrea cut her eyes at her.*

*"Girl, please." Nijah waved her off, knowing the threat was empty.*

*"Okay, Aúrea. I can see the baby's head. One more big push is all it should take."*

Aúrea *sucked in a huge breath, squeezing my hand again, then pushed with all her might.*

*"It's a boy," the doctor exclaimed.*

"Are you really watching that video again?"

Aúrea came into the room, interrupting my view of the television.

"Sure am," I admitted taking the remote and powering off the television. It had been a year ago today that Aúrea gave birth to my baby boy. Since she had him, I found myself watching the video of her giving birth every so often. I had been so into the video that I could sense everything that took place that day, which was why I hadn't heard her walk into the room.

My son's birth was a huge milestone in my life, just like me getting out of the drug game had been. His birth into the world was the moment I didn't mind repeating, though.

"Best day of both our lives, huh?" she beamed, taking a seat next to me.

"*One* of the best days. Where's my Junior, anyway? He has a party to be getting ready for." Leaning over, I kissed her cheek.

"He's napping. The party isn't for another four hours. He needs to rest so he can wear himself out."

"You always trying to wear my boy out," I chuckled.

"No, he does it to himself. P. J. is a ball of energy and a little terror," she giggled.

P. J., short for Prentice Junior, *was* a ball of energy and a little terror, and that's because his ass was spoiled. He had all the women in his life wrapped around his finger. They let him get away with anything, including his mother, sitting next to me. Between Aúrea, my mom, Nijah, and Prima, my son was loved on left and right. At only 1 year old, he was eating that shit up.

"Wait until he gets some cake and ice cream. Then he's *really* gonna be turnt."

"I know," she exaggerated, sighing like she was already exhausted.

"You love to act like he wears you out when you one of the main reasons he so spoiled." I took my arm, throwing it over her shoulder, pulling her into me.

"And you made him rough. He thinks he's a boxer and stuntman."

"He's a boy. He's supposed to be rough and tough."

"I agree, but it still baffles me how he's going through a terrible two-phase at 1."

"All right, it's time for you to get off my boy." I sucked my teeth, and she laughed.

"How long do we have before everybody gets here? I know a few more people are coming to set up—when are they coming?" I asked her. There were already a few people in the backyard setting up. P. J.'s party was a carnival theme, so there were way more decorations to go up, including a couple of rides. My son's first birthday was going to be lit, and the $25,000 bill was proof of it.

"Um, about another hour or so," she shrugged.

"You have anything else you need to do?"

"No. Your mother and Nijah have taken over. Told me to take my ass in the house," she pouted.

"Oh, so that's why you're in here? It wasn't to come to check on your son and man?"

"I would have done that, regardless."

"So, are you upset they took over?" She needed to be honest with me. If the answer were yes, I'd go outside and check both my mom *and* Nijah. I knew they were excited about P. J.'s first birthday just as much as we were. However, he was *our* son, and if anyone should have been running shit for his first birthday party, it was his mother.

"Oh yes, I'm fine. The things I'm worried about directing won't be here for a while. When they come, both your mom and Nijah will be stomping in here with attitudes because they will *not* get to control that," she said seriously, and that shit brought a grin across my face.

Aúrea knew how important it was for them to feel like part of this process, so she let them have a piece of it without allowing them to take her moment.

"You the shit, you know that, right?"

"So are you." She puckered up, waiting for me to kiss her lips, and without hesitation, I pressed mine to hers.

"Since we have time, I think you should come ride my dick."

"Really, Prentice?" She sat up and popped me in the chest. Not hard, of course.

"What?" My crooked grin was all it took to remove the little frown she had on her face.

"Come on," she huffed, standing, taking a few steps away from me and the sofa.

"Oh, shit, you gon' do it?" I leaped up, excitedly rubbing my hands together.

She looked at me over her left shoulder, grinning.

"Not if you don't hurry up."

"Shit, you ain't gotta tell me twice."

Stepping on the cushion of the couch, I hopped over it and rushed to her, picking her up bridal style as she giggled uncontrollably in my arms.

"You better not drop me." She held me tightly as I practically ran up the stairs carrying her.

"Never."

"You don't think y'all went overboard?" Mr. Lewis came up to me and asked as we stood at the door of my backyard watching the party.

"Nah, why you say that?" I asked him.

"Because P. J. is 1. He won't remember none of this shit." He shook his head like he was in disbelief, making me laugh.

"It's cool. Aúrea wanted to go all out for his first, so I told her she didn't have a budget. This is what she came up with. Even though it's a lot for a 1-year-old, you gotta admit it's fun as hell for us adults."

"Yeah, you got me there. My ass hasn't been on a Ferris wheel in forever. Your mother convinced me to get on that one with her."

Mr. Lewis and my mom had grown close since my party. I wasn't sure if they were at the point of bumping uglies yet, and I didn't even want to know if they were. It wasn't surprising that them growing close didn't bother me because for once in my mother's life, she liked a man who was actually good for her.

"So business is good, I take it."

"Business is great. Will be even better once we get that second restaurant opened."

"I meet with the contractor in two weeks," he informed me.

My consultation business was booming. My last consult had made my client a whole lot of bread, $2 million to be exact, and he wasted no time telling his other rich friends that it was me who helped him. After that, I was getting clients left and right. With the money I gained, I helped my mother open another business, plus invested in Mr. Lewis's second restaurant across town. Everyone I loved was eating real good, and I couldn't be happier.

"All right, let me get my ass back over here and make sure these cooks ain't fucking up the food."

"You know you aren't the chef, right?"

"Cooking is what I do. Besides, it's *my* restaurant catering this shindig . . . You know if my name on it, it gotta be right."

He extended his hand to me, and we embraced before he hurried off.

"What the old man was talking 'bout?" Sonic asked, walking up, giving me dap.

"The food," I chuckled.

"He refuses to let them cooks fuck up. Aye, bro, this a nice-ass party for nephew. When I have my shorty, I'm gon' have to steal this theme. I'ma wait 'til he or she about 4 or 5, though, so they remember. I refuse to spend a grip, and it goes unappreciated."

"Nigga, whatever. So you and Nijah planning to have a little one?"

That's right, Sonic and Nijah were official. Had been since the night of my party. She decided to stick around, claiming that living in L.A. without Aúrea was not possible, so we all took a trip to L.A., cleaned out her apartment, and she moved into Aúrea's old place.

"Nah, we not planning it. We also not opposed to it happening. P. J. run me crazy enough, and he ain't even mine. So I can only imagine what my own shorty would do."

"Prentissss!" The soft yet loud tone of my name being dragged out drew near as my eyes settled on Prima and my son rushing toward us.

"What's up, baby girl?" I picked her up, kissing on her cheek.

"Hi, Uncle Sonic. Prentissss, can you come get on the rides with us?" Prima spoke, batting her pretty, long lashes at me.

"Which one?"

"The one over there that twists fast." She pointed.

"Ah, hell no!" Sonic spoke up as he too caught wind of the ride she was talking about. That shit was bound to make me throw up. I didn't know why Aúrea ordered that shit, anyway.

"P. J. is too small for that ride, Prima, and I don't like going in fast circles."

"It's his party. He can get on anything he wants to, and he wants to get on that ride with you and me." She placed her hands on her invisible hips.

"This my cue to dip," Sonic chuckled. He patted the top of P. J.'s head before leaving my ass there with my sister and son.

"Prima, not that ride, okay? I'll get on any other ride with you." Her bottom lip poked out, which was how she usually got me to do whatever she wanted me to. This was one thing I wasn't budging on, though. I picked her up, placing her on my left side, then lifted my son and put him on my right. Carrying both their asses toward the bumper cars, *this* was the ride we were getting on, and they both were gonna like it.

"What's wrong with her?" Aúrea asked, stepping up to us, kissing my lips. She noticed Prima's attitude.

"She wants to get on that death trap of a ride you ordered with my son and me, and it's not happening."

"Ugh," Prima groaned, causing Aúrea and me to laugh.

"It's not a death trap. *That* ride isn't for the kids. It's for the adults who aren't scared," Aúrea informed me.

"So, I guess your ass got on there?" My brows rose in question.

"Sure did. Me and Nijah." She said that shit like she was supposed to get a reward.

"See, Prentice?" Prima cut in wiggling out of my arms. I let her down like she wanted me to.

"You still not getting on there." I cut my eyes back to my little sister.

"Mommy will let me," she sassed.

"No, she won't, Prima."

I was seriously going back and forth with my little sister, which shouldn't have been the case because *I* was the man and in charge.

"Prima, how about we ride the bumper cars first? Then you can find your mom to see if it's okay to get on the ride. If she says yes, I'll get on with you."

"No, you won't, and she's not getting on that," I emphasized again. Both Aúrea and Prima were trying to test my gangsta.

"Fine, can it be girls against boys?" Prima asked.

"Yes, we will beat them."

"Oh, all right. It's like that? Come on, son, let's show them who the *real* drivers are around these parts." P. J. giggled as we all headed to the cars.

Prima and Aúrea weren't giving any mercy to me and P. J., so my plan to let them win went out the window. We smoked they ass. I wouldn't be surprised if my little sister woke up with whiplash in the morning.

"Can I get everyone's attention?" I spoke into the mic. The party was still going, but there was one thing I needed to do before our guests began making their way out.

As in any time I asked for a room to pay attention to me, everyone in attendance did so without question.

"First off, we want to thank all of you for attending our son's first birthday. We hope you all are enjoying yourselves. As you know, the food came from Mr. Lewis's place, so when you get the chance, stop by and check him out. He's also opening a restaurant downtown soon, so we want to see all of you at the grand opening."

Making eye contact with Mr. Lewis, he mouthed, "Thank you," to me, which I acknowledged with a head nod.

"Babe, come up here." I shifted my attention to Aúrea, who was standing, holding our son. She passed him to my mother as she made her way to where I stood.

"Y'all give my woman a round of applause. She put all this shit together." Everyone cheered for her, including me.

"All right. All right," she spoke, waving off the applause. I loved seeing her smile and blush.

"Aúrea, since the day you came back into my life, I've been the happiest man alive. Then you gave me my son, and I didn't think I could get any happier, but I can. I will, if you do one last thing for me."

"Anything," she breathed out. Everyone simultaneously said *Ahh,* making the two of us chuckle.

"From the day I first laid eyes on you, I knew I was meant to be yours, and you mine. Only thing left to do is make this official by giving you my last name." I removed the small ring box from my pocket as I eased to my right knee.

"Aúrea Belle Shepard, will you continue adding to the joy you bring me every day as my wife?"

"Yes," she shouted, leaping into my arms, making both of us fall back as she placed multiple kisses on my face, and all our friends and family applauded.

Life was good, and from here on out, it would only get better.

# *The End*